The
First
Law

A novel where spiritual energy evolves

Richard L. Ragle

MedArt Publications

© 2010 Richard L. Ragle All Rights Reserved.

ISBN 978-0-615-39621-7

First print August 2010.

Printed in the USA

This book is dedicated to God.
Thank you for the feeling of Love.
I manifest it in action as creativity.
Whether creating a book, a sculpture, or
a friendship.
When in love, my energy expands.

I wish to thank the following people for their
inspiration and help in this work:

Michelle Izmaylov, Maggie Carter
Kristine Davis, Nicolass Oving,
Lisa Powell, Keith Moen, Cheryl Haynes,
Stephanie Lucas and Susie Thomen.

To these, and all my other friends and family,
I love you.

When death is proximate; Love becomes sacrosanct.

Prologue

"Are you ready?"

"With you?" Dersti teased. "How can anyone be ready when you keep coming up with new things to throw at me?"

Leydon smiled and tightened the straps around his shoulders. Glancing at Dersti, he sighed softly.

There is such a thing as loving someone to the point you would die for them, and this is an interesting lifestyle. The feeling of gratitude that you walk around with in your heart is a gift! All the love and acceptance you ever dreamed possible is palpable, so easy to feel. As if all the love you ever felt for everyone and everything dwells, swells, and blossoms in your heart. It's there within easy reach, with no blocks or mental machinations to stir hesitation in feeling love. You feel happy, eternally grateful. You smile for no and every reason.

"Come and help me," Leydon said, opening the force field door of the hovercraft. The door hissed open, and he and Dersti peered out upon the endless green plains carpeting the earth 5,000 meters below them.

There is intellectual knowledge of love. You know that is what you want to feel. And then there is emotional and spiritual knowledge of love. That "AH-HA" moment that floods your conscience when your heart fully opens to love. It is no longer an intellectual concept but a throbbing necessity, true and present, in your heart!

"Ready?" he yelled above the rush of wind.

She nodded and squeezed his hand.

You awaken in love to a glorious sunrise washed with creamy reds and smeared with orange. Your days are like a rose bush. You're aware the perfect rose may have a thorn, but you mostly gaze in awe and simply accept, that a thorn bush has perfect and beautiful roses! And you feel grateful for the roses, which glow and darken with mystery and passion in the crimson sunset of love. Then you sleep and dream upon pink clouds of love. Day after day, you feel gratitude for love.

Leydon dove first from the hov, followed by Dersti. Hard wind whipped their bodies as they sped to around 120 mph. Dersti, who had only been skydiving twice before, may have screamed. But her shriek of joy was lost in their earthly descent.

Love given by grace can be lost by ego. If you choose to stay in love and it is a choice, love becomes who you are. And love is not sheltered in any one heart; it spreads in ripples to the person who opened your heart to love and beyond, until those around you can feel the love that radiates from you! Once your heart feels the love of the beloved and senses how glorious love feels, you feel it for others. A glow surrounds, envelops, encompasses you.

Dersti held out her arms to Leydon. They linked hands and twirled together through the air, breathing the sky and the clouds and each other. Separating, both spread their arms and legs so the webbing on their suits caught the air. They glided down, spiraling around each other, watching one another's beaming smiles. The wind fluttered grinning cheeks, just as it ruffled the webbing of the suits allowing flight.

You feel it, and others see it. Soon the feeling of love spreads to even more distant others, for it is the most contagious feeling in the world. God created us in love, and our brains are hardwired for the feeling of love. It becomes a journey of exploring love in everything. From the soft lips of your lover to the curl of a rose petal. Love glitters in every living creation. Even within the perfection of the thorn.

As the ground rapidly approached they shared a quick

10

nod of acknowledgment, both pulled their parachutes. What was the rapid, gliding flight of two flying squirrels, swiftly transformed into the slow, graceful descent of two dandelion seeds, floating at the whim of the wind.

Chapter 1

On Miracles and Odd Happenings

Tail whipping back and forth like a fan, Zeus peered up and grinned at Logan in a silent thank-you for the walk. What a smile! A celebration of life, really. When Zeus pulled back those furry white cheeks, he revealed much more than bright teeth and big dimples; he revealed his soul, which was far more beautiful than his exterior.

A fluffy white Samoyed, Zeus was the perfect picture of agility, beauty and dignity. His compact, muscular body wiggled as he padded along the path. Lips curled into a perpetual smile, he always seemed to find a reason to smile and fan the fuzzy tail that curled over his back. Endearing black eyes touched up with a natural hint of black eyeliner and a black button nose rounded off the image. Zeus was more than man's best friend; he was family. And what a family Logan, Zeus and second Samoyed, Loki, were.

Pale wisps of distant sunshine filtered through heavy clouds. Thunder grumbled across the sky every once in a while that misty morning in New Mexico. The trio was wandering through the Sandia Mountains situated between Albuquerque and Santa Fe. Logan paused for a moment and wiped a few rogue raindrops from his face. As far as his piercing eyes could see, the mountains all around him rippled away into distant mist. A nuzzle at his leg drew him back to the present.

Logan loved both his dogs, but Zeus was special. Zeus, whose nose was now buried in the leg of Logan's pants, elevated his human friend to a new understanding of the meaning of love. Of course, Logan had plenty of girlfriends and had even been married before meeting the Samoyed. But it was Zeus who opened his heart to the true meaning of what it felt like to love and to be loved unconditionally.

Life for Logan didn't get much better than a stroll through the hidden paths of the mountains with his dogs, having dinner with his friends, and enjoying the spirituality he felt in AA meetings. Yet what dramatic changes these simple pleasures seemed to Logan. Having grown up poor in the system of an alcoholic family, luxuries such as peaceful walks were hard to come by. One of the stories he rarely related was how his mother had quit buying toilet paper in order to save money for vodka. She replaced the roll with two buckets in the bathroom. One bucket was filled with worn rags and torn stretches of old sheets, and the other bucket brimmed with water and bleach. You would pick a rag, any rag, and use it to wipe your ass. Plop the rag into the bleach water and you're free to go. Logan sort of understood the concept but was revolted when he realized his mother washed the dirtied rags and reused them. Forced to get a regular job at fourteen, he soon started to buy his own toilet paper. And so the seeds of one of the first big lessons of his childhood were planted: money could change his life and ultimately make him happy.

Because he grew up in an alcoholic family, his main survival tactics became self-reliance and determination. There were benefits to those traits, and they carried him through medical school until he was eventually board certified in Family Practice medicine. But there were also downsides. In striking out on his own he succumbed to the very plague that gnawed at his family's core. He became an alcoholic himself.

Thank God that during Logan's internship it dawned on him that in a couple years he would be in practice and be the one making life and death decisions. One evening while downing a foaming mug he realized he could barely stand, let alone fiddle with the responsibility of a patient's life. He was terrified by the very idea of it and admitted defeat. Powerless over alcohol and acknowledging his need for help, he sought out treatment and got sober. That was 24 years ago.

Often he would wander outside and lean against the wooden walls of his mountain retreat in the cold night and summon the distant memories. He did not regret the past nor his parents' choices. For everything that happened to him helped shape his character and made him into the understanding man he was today. Today, he liked himself. He was in a profession that enabled him to make money, although money alone no longer made him happy. Had he not experienced that one revelation, he might still be trapped in the mental prison of believing that money equated to happiness. And at times being able to buy enough toilet paper to sustain his dignity folded his lips into a smile, he knew it was love that equaled happiness.

Logan paused for a moment on the path and quietly called out so his dogs would wait for him. Loki plopped down where she stood and laid her elegant head on her paws. Zeus padded back at once and rubbed his body against Logan's legs. The man ran his coarse fingers through his friend's silken fur and struggled to catch his breath.

His body was starting to give out. Whether it was damage done from his drinking and drugging years, the overwhelming environmental pollution, Vertig's syndrome, or just plain wear and tear, he wasn't certain. Although the scientist in him couldn't help but correlate cause and effect, he knew it was useless to try to analyze what he had done right or wrong through the years. He realized there were just too many factors involved to ever obtain a clear understanding. The greenhouse effect, polluted air and asthma were all contributing factors that haunted him like wraiths every day of his childhood. There were also, of course, other factors. Like growing up in an alcoholic family. Being abused as a child. Living on a raped, battered, dying planet. And then there was that feeling, almost as if he was from a different time and space, which just couldn't be ignored.

The current mystery in his life was inexplicable. He sometimes felt when something in his body would give out or change, something else would be enhanced. Every physical trauma bestowed a spiritual gift. As Logan leaned forward to stretch his sore back, a low moan escaped his lips. He had two herniated discs in his back and they were a constant bother. For years he tried everything from acupuncture to back surgery—not just once but twice—yet still had chronic pain. He knew pain was a motivator for personal growth. The spiritual and emotional pain of his alcoholism had, for instance, motivated him to carry out the work necessary to obtain new heights of spiritual growth. The physical pain writhing in his back was motivating him to grow. He engaged himself in more prayer and meditation than ever before. He couldn't work as hard at his job in medicine, but the "gift" related to this was that his life had slowed down. For the first time in his life he was able to appreciate simple meditation, walks with his dogs and the misty scent of roses in the morning dew.

He had become a believer in gifts. Often he had seen that whenever the shit hit the fan in his life, there would always be a forthcoming gift if he remained observant for it. One of the unexplainable gifts granted to him lately was that he had started to see auras. Over the last couple of years his ability to see the distinct colors and layers in the aura enveloping every living being had become more refined. He appreciated this gift, but the scientist in him also wanted to make sure it wasn't the manifestation of a brain tumor! Remembering his appointment with his doctor later that morning, he whistled to his dogs to follow him home beneath the snarling cumulus clouds sweeping across the sky.

*****

"Doctor," Logan said.

"Doctor," Warren repeated.

Warren Cloud was one of Logan's best friends. Ever since they struggled and triumphed through medical school together, it became an inside joke between them to address one another in this manner. Although attending medical school was a brutal and humbling process, they knew that someday they would become doctors if only they could endure the inhumane system. There were days, though, when they had to do silly little things like calling each other 'doctor' in order to remind themselves what all the trauma was actually for. That, and enjoying an occasional evening out. The best nights were those they couldn't recall the following morning.

"So, what do you think?"

Logan had already given his friend the history of his latest condition and told him that sometimes seeing colorful auras surrounding someone made it hard for him to concentrate while speaking with that individual.

"Well, your funduscopic exam, MRI and visual acuity all seem normal." Warren paused. "How badly do the colors bother you?" he added.

"Not too much, I guess. What scares me most is that as time goes on the colors seem to be getting brighter and more defined."

"So do you see auras in most people?"

"Yes . . . everybody, in fact. Some I have to really focus on, but others are like walking neon rainbows."

"So what do they look like? The auras, I mean."

Logan leaned back and kneaded his crinkled forehead with his fingers. "The colors are transparent, so when I look at someone directly I can easily see their face and form. It's kind of like a halo of light, I guess. There are usually multiple layers of light, and they totally surround and engulf the physical body. The light is contoured to the form of the human body, and when we move or lift an arm the aura moves right along with us. For example, when your arms are down at your side the aura is shaped like an egg around you. When I look at someone's face, their face is free of color, but the periphery is where I see color."

"Seems like the light is polarized," Warren added.

"That's right, and the light seems to radiate out in straight lines from the body. So when you're looking directly at someone you don't see the colors. It's only when you look at someone in profile—that is, when the light is at a 90° angle to your line of sight—that you can see his or her aura. So here's another way to explain it; it's like looking at a cactus with spines coming out in all directions. When you look directly at the cactus, you can't really see those spines coming straight at you but can easily see the spines coming out from the sides. Does that make sense?"

"Interesting," Warren said thoughtfully. "It does make sense," he added with a glitter in his brilliant sapphire eyes.

Logan sat up a little straighter. "Oh, one more important point. While there are many different layers of light with many different colors, everyone seems to have a color that dominates their aura. For example, mine is an emerald green with purple streaks spiraling out from the edges. And the exact colors and intensity change with our emotional condition."

Warren's lips folded into a smirk. "So, dare I ask what you see in my aura?"

"Black! Lots of black."

"Hey, eat shit!"

18

"Oh, I'm just kidding!" Logan said with a chuckle. "I knew you were going to ask and I could hardly wait to answer."

"You're just a funny guy," Warren mumbled.

"Yeah, I've been told so. That's exactly what my wife said when we were getting divorced."

"Well, all right, enough of that. What do you really see in my aura?" Warren asked again with a hopeful smile.

"The outermost, predominant layer has a reddish-orange hue, and then you have many layers underneath of varying colors. It's really quite attractive," Logan murmured sensuously with a sly grin.

"Oh, of course it's gorgeous," Warren said, pride dripping from his tone. "What do the different colors mean?"

"Can't say I've studied that much yet, though I do have a book on color therapy. Did you know that some people have made color therapy into a whole field of serious study? Anyway, I know blue is a color of calm and red is supposed to be a color symbolizing energy or anger. I looked mine up and found out that emerald green is supposed to be the color of healing," Logan said proudly.

"Well, I guess red makes sense for me right now since I'm fired up about my economic situation," Warren gruffly explained.

"I wouldn't lose sleep over it, especially since I don't think the red color means you're a bad person."

"I know, and I'm sorry I sounded a little defensive. Anyway, let's get back to the topic at hand. Like so many things in medicine, it really boils down to how much the condition bothers you. After all, the treatment could be worse than the disease. You know some New Age guru would give his left nut to be able to see auras!"

The friends broke into laughter.

"I think you're right," Logan agreed, still chuckling. "I think it would be different if I had always been able to see auras and learned to live with it, but the rapid onset has sort of got me freaked out. In a way, I feel blessed to have been given this gift. But in another way, I also feel self-conscious about it. What the hell does all this mean, you know?"

As often is the case with friends, the discussion diverged into general chatting and catching up afterwards. It was finally decided to use one of the best treatments in medicine, especially when the diagnosis is unclear. "Tincture of time" would be the treatment for Logan's ailment, and they enveloped each other in a hug before Logan left for home.

Chapter 2

Mechanics and Chemistry

Logan was halfway home when his Porsche hovercraft lurched angrily once and then began to lose altitude. The hunched clouds growling over, black with the promise of a violent storm, sent shivers along his spine. He snapped his head around in search of a road on the ground below. Pinpointing a narrow path, he deployed his wheels and hit the backup power system. The hybrid gline, solar, and electric engine—the very latest market version—kicked in and thankfully operated perfectly. Logan peered up at the sky as another rumble of thunder split the angry clouds. Quickly weighing the advantages of going home against those of heading to the mechanic lest something else go wrong with the Porsche, he decided on the latter and adjusted his direction accordingly.

His mechanic, Marc, was on his way home when Logan pulled in for a quick inspection. Marc, in contrast to the trim and athletic Logan, was more belly than legs and with a wide grin to match his girth. He feigned a grumpy pout when the Porsche pulled in but didn't refuse Logan service. It was one of the things Logan liked about being a doctor; some people tended to treat you with a little more respect than usual and would fit you into their busy schedules.

There was the slight matter of being charged double or triple for the same service, but still, it was nice to be treated special.

After plugging the car's CPU into his analytic computer Marc quickly found the problem.

"Looks like the main chip in the mag-drive system is out. The chip's pretty easy to replace, but balancing the pole reciprocators can take the computer a couple hours to do. You understand how the mag-drive system works?" Marc asked.

"*How* it works? Well, I know it makes the car hover," Logan mumbled sheepishly.

"I hope you're better in medicine than you are in mechanics," Marc said, patting Logan's shoulder with a smile. The mechanic was also a patient of Dr. Logan Rainell, and they had known each other for years. Logan smirked back; the lighthearted banter was expected.

"Okay, first off you have two tri-analine magnets, one at each end of the car. The CPU has a sensor in it that analyzes the magnetic force of the earth's North and South Pole about a million times a second. It then sends electricity to the magnets at a cycle that is just opposite that of the earth's magnetic pole. That's what makes you hover. Are you still following?"

Logan adjusted his features into a perfect blank look. "Uh . . ." he drawled with a devious grin and a flicker in his bright blue eyes.

Marc rolled his eyes. "Alright, let me put this in terms you'll understand," he enunciated. "There are two magnets. Two mag-nets. Still following? Okay. So you have two magnets..."

"Oh, come on!" Logan interrupted with a laugh. "I get it, I get it. Keep going."

"Well, let's see . . . sending current to either the front or back magnet that is just slightly out of phase with the earth's magnetic pole will pull you either forward or backward. It's incredibly complex for the computer to analyze. I'm still amazed someone figured out the whole system."

"I wish I'd bought stock in Micro-dyn," Logan said with a sigh.

"I wish you had, too. I had been watching their R&D for a while and bought stock just before they came out with the mag-drive system. Now I don't need to work; I do so just to keep busy. I've got everything paid off, a huge principal, and live off the interest."

"Good job, Marc! Boy, that's one of those things that comes along maybe once every other lifetime."

"Yeah, it was pretty lucky," Marc said as he exhaled on his precisely cut fingernails and polished them on his shirt with pride. "Now then, about your hover. Seems like one of the magnetic bearings in the hybrid engine's electric generator has a crack in the magnet. 'Course you're still getting around 200,000 rpm, which is plenty of electrical output, but when that bearing goes—"

"I'll fall from the sky like a rock!" Logan interrupted.

"Nothing quite that dramatic," Marc reassured him. "The battery system's got enough juice to make sure you can land safely, but once that happens you'll be grounded until you get it fixed.

"There is some good news. The computer that balances the electricity between the two hover magnets is working well and the micro-engine is charging the mag-drive battery very efficiently. Even with the crack, it looks like you're averaging 232 mpg."

"Cool! I guess that sounds about right, but I still go through about three gallons of gline a month. And at its price, that's about two gallons too much."

Marc dug his fingers under his broad belt and wriggled his hips to pull up his pants a little. "You know doc, you're the only customer I have that calls that stuff by its real name. Everybody else still says gas," he said with a chuckle. Then he called out in a booming voice, "Roscoe!"

Moments later a man in oily clothes emerged from behind a sheet slung across the back of the garage. His fingers coiled around a heavy wrench, and Logan could not help but think how finely the man seemed to live up to his namesake.

"Roscoe, this is Dr. Logan Rainell," Marc said. "Doc, this is Roscoe."

"Good to meet you," Logan replied, raising his hand to shake. But when he noticed the sticky grease smeared over Roscoe's palms, he had second thoughts.

Roscoe grunted something that Logan assumed was a greeting.

Marc wrapped one thick arm around Logan's shoulders. "Listen, doc, I've got a favor to ask. Would you explain to Roscoe how they make gline?"

Logan blinked again, this time in genuine surprise. "Of course. Well, it's all really a very complex technical application of simple chemistry, and I'll just give you the basics.

"You know how gasoline used to come entirely from natural oil resources? Well, over the last few hundred years we've pretty much used up those resources. So they started to add alcohol, from corn fermentation, to gasoline in order to extend existing supplies." Logan paused. "Do you know what fermentation is?"

"I'm not an idiot," Roscoe said slowly with a pronounced Arkansas accent.

"Of course not! No offense meant," Logan said quickly, wondering what he'd gotten into. "Anyway, it all proceeded just fine for a while until they figured out how much gasoline was used in cultivating the fields and processing the corn into alcohol. Then they realized they used just as much gasoline as they saved and, in some cases,

24

even more. That's when they got the organic chemists involved."

"Yup, makes sense."

"So here's the part where it gets pretty tricky, but I'll make a long story short. Basically, the molecule that makes up wood, straw, old leaves, grass cuttings and all that kind of stuff is called cellulose. There are many different types of sugar, but the type of sugar we use in our bodies and one of the sugars used in fermentation is glucose. It took years, but after a while chemists found a way to take wood, old leaves or straw, put the materials into large vats, and break down the large chains of cellulose molecules, which are usually linked together to form wood, into single molecules of cellulose. Then they chemically found a way to convert those cellulose molecules into glucose molecules, which they ferment with yeast to make alcohol. That way, they end up with way more energy than they use to make it.

"They slowly kept increasing the amount of ethanol they put in gasoline so that it's now 90% ethanol and only 10% gasoline. At some point they changed the name to "gline," a combination of glucose and gasoline. Which is chemically not correct, but it sounds pretty good!" Logan paused and glanced between Marc and Roscoe. "Did that make sense?"

"Yup," Roscoe mumbled. As he turned to walk away, he added, "Gd eat ch."

Logan's eyes wandered over uncertainly to meet Marc's. "Good to meet you," the mechanic clarified.

"You too," Logan called out at Roscoe's retreating back. When the assistant had disappeared behind the sheet, Logan whispered to Marc, "Okay, so what was that all about?"

"See, Roscoe asked me the other day about making gline. I couldn't recall the exact details but remembered the time you told me about gline, so I figured . . ."

25

"How'd I do?"

"Perfect!"

Logan nodded towards the sheet that now concealed Roscoe, still a little perplexed. Marc seemed to understand and said, "Roscoe? Oh, he's a good ol' boy who is just a little slow. Plus he's from Arkansas, so you gotta give him a break. You know Arkansas: they've got great quartz crystals, Roscoe and that president."

They broke into laughter.

Chapter 3

Gramps

After arranging to leave his hover overnight with Marc, Logan set out on the short walk home. He thought about walking, the oldest form of transportation, and mankind's dependency on fossil fuels and the damage done by their use while winding his way through the mountain path. Since he lived in the Sandia Mountains east of Albuquerque, he had researched the area and knew that at one time the land had been considered a "high mountain desert" and had over 300 days of sunlight per year. Now because of the greenhouse effect, the East Mountain area was deemed a temperate rainforest. He enjoyed botany and liked the plants and greenery that abounded. Yet Logan also dreamed of what it would be like to see blue sky, wide and glittering with the promise of sunshine, for more than the 60 days per year they presently enjoyed.

Even then it wasn't a clear aquamarine expanse; the sky was usually dotted with towering cumulus clouds that would extend up to 30,000 feet. The thunder and lightning shows were, though spectacular, sometimes too intense. Too often Logan would jolt awake in his bed in the early morning hours, roused by the rolling drums of the storm. Other nights, it would be too loud to even sleep. He would then stand out on his deck to enjoy the show, though he couldn't help feeling that the heavens were being "rent asunder" as lightning grappled across the blackened clouds. It was ironic that mankind had invested enormous amounts of time and money into the development of solar power while burning up so much fossil fuel and taking such poor care of the air quality that solar power was rendered useless in many areas due to cloud cover. It saddened him to think how humans had done such a shit-poor job of taking care of earth. Although he was a doctor and trained in science, he found a deep truth in the beliefs of some of the ancient indigenous cultures that the earth was alive. Recognizing that also meant understanding that just as a sick human needs to be cared for and nurtured, so too does the earth. He only hoped it wasn't too late. On the other hand, he also believed in cycles and that the cycles the earth dealt with could be millions of years long.

He paused to consider an oddly shaped rock on the path. Kneeling with only a slight throb of protest from his back, Logan lifted the stone and turned it over in his hand. It was smooth, with notches on the sides, and unlike most rocks in the area. It reminded him of another unique object in his past, a frog.

When Logan was a child, his grandfather had many antiquated teaching objects he called "books." These strange collections of wafer-thin sheets called paper had wonderful pictures of dinosaurs and prehistoric creatures. He saw paintings of prehistoric rain forests and noted how similar the tangled growths of trees and plants seemed with the present day forests. Sadly, the biggest difference was in animal life. So many of the old species were extinct now. When he was a small child, his grandfather would often invite him to sit on his lap late into the evening hours while he told him tales about animals that were alive when he was young, like frogs. Logan had never seen one, but Gramps showed him a picture in a book and said he'd been lucky enough to have one as a pet when he was a boy. Gramps told him his frog's name was "Roo," as in kangaroo, because it could jump so far. It belonged to a species called a Bullfrog, though Logan never understood this as a boy. The frog didn't have horns, and it wasn't big like a bull. He always thought Jumpfrog or Smilefrog would have been a better name for this type of frog. But whatever its name, he was always sad when he remembered there were no more left. He asked his grandfather about why frogs had disappeared. Besides the usual reasons, which included habitat destruction, parasites and pollution, his grandfather also thought there was a more insidious cause.

Grandfather said their family was part Ute Indian and was originally from the region of Ouray, Colorado. According to family lore, many generations ago a German immigrant had settled in southern Colorado and married a Ute woman. Consequently, many Native American beliefs had been passed down in the family. One of these beliefs was that we are all one and that we are all part of a greater being. His grandfather enjoyed listening to the delicate classical music of Beethoven and Mozart. Grandfather used to say that no one was unto themselves. Everyone was "like a single note in a grand symphony." According to our family's sayings, each person had their place and no one "note" was more important than any other. And while no single note creates a symphony alone, it is quickly noticeable if one note is missing. Logan's grandfather said the Native Americans believed that everything in the natural world was part of a greater whole. The loss of any part would affect the whole. They not only believed in these principles; they acted upon them. When they killed a deer, they would thank the deer for its sacrifice and let the deer know it would live long as part of

29

the hunter. When they ate the deer, the protein would become part of them in more than physical terms and the deer's spirit would live on in each man. At times, though, such beliefs led to rather gruesome rituals like eating the heart of a great warrior to obtain his courage.

As a young boy, grandfather taught Logan we are all C.P.A.'s. What we do either "Creates," "Promotes," or "Allows" something to happen; hence, each individual is responsible for everything that happens in his or her life. Gramps also taught Logan that thoughts precede action. That God's thoughts collected energy into matter. That human thoughts would either support and promote the continued existence of a creature or would not. Gramps often said that "what you think about, you become or create." It became his idea, then, that the frogs died out because people stopped thinking they had a place in the world. People were more interested in hover cars, mining the moon or the Mars colony. Yet to truly live in harmony, Gramps said there had to be a balance between the physical and the spiritual world. People had to think enough about frogs to keep their spirit energy alive, especially because the loss of one species always affects many others. And although Logan had never seen a real frog, he missed them. Frogs would always have a place in his spiritual world.

Chapter 4

Cycles

Logan wasn't far from home when he walked across a boggy patch of plants on the path and noticed it was spongier than usual. Wondering why, he padded a few steps forward and found the answer. As he stepped down, several large farts of methane gas erupted beneath his feet in a gaseous cacophony. Which made sense, of course, since decomposing plant and animal life made gas and, given enough time and pressure, would turn into coal or oil deposits. He knelt and traced his fingers along the ground, beaming with the secret knowledge that he was witnessing one of the earth's cycles.

The first law of thermodynamics states that energy is not destroyed, it changes to different states of matter. And what a perfect example this was. These decomposing plants were changing from physical to gaseous state of matter. About 4.5 billion years ago when the earth was new there was so much carbon dioxide in the air that it created a dense greenhouse effect that warmed and moistened the planet and supported huge quantities of flora and fauna. Over millions and millions of years, the carbon dioxide levels in the atmosphere decreased as the carbon became bound up in a vast quantity of plants and animals. Then a large asteroid hit the Yucatan Peninsula 65 million years ago, causing a sweep of extinction worldwide across many species. Over millions of years this large mass of dead plant and animal life compressed and formed huge coal and oil deposits.

Eventually humans increased in intellectual capacity, which culminated in their ability to mine and utilize the oil and coal fields for their own means and ends. Now mankind has used up almost all of the fossil fuels of earth. Burning these fuels released the carbon trapped in decaying remains back into the air in its gaseous state as carbon dioxide. The increase in carbon dioxide and other forms of pollution caused another warm and wet greenhouse effect. Plants thrive in high carbon dioxide environments and so plant life is now abundant in New Mexico. That which was once a rainforest, became a desert, is now a rain forest again.

Logan knew this was part of earth's life cycle. There would eventually be another mass extinction, the carbon would turn to coal and oil and the next culture of industry would utilize it. After all, the first law of thermodynamics is a universal fundamental. He chuckled as he released his own methane in harmony with his footsteps.

Chapter 5

Love

Two bouncing bodies danced around him as Logan entered his home. Zeus and Loki greeted him with wagging tails and happy, smiling faces. They taught him so much about love. Dogs never had to decide if they wanted to show love. If they felt it, you knew it! His return home was always heralded by a five minute love fest by the front door, which was always welcome. When married, the first thing he often heard on his return was, "Take out the trash!"

Wagging tails. Excited yips. Chuffs and barks. He would always match their excitement with soft, sweet talk and plenty of scratching. But, inevitably both Zeus and Loki would be belly-up after about three minutes, legs dangling in the air and wagging tails now polishing the wooden floor.

It was then that he could really see their auras. He was always curious about the differences between the auras of his dogs and those of people. Human auras tended to be thicker and had different color layers. On the other hand, dogs and other animals tended to have smaller auras that were golden in color. But there were also several similarities. When happy or excited, the aura colors would brighten and swell in size as if spreading out to more fully encompass the individual.

Logan noticed that when people or dogs felt love for another, colorful fingers of light from one aura would reach out and intermingle with the other person's aura. Fingers of light from both auras would intertwine and dance in the air. After observing them for some while, he came to call the fingers of light that developed, *lingers*.

Not surprisingly, such *lingers* were abundant as they all greeted each other. Logan knelt to say hello and ran his fingers through his dogs' fluffy fur. Zeus pressed close to his friend's body and sniffed his hand, while Loki licked his arm. They liked to smell his breath to see where he had been, what he had eaten and what his general state of health was. But they soon settled down for more serious loving. Loki loved the physical contact of having her belly scratched. Zeus, on the other hand, seemed to enjoy more esoteric contact and liked to have his belly tickled. Logan began by allowing his fingers to dance along Zeus's belly in random sweeps of motion, but eventually he would lift his fingers so that only the lingers of his aura would be making contact with Zeus's belly. Zeus's eyelids would droop over his wide, dark eyes. His tail would pause in its ceaseless wagging and he would seem blissful. If Logan lifted his hand higher so the lingers no longer made contact with Zeus's belly, the Samoyed's eyes would lazily slide open and he would turn and twist his head to see what had happened. Once eye contact was made, the tail would start polishing the floor again to see if he could con his way into getting some more attention through the sheer blessing of his cuteness. Poor Zeus . . . how he suffered! Getting his belly tickled with aural lingers—the poor guy was abused!

The joyful reunion was interrupted by the gentle beep of a tel-chip, which was attached to the mastoid bone behind Logan's ear. He told it to save the message and decided he would call right back. At times he felt like he was a slave to the tel-chip. His doctor friends nicknamed it the electronic

34

dog leash, though he was glad he could remove his. He knew of some people—mostly drug dealers and stockbrokers—who had theirs permanently implanted onto the mastoid process. Bone conduction was the term officially used when the vibrations produced by the tel-chip traveled through the bone to the inner ear and produced sound. Historically, it had been part of the physical examination to determine hearing loss. A doctor would take a vibrating tuning fork, touch the end of the handle to the mastoid process behind the ear and then hold the vibrating tuning fork in front of the ear. He could then subjectively compare the change in hearing between bone conduction and air conduction. The tel-chip was another piece of technology Logan wished he had bought stock in. He finished giving belly scratches and tickles to his dogs and told the tel-chip to return the call.

Chapter 6

Love Number One

"I.C.U. Nurse Puckett speaking."

"This is Dr. Rainell. Did you call?"

"Oh, hi doc. Hold on, let me get her."

There was a pause for a few moments, and Logan listened to the soft sound of silence across the line.

"Hi Logan, this is Kersti."

Kersti Craddock was one of Logan's high school sweethearts, but he had loved her since the fifth grade. She seemed like such a clever little creature even then, always near the front of the classroom with her face reflecting the glow of her electronic reader. It amazed him how she was as beautiful now as she was 30 years ago in high school. He did not believe in coincidence, and the fact that they now worked at the same hospital was a nudge from God suggesting that he complete an amends that was long overdue.

Back when they were dating, she seemed like everything he could ever look for in a girl, even aside from her perfect physical attributes. Dark chestnut hair, black in certain light and brown in another, cascaded along her shoulders like a waterfall. Her glittering hazel eyes glowed blue in just the right luminescence.

When they hugged, his chin would rest on her head and scoop out a small valley in her hair. She used to say she felt like a baby bird being cuddled and protected. He loved to snuggle with her. She was intelligent and loving. They often murmured sweet nothings to one another late into the night. When they kissed, she tasted and smelled so good! He thought she was perfect and was deeply in love with her.

Yet he felt a bond with her that permeated deeper than her almond skin and went beyond physical beauty and carnal attraction. He loved her very soul, which confused him because it seemed so important and so special and so beautiful and yet . . . never had he heard another man speak of a woman's soul. Logan was so lost. He had no one he could talk to about his feelings. No one in his family, certainly. The best advice other guys could offer was, "Fuck 'em and forget 'em." But he knew he could never do that to her. Never! Still, he realized that as their relationship progressed she might expect it to turn sexual. Logan was a virgin, which—judging from the way his friends spoke—was abnormal. He felt ashamed of himself for it. No adults in his life had ever discussed love and sex with him, and he was uncertain and afraid. So whenever Kersti would begin to whisper sweetly in his ear or cuddle against him to elevate the atmosphere of intimacy, he would get another beer or light a joint. Evading her affections was the only way he knew to deal with the overwhelming emotions frothing within his own soul. The beer and joints numbed his fear and confusion but drove a wedge between them. Ashamed, confused and drugged, Logan quit calling her. He eventually moved from Colorado and lost contact with her. But he had always deeply missed her. Always thought of her. Always wondered what could have been. Whenever he remembered how he had treated her, a knife of guilt jabbed his heart. She did not deserve to be treated that way, and the way he ended their relationship was cruel.

He had thought of her endlessly for the past two weeks ever since she was introduced as one of the new I.C.U. nurses. After asking around, he found out she was married and had two teenagers. He knew he had to make amends as soon as possible, or he would go nuts!

Kersti had also deeply loved Logan. As a girl she would write in her journal in neat, curly scripture: *I love Logan Rainell and I don't know why.* When her mother found out, she got mad at her daughter and admonished. "It's only puppy love," her mother would say. "You don't know what true love is yet!" And maybe Kersti didn't have her mother's experience, but within her secret heart, she *knew*. She didn't know why, but she loved him. Truly and deeply. And when he disappeared from her life, she was crushed. And pissed.

But she never had the courage to call him either, as they were both so young. Kersti always thought of him, though, and still loved him even though he had treated her with such disrespect. Years later when she was already married with two kids, she had a vision of him with alcohol. It came in a dream, and she woke with a fluttering heart and a terrible illness somewhere in the pit of her stomach. Kersti wondered if Logan was in trouble. She was mad at him, but also worried about him and some distant part of her loved him even still.

When she saw him again in the hospital, he had transformed and become a very different boy. Not a boy, she realized, but a man now. Logan was a physician, tall and muscular, and still so handsome. Still with that long, sandy-blond hair. And those bright blue eyes. Always glittering, those eyes. She felt strangely conflicted. A part of her wanted to tear into that man like a wildcat with years of repressed rage. But there was another part that still heard a small voice whisper, "I love him, and I don't know why."

Torn between anger and love, she had also been

thinking of him for the past two weeks since their lives had intersected once again. And what a curious crossroads it was. Kersti finally decided it would boil down to their first few interactions. If he was still a jerk, she would admit her mother was right. Just puppy love. Nothing real. But if there was a changed man behind those eyes now . . .

*****

"Good evening, Kersti," he said formally, though he couldn't help but slip a little affection into his voice.

Kersti's response was professional. "I'm calling regarding Elizabeth Wagnar. Some members of her family are here and the rest will arrive in a couple of hours."

There was a whisper of static across the line.

"Have you eaten yet?" Logan asked boldly.

Kersti hesitated. "No," she said, and after another pause, "I haven't."

"Could I buy you dinner or a cup of coffee or something?"

"Well . . . I *am* hungry."

"Good! I'm on the east side of the mountain, but I'll hover over and see you in a little while." Logan tapped off the tel-chip while his stomach did flip-flop's from anxiety.

Since he lived on the other side of the mountain and was somewhat isolated, he was lucky his nearest neighbor, who was also a doctor, had a hov he could borrow. Anxious as he was for the imminent reunion, he also couldn't wait to see Kersti again. Taking off and rapidly clearing the top of the forest, he was surprised to see a rare break in the clouds. As he cleared the clouds above the mountains, he became part of a glorious sunset splashed across the sky. Above, spread a royal blue sky and a layer of bright orange clouds mottled with dark red blotches. Hunched at the horizon, the yellow sun dipped halfway out of sight. The domed acrylic canopy of the hovercraft reflected the orange and yellow light into the interior, painting a warm glow over everything. For a long while, Logan was awestruck by the beauty. Then he cleared the Albuquerque side of the mountains, dipped below the clouds and emerged back into the haze. The G.P.S. in the hov brought him down right on the hospital's rooftop landing pad.

Just as Logan was walking into the I.C.U., Kersti was walking out.

"Hi Kersti."

"Hello, Logan," she replied, allowing her steps to drift towards the cafeteria. "The rest of Elizabeth's family are on their way in, so I'm going off shift for dinner. I told the I.C.U. to tell you I would be in the cafeteria. I hope your interaction with them won't be too difficult. I think they—or should I say she, Elizabeth's sister—have finally realized her condition is terminal."

"Sometimes I have a hard time with people who think mainstream medicine is inherently evil," Logan said softly, voice weary with memories. "They think herbs and vitamins can cure anything. I think I finally made an impact on her family when I described my belief that all aspects of medicine work some of the time but that none of them work all of the time. I told them I believe medicine is a long continuum. On one end lies perfect health and on the other is death. As you drift away from perfect health, herbs, acupuncture, vibrational energy work, osteopathic and chiropractic adjustments are good options to keep optimal health. If your health declines, prescription medicines and surgery may be needed to maintain health. As you get worse and closer to death nothing is going to help. Still, it amazes me how some people think if they just find the right combination of herbs it will cure metastatic cancer. You won't believe this, but Elizabeth's sister did back flips— almost literally, I swear—trying to get her chiropractor on

41

staff here to take care of Elizabeth. Chiropractors don't have a full range of medical training. You know, I've worked with her chiropractor for many years and not only like him as a man but also respect his knowledge of herbs and natural therapeutics. But I get frustrated and upset when I see how cases like this are handled."

"Okay," he added with a chuckle as he gently held her elbow. "Thank you for letting me rant and rave. I've wanted to say all that for a while."

"Oh, you're doing such a good job and I didn't want to interrupt," Kersti said with a small smile. She tried to focus on Logan's face, but her eyes darted away in confusion. Because she'd seen Logan smile just now, she couldn't help but immerse herself in old memories. His lips creased at the corners and curved slightly, eyes glowing . . . it was the same smile she had known as a child. But there was something more to this smile. Something more peaceful. Perhaps he was a different and even a better man.

"Kersti?"

She suddenly noticed he was staring at her. His lips folded into another smile. She knew why; she had stopped in the middle of the hallway, just blankly absorbing his features. "I'm fine," she said quickly. "I want you to tell me more about this case. I really like Elizabeth and her husband, Everett."

"Oh. Alright . . . I agree they're wonderful people. They are actually two of my favorite patients. Besides raising three wonderful kids, they've done a lot for the community. They sit on boards and are major contributors of both time and money to philanthropic organizations around town. And they both volunteer in hospitals. I've seen them around sometimes when they read to the older patients and play holographic games with the younger ones. You should see Everett play some of these holo games! Here the guy is in his eighties and he'll have his V.R. eyepiece on and be bouncing

42

around the room in his spaceship shooting down aliens! Elizabeth will play too, though she's usually not as animated.

"You won't believe what happened one time, though! A while back a little boy who was dying of a cancer resistant to nanobots said he wanted to see Elizabeth play against Everett. And not just have two teams play against the computer; he wanted them to play against each other. He wanted Elizabeth to be the evil alien and Everett to be the hero from the united federation. Well, here's what happened: Elizabeth sat down in a big armchair in the room, slapped on her V.R. Eyepiece and placed her hands on the V.R. control panel of the spaceship. Her sweet face morphed into an evil look like some demon had possessed her and whenever she shot something down she made a low, evil laugh . . . sort of like *huh!huh!huh!* Everett did his usual bounce and weave around the room, but Elizabeth gave him a good run for his money. Everett came out on top in the end, but all the doctors and nurses on the floor were watching. I've never laughed so hard in my life!" Logan finished, laughing just from the memory. Hearing him laugh after so long made Kersti's heart melt—just a little.

Kersti, you should see Elizabeth's aura, Logan thought. It was vibrantly layered with many colors and almost twice as thick as her body size. The inner layers glowed with every color of the rainbow—reds, oranges, yellows, greens, blues, a little indigo, and even some violet sprinkled in. There were probably 20 distinct layers! When they coalesced, the colors would blend and weave hues he had never seen or even dreamed could exist. Each color flamed with an internal light. The intensity reminded him of the stained glass windows at the National Cathedral in Washington D.C. on a bright, sunny day.

The outer edge of her aura was the most brilliant of all. It flared with a bright golden color that undulated in constant motion and looked like molten gold in a stream bed rippling over pebbles. To top it off, the *tour de force,* her lavender lingers flashed from the edges of her golden aura. They would brighten with bursts of light at times of emotional activity. He had noticed such activity in other people's auras, but Elizabeth's was quite pronounced.

Once Logan noticed Elizabeth in the waiting room when no one was around. Her aura was quiet, and not flickering with much activity. When he entered the room, though, not only did her aura brighten but also long lingers reached out to him, almost pleading for his own lingers to reciprocate. His responded immediately and "linger hugged" as they got closer. When Logan finally crossed the room and stood close to her, he felt warm and comforted and wondered what they looked like from a distance. He supposed it was probably similar to the way it looked when she was with her husband. It was interesting to observe that whenever they were together their auras would blend, brighten and dance together in a spectacular swirl of color. It was a good lesson in mixing primary colors! From a distance, the caress of her golden bands against his blue ones would make both appear temporarily green. It also seemed that for a period of time after they separated both of their auras remained brighter. Each would also share some of the colors of the other person. Over time, though, each person's aura would return to the way it looked prior to contact.

"Anyway," Logan said, snapping back to the present conversation, "you asked about her condition. Let's see . . . well, Elizabeth was in my office about a year ago with an unusual skin lesion. Thank God I did a biopsy and covered my butt legally, though in retrospect it didn't really make much of a difference. The biopsy turned out to be an amelanotic melanoma."

"I saw that in the chart but don't know what it is," Kersti admitted.

"Join the crowd," Logan said. "Not many people have

even heard of it because it's exceedingly rare. You know, regular malignant melanoma is a cancer of the skin cells that produce melanin, which is the substance that gives us the color in our skin. So, normally, a melanoma lesion is black, blue or even has areas of red on a black or blue background. But what's important is it's obviously noticeable because of the dark color. The amelanotic melanoma lacks all of those colors, and hers was a tan, bumpy lesion about the size of a quarter on her right shoulder. It had gotten so big because it lacked the colors that would usually make a doctor suspicious. The chiropractor ignored it. I was worried when I saw it but didn't know what it was, so the dermatologist and I did a full workup. After a wide excision and a lymph node exam, we received the pathology report and the true diagnosis. Maybe that would have helped, but here's the terrible part: Her family refused our recommendations and said they were going to seek care with her chiropractor. I pleaded and pleaded with her to not proceed that way. Finally, she came in with her sister one time."

"Oh, God!" Kersti moaned softly.

"Exactly! And she proceeded to give me an earful about how they had the right to seek any care they want. I agreed with her but went over all of the risks again, all to no avail. Unfortunately, the whole family and especially her sister seem to have an inordinate amount of influence over Elizabeth. She'll practically do anything they say. Anyway, the next time I saw Elizabeth was two weeks ago in the E.R. after she had a seizure. The magnetic holograph showed that metastasis had spread to her liver, lungs and brain. When the nanobots failed to remove all the cancer, we realized the condition was terminal."

They had by now reached the cafeteria. Both grew quiet as they waited in the food line with their trays. Since he was physically close to Kersti, Logan allowed himself to be entranced watching their auras interact and dance with brilliance. Their auras together were magnificent! It was only after a long pause that Kersti spoke again.

"Do you have a hard time dealing with people who are dying?"

"I used to," Logan admitted softly, "but not anymore. I now find it an honor to be in someone's company when they are dying. You know, when I was an undergraduate I had a work study job at O.M.I.—that's the Office of Medical Investigators. We performed autopsies on all of the questionable deaths in the state. All the murders, suicides and accidental deaths. It was really the best anatomy class I ever had. I was actually bored with anatomy class in medical school; in fact, I hated it! In med school, the bodies don't look real. All of the tissue is a dull tan color, and the bodies smell like formaldehyde! Fresh bodies have definite color and texture changes between tissues. The heart is red like a muscle should be, the liver is brown and the lungs are a tan-pink. Blood is red. I hope all this doesn't sound terribly strange, but it's really all a very interesting process. It's just too bad that when they preserve bodies with formaldehyde, everything turns gray and loses its individual texture; by the end, everything feels like tanned leather.

"On the other hand," he emphasized, "at least there are no maggots crawling up your arms while you're trying to work. I remember one time in the decomp room—that's short for "decomposition"—we were working as fast as we could and still had maggots flooding up the walls to the doorknob by the time we were done. We had them swarming up our arms to our shoulders, which is when we got worried because the decomp suits are open at the neck. We had to keep shaking our arms to get them to drop off. Maggots," Logan spat, cringing. "There's nothing like them. Hey, by the way, are you going to eat your rice?"

Kersti's left eye twitched. "Very funny," she mumbled. "Now I've practically lost my appetite."

46

"Just a little O.M.I. humor," Logan said, beaming. "You don't want to get me started on my O.M.I. Stories!"

"Well, yeah," Kersti said, breaking into a silly accent. "That's kind of the idea, not getting you started."

"Well, fine," Logan said indignantly.

"O-kay."

"Fine, then."

"All right."

Silence lingered for a few moments until they both burst out laughing. Kersti slid her tray into his, remembering the casual way they used to banter back and forth, and smiled. For a brief instant their arms touched. Logan lost his concentration and a chill trickled up his spine as he noticed the vibrant emerald green and deep indigo blue of her aura. Her lingers reached out, as did his, and together they swirled and played there in the lunch line. Logan felt like a deer trapped in the burning headlights of a car. He also felt overwhelmed with love for her, and it became an effort simply to walk down the food line.

"Where was I?" he said quickly, meaning more than his words let on. "One of the beliefs I formed while doing autopsies was that we are this wonderfully complex biological package that carries something else around, our soul. You've probably had the experience of knowing someone you were close to and being present when they died. They always look different in those last few moments, and you know something's changed."

"Besides that they're dead, you mean," she whispered. A distant look in her eyes, but she was smiling.

Smiling back, he couldn't help but think how beautiful she was. Forcing his mind to momentarily abandon that track of thought, Logan added, "And besides the fact that their facial muscles are completely without muscle tone for the first time in their life. But that's not what I really mean. There's something else, something different." He thought for the first time that he had not seen anyone die since he had been given this gift of seeing auras. A shard of deep sadness cut through his heart as he realized this would soon change with Elizabeth's death.

"I do know what you mean," Kersti said gently. "It's like the light, or their spirit, has left."

"Funny you should put it that way . . . "

"What do you mean?"

"Oh, nothing much. I was just thinking of something."

"And you're not going to tell me?" Kersti said with a wicked grin.

"No, it's not that I don't want to tell you. It's just that it's sort of an incomplete thought."

"All I have are incomplete thoughts, so one more will fit right in!" Kersti said, laughing. "Hell, it might just complete one of my partial thoughts and then we'll have a single complete thought!"

"That sounds dangerous."

"It might be," Kersti said. The dark charm still glowed in her smile.

"I heard somewhere," Logan said, remembering his AA meetings, which he didn't quite feel she needed to know about just yet, "that we are not physical creatures trying to learn a spiritual existence, but rather, we are spiritual creatures who are trying to learn from a physical existence."

"I like that. It takes the pressure off, you know? If we're already spiritual beings, all we have to do is learn from this physical plane as best as we can."

"Exactly," Logan agreed. "I was talking earlier about what an honor it is to be with someone who is dying. For me, it's about sharing one of the most intimate events a person can experience. Most people I've been with during the dying process have been fearful to a lesser or greater extent of death. It seems like all of them, regardless of their spiritual level of awareness, have a moment of clarity just before they die. When everything becomes clear and the fear goes away. Maybe questions are answered. Maybe they see loved ones. But for that brief moment they seem blissful."

"I've heard scientists say it's all because of a sudden release of endorphins, dopamine, blah, blah, blah," he added sarcastically. "But I think there's something more to it. I doubt that the scientists who are coming up with those theories have actually sat with 100 or more people during the dying process. That's one of the concerns I have regarding suicide, aside from all of the religious concerns. What if many of the questions you have about your life are answered in that final moment of clarity? The act of suicide may rob you of those answers. If it does, are the lessons of this life lost? Do you have to come back and do it again?"

They had found a table and set down their trays. Logan paused to chew a bite of food and wondered if he was being too philosophical. "Since you're a nurse, you must have seen some interesting death experiences, too," he said, hoping she didn't think he was completely nuts.

Chapter 7

Amends

Kersti was feeling playful.

"Yeah, yeah, enough about philosophical death," she said with a smile. "Let's hear more stories about maggots and autopsies."Logan tried to speak but suddenly felt as if his voice had caught in his throat. He couldn't find the words, any words, to say to Kersti. After their long separation, he realized that simply seeing her was enough. Any speech seemed like too much and would shatter the lasting spiritual blessing of that moment.

"I have really missed you," he said softly at last.

"I've . . . I've missed you, too," Kersti replied, surprised by the abrupt change in topic. Uncertain as to Logan's intentions, she tried to steer the conversation back to their earlier discussion. "I agree with what you said and have had similar experiences. While you were talking, I was thinking about how this is one of those topics that cannot be fully appreciated by people who have not experienced it for themselves, even when someone else is describing it." She faltered, still impacted by the emotion in Logan's voice only a few moments earlier. Not entirely certain if she wanted to return to the emotional part of the conversation, she said instead, "I hope that when I die, I'm not in a hospital—or, even worse, a nursing home."

Following her lead, Logan said, "I'll second that motion. My grandfather used to tell me stories about how Native Americans looked at death differently from us and were not afraid of it. They seemed to somehow know when their time was up, and when that moment came they would say goodbye to their loved ones, go sit beneath their favorite tree on the mountain and consciously release their spirit. I don't know if I'm that spiritually evolved, but I think that is way cool!"

"That does sound like a nice, peaceful way to die," Kersti quietly agreed.

They lapsed into silence as they continued to eat. Fully absorbed in distant memories, Kersti picked at her meal with a fork but barely lifted the utensil to her lips. Logan stabbed his food a few times as well, but he was watching Kersti more than his own plate. Her gentle eyes lingered on her plate, and it almost seemed as if she was avoiding his gaze. After a few minutes, Logan broke the silence.

"Seriously, I do want to say something about us."

Kersti set her fork down, but her eyes remained fixed on her food as if some secret of the universe was buried in the mashed potatoes.

"Kersti?"

Her gaze flickered up and met his. She seemed calm enough to Logan, but little did he know that her composed appearance belied bubbling anxiety.

"First off, I want to set your mind at ease. I know you're married, and I don't want you to mistake this as a come-on. But as I mentioned, over the years I have thought of you often. I have regretted the way I ended our relationship. It goes without saying that I was just a kid and, in hindsight, it was obvious I had a problem with alcohol and drugs. Whenever we had the opportunity to increase our . . . well, our *intimacy*, though I'm not just referring to physical contact, I would jump up for another beer. Aside from the fact that I was a virgin and scared to death that I might look like I didn't know what I was doing, there's something else you need to know to understand my actions."

Logan paused for a moment, searching Kersti's eyes for signs of disgust that he was bringing up the past. Yet he saw nothing but a glow in the deep pools of her eyes and knew he could go on. "I grew up in an alcoholic family where having feelings—or, God forbid, talking about feelings—was something I never learned how to do," he continued quickly before he lost the nerve to tell Kersti what he meant to say years ago. "I have been clean and sober now for 24 years, and over these past years I have struggled to get in touch with my feelings. So I want to apologize to you about how I behaved. I was wrong and can see how my behavior was very hurtful to you. We g-got . . . we got along so well," he choked out, feeling a threatening lump swell in his throat. "I loved you so much, and then I just stopped calling you. Didn't tell you it was over, didn't tell you to go fly a kite, d-didn't . . . I didn't tell you anything. I just disappeared from your life."

Eyes wet and glistening, Logan mopped up streaks of hot tears from his face with a sleeve. "I-I don't want to sound like I'm making excuses now," he said quietly, struggling to keep the pain from his voice, "but at the time it was all I knew how to do. That was what was modeled to me in my family. When you had a problem with someone, you didn't talk to them about it. In my family, you were taught to give them the cold shoulder and disappear. That was done to me time and time again, and I know how painful it is to be on the receiving end of it. It's sad that as much as I hated it being done to me, that's exactly what I did to you. To you, Kersti, the only person I ever truly loved. The only one who touched me deeper than any physical brush of fingers on skin or words in your ear. You touched my soul, and all I could do to thank you was hurt you. I am sorry! So sorry, Kersti, and I can't even begin to . . . but, no. I can't believe myself; I'm starting to sound like the victim when in fact I am the perpetrator. But I guess that's how this dynamic works. The victims turn into perpetrators!" his voice laden with passion and lips trembling.

Quickly realizing his emotions had overwhelmed him, Logan squirmed in his chair and composed himself. "Anyway," he said softly, "the bottom line and the thing I wanted to say is that I have always loved you." Tears rolled along Logan's cheeks, tracing small rivulets along his cheekbones. His heart thundered a terrible tattoo within his chest as he hoped beyond hope that somehow Kersti would understand and forgive him. "Please, I . . . I would never do anything to hurt you. What I did back then was not your fault. I want you to know that, and I want to apologize."

There was a long, disconcerting pause. Kersti blinked and the hazel in her eyes seemed to recede. Was it fear he saw in her eyes? Hatred, even? Had he only compounded his woes and trapped his heart forever in a dark void, never to know that Kersti—his beautiful love once and always—had forgiven him? Logan almost gasped when her small hand reached across the table to gently touch his cheek. She rubbed the tears glazing his cheeks into his skin like they were part of a precious anointment. Her lips parted, and at first only a single soft breath escaped. Then she whispered, her own eyes shining with tears, "Thank you for saying that." She paused before continuing in a voice that quivered with sobs, "I thought I was going crazy at times. I loved you so much and didn't understand what happened. I thought I had done something wrong and didn't know what to do. Eventually, the pain lessened and life went on. But I carried the wounds in my heart . . . until now. Thank you for . . . everything."

Logan's fingers slowly glided along her arm until his hand was pressed over her own. He gently held her hand against his cheek and wove his fingers among hers. Silent tears rolled down both faces.

As if suddenly connected in mind and spirit, they both stood and hugged. Oh, God! What a hug it was! They were like two magnets united together! Unbreakable! The heat and energy they felt between them was intense. Logan pressed against her in awe, holding her and watching their two auras mix and—

The emotional bond was suddenly shattered by the electronic chirp of both their tel-chips. "I'll be right there," Kersti said to the chip. For Logan's sake she explained, "That was the I.C.U. The rest of Elizabeth's family has arrived."

"I know," he said, having received the same message. "I'm glad we had lunch and I got to make amends."

"Me, too," Kersti said, beaming. "Let's do it again sometime."

"You mean I have to say all that again?"

"No silly. Let's have lunch again," Kersti replied coyly.

"Oh. I can do that!"

"Though after all this time, I should make you apologize again!"

They shared another wonderfully healing hug, and Logan realized he did not want to let go. When he did finally release Kersti, she just kept clutching him as if he was her very lifeline. With a soft sigh he realized he was forgiven, and he hugged her again and even harder.

Chapter 8

The First Death

Elizabeth's family was already in the waiting room by the time Logan and Kersti approached the I.C.U. There were six relatives in all, yet aside from one woman who was quite tearful and being comforted by another they all somehow seemed out of place surrounded by the stark white hospital walls. A couple of relatives were huddled in a corner, reading magazines and chatting softly. A small man sitting alone caught Logan's eye; though his face was wrinkled and faded, he was staring up at the ceiling with a sharp, clear gaze and seemed deep in thought. And of course there was Elizabeth's sister, dominating the center of the room with a cold, defiant stare. Her hands were folded into neat fists and pressed against her hips; she seemed very much in control. But in her eyes—in all their eyes—there glittered a distant sadness that stirred Logan's soul. His heart went out to them in empathy, and he couldn't help but think that here, in front of him, is the microcosm in the way people deal with death and dying. Denial, anger, depression, bargaining and hopefully at some point, acceptance.

He hadn't noticed that Kersti's hand had found his until she suddenly gently squeezed his fingers in silent support. Their eyes met for a brief moment before her shy gaze flitted away and focused on an interesting panel on the floor. A soft blush painted her cheeks, though she did not release his hand for another few moments. With a smile to her, he at last went into the waiting room and said hello.

The small man's crystal eyes immediately locked with Logan's. "How is she doing?" he asked.

Logan gave a small, sympathetic smile and shrugged his shoulders slightly. "About the same."

Although he did not share it with the family as doing so would be breaking Elizabeth's confidentiality, he remembered a conversation he and Elizabeth had last week. *"They are still scrambling around trying to find a new combination of herbs that will help me, and I'm sitting here dying!"* she had said. The dying process was difficult for everyone, but watching her family stuck in denial was particularly awful.

In fact, he remembered that conversation as if it were only yesterday. Hazy, yellow morning light leaked through the open window that morning. The air was thick with moisture and smelled like fresh dew. Logan sat on Elizabeth's bed and quietly held her hand as they spoke.

"You know, I'm going to miss that," she said faintly.

"What's that?"

"Dew. The tickle of dew in my nose first thing in the morning."

"I-I know you will," Logan barely choked out, thinking how much he loved the smell of a dew-saturated morning.

Elizabeth slowly rolled over to lie on her side, her frail body out of place beneath the heavy covers. Her gaze was distant yet intent. She peered out the window, inundated with thoughts.

"I think Everett knows . . ."

"Knows what?"

"That I'm dying," she said bluntly. "But I don't think the others have a clue."

Logan shifted on the bed to make eye contact, and Elizabeth turned to meet his gaze. The withered sadness of her faded irises seemed to veil a distant glow, the glow of a loving spirit.

"Many years ago a Dr. Elizabeth Kubler-Ross wrote a landmark book called *On Death and Dying*," Logan said. "We still refer to it today. She said that every dying person and everyone in that person's family goes through five stages of grieving. There's denial—"No, this can't be happening! Not to me! Not now!""

"That's where most of my family is," Elizabeth whispered. She glanced at the window again.

"Seems like it, huh?" Logan agreed sympathetically. "And then there's anger—'How could God do this to me? I will not let it happen! I'll fight with every ounce of strength I have—'"

"That's where my sister is," she interjected.

"Is it ever!" Logan agreed.

Her eyes flickered back to his face and roved across it, tracing the outlines of his cheekbones and nose and the loose strands of hair curled across his forehead. Curling her lips into a smile, she mouthed something inaudible.

"Could you repeat that?" Logan asked.

"Is she giving you headaches?"

Logan flushed with embarrassment. "No, she's fine." Elizabeth pursed her lips in a mock pout, and he added, "No, really, it's alright. As I was saying, there's also bargaining —'Okay, just get me through this and I'll change. I'll be better. I'll give God 30% of the net profits!'"

Elizabeth laughed and Logan beamed at her happiness. The laugh morphed into a cough, and suddenly she was hacking into a handkerchief clutched in her thin fingers.

"Are you okay?" Logan asked gently. His hand twitched forward to rest on her shoulder. It was a comforting gesture for her, but the angled bones protruding into his palm startled him. Elizabeth had always seemed small; now her body was slowly wasting into dust.

"Yes, I'm alright," she said, setting down the hankie. She managed a smile. "You never told me I could buy myself out of this condition."

"I wish you could," he whispered, squeezing her hand. "I would donate." Each frail bone in her tiny pale fingers dug into his skin. "Amazingly, people really think that way when they are stuck in the bargaining stage," he added. "And then comes depression—'I've been good all my life, it's not fair, it's just not fair.' Then an agonizing depression ensues."

Her lips folded into another weak smile. "Well doc, I've identified some of my family in each of those stages."

"Hopefully at some point everyone will reach acceptance. 'I am going to die,' they'll say. 'I don't have to like it, but I accept that there can be no other outcome.' When people reach acceptance, they stop wasting their time and energy and focus on what is most important—the love shared and given to them by their family members. Acceptance rescues people from the struggle against death and allows them to feel love for those around them again."

Their eyes locked once more. The glow was brighter, glistening, and Logan knew it was understanding he saw in her gaze.

"Logan?"

She rarely called him by his first name. It was usually 'doc" or "doctor" out of respect for his profession. He knew this was to get his attention.

"Yes Elizabeth?"

"Will . . . will you do something to help them? Please, talk to them . . ."

"We can worry about them later," he said. "Right now, focus on yourself."

"Logan." Her fingers danced across his palm, gently stroking the creases in his skin. "Please. Talk to them. I want them to understand." She paused, catching her breath. "I only want them to understand," she whispered.

He nodded. "I will, Elizabeth."

"That's fine, that's good, I only want . . ."

She couldn't go on.

Logan was about to speak when he found himself simply staring at her. Elizabeth's aura was flicking like a faint flame caught in a sudden draft.

"I want to see them," she said. "I want them to come here on their own terms and understand. I want them to forgive themselves; none of this is their fault. Because they blame themselves. They say it's their fault, *theirs*, theirs alone and if only they had acted faster or otherwise then things would be different."

Eyes closed and lips slightly open, she murmured something beneath her breath.

"But I want them to know. And understand. There is life beyond death, and this is only the beginning for me. Denial will only hurt them. *Plague them.*"

Lifting one hand, she traced an invisible sign in the air that held some secret meaning for her alone and no other living soul.

"In understanding lies love. In faith lies hope."

The outer edge of her aura burned with a flaming fervor, while the inner edge flickered.

"In hope . . . in love . . ."

Elizabeth fell back onto the covers, still murmuring to herself. Logan watched as her aura settled into its usual sleepy state, curled up peacefully around this beautiful woman.

His fingers roamed to the tel-chip . . .

"I love you."

Logan froze. "What?"

She laughed, so faintly he could barely hear. "That's what I want to tell them. It's all I have left to say. If only they would come and I could say those words, I'll begin my next journey in peace."

In a sudden spasm, her fingers dug into the linens encasing her in a silken cocoon. Eyelids fluttering, her mouth twitched in pain. Logan wondered if beyond that physical agony she could still feel the peaceful soul that always was and *is* Elizabeth. Or perhaps she felt tortured and tormented by the nearly ceaseless pain.

"And if only I could say that . . . if only I could tell them I love them. That I forgive them. That I have always, *always* loved and forgiven them. If I could say that, we could all move on to life. To love. To peace."

She paused.

"Logan. My doctor. My friend. Convince them."

His warm hands blanketed her cold ones. "I will, Elizabeth. I swear I will."

"Amen, love. And thank you."

She pressed a kiss to his hand and lay back on her pillow, hair billowing in a cloud about her head. Smiling, at peace, in love with life. With the universe. With the beyond.

"I swear, Elizabeth," he breathed.

*****

Logan sat down with the family and lovingly, though honestly, told them that Elizabeth was dying and nothing more could be done. He started to cry with them when he told them what a wonderful person she was and how much he would miss her. Wiping away the tears, he proceeded to tell them that sometimes dying people stay around in order to give the families they are leaving behind time to get used to the fact that they are indeed dying. This, he believed, was precisely what was happening with Elizabeth. Sometimes the best thing families can do is simply to tell their dying loved ones how much they love them, what they've meant to them and they will miss them, but it is okay for them to let go. Logan explained that everyone reaches that understanding in their own fashion and in their own time, and there's no easy or perfect way to say it. But it really helps the dying to hear those things and makes their passing easier. He added, "It's a strange way to look at it, but it's meant to show the dying person that you've come to terms with their death and so are, in a way, giving him or her permission to die. Which helps the dying, because they are worried about you!"

Evidently, this discussion helped.

"We talked about what you said, doctor, and most of us agreed that you're right," the eldest daughter said. "And even if you're wrong, what harm is there in telling her how much we love her, what she's meant . . . ." She paused for a few deep breaths, and when she went on her voice was shaking with emotion. "So we've just finished going in one by one and saying goodbye."

"I'm so glad you decided to do that," Logan said with relief. "How did it go?"

They went on to tell him what their experiences were like. Some of them cried while pouring forth memories while others remained as objective as if they were presenting a book report. Logan couldn't help but think how while death is such a natural and important part of life, most of us have no training for or even an understanding of the dying process. It happens to everyone, yet most of us spend the majority of our lives thinking that somehow we will outmaneuver the grim reaper. *Even I do it*, Logan thought. After all, it was so culturally ingrained in our society—the notion of the grim reaper! Why not the "joyful reaper?" Or the "new adventure guide?" Most of us avoid even thinking about death. When our thoughts do alight upon it, we tend to put death in such a negative light that it's no wonder we try to avoid it. Then when it comes our time to die or a loved one is dying, we don't have a clue as to how to handle the situation because we've never discussed it and barely thought about it.

When each had finished sharing, Logan thanked every family member for having the courage to accept Elizabeth's new journey and telling her so. "It takes a lot of courage to do what you did for Elizabeth and for yourselves. Thank you again!" Then he excused himself to see Elizabeth.

The hospital's I.C.U. was set up as a semicircle. A crescent-shaped desk with an elevated panel around its circumference stood in the center of the room. The small raised section of the desk held all the monitors for the hospital rooms. Logan remembered pictures of older hospitals where an entire wall would be allocated for the monitors of an I.C.U. Also following the semicircle design were the patient rooms of the care unit, which were located along the outer perimeter of this larger space. A glass wall complete with a sliding glass door separated the patients' rooms from the nurse's desk and monitors. From the nurse's desk, it was easy to look out and see each patient. Patients could get privacy by shutting the glass door and activating the window tint. But unless the patient was taking a bath or having a medical procedure done, they usually kept the windows clear and the door open.

Logan sat at the desk and examined Elizabeth's chart and latest lab tests on the monitor. He glanced into Elizabeth's room and saw Kersti adjusting the telemetry unit. Everett, Elizabeth's husband, was sitting beside his wife and holding her hand. They both looked tearful. Her lips were moving, but she must have been speaking softly because Logan heard nothing.

Kersti soon finished what she was doing and, leaving the door open, walked towards Logan. An enigmatic look was plastered across her face.

"What's happening?" Logan asked with concern.

"Elizabeth told Everett what all of the kids and the family said to her," she explained, her voice somewhat pained. "They were both crying. Elizabeth said she was so grateful that her family had come to see and accept the truth about the situation. Before Everett arrived, she and I had a nice conversation. She wanted me to thank you for what she assumed was your part in her family finally accepting that she was dying. Elizabeth said s-she . . . she loves you" Kersti choked out, eyes swollen with tears. "I told her you would be right in and she could thank you herself. She said that would be okay, but when she spoke it was in a funny, dreamlike tone of voice. I was going to call—"

Kersti froze in mid-sentence when they both heard a loud gasp from Everett. "Oh, baby . . . please, Elizabeth . . . please, not now!" he sobbed.

Logan looked up in time to see Elizabeth's lips form the word *yes*. She fumbled with something on her finger for a moment, and Logan recognized it as her wedding ring. She placed it in her husband's hand and closed his fingers around it. "It is time," she said. "Remember always that I love you. You have given me my children and 63 years of life with you. I will always be with you. Always!" One of her trembling hands rested on his cheek, and she stroked his face one last time. Smiling faintly, she squeezed his hand and closed her eyes. Everett slumped onto her bed and quietly cried.

A sudden flatline buzz from a monitor startled Logan and Kersti. They realized that all of the readings on Elizabeth's monitor were at zero. They exchanged a tearful glance. Neither remembered ever witnessing such a sweet, peaceful death. Kersti was awed not only at the way Elizabeth just died but also at the memory of the conversation she shared with Logan over lunch about being able to consciously release one's spirit. It was a little spooky for her to witness exactly that and only a few hours later. For his part, Logan was grateful they had gotten a "do not resuscitate" order, a D.N.R. No one would go in and do sonic chest compressions, electric cardioversion, or any other number of procedures that would accomplish little aside from causing total chaos and disrupting this beautiful, peaceful and loving death. A strange sort of deep love for Elizabeth seized him. He felt how much he would miss her; a single tear rolled down his cheek. He felt honored to be part of this culmination of her life.

What happened next shocked him. The aura encasing Elizabeth intensified in brightness and enlarged in size until it filled the entire room. It was so bright that Logan was forced to squint. The brightness continued to expanded out and passed through the walls of the room. Within seconds the colorful aura around Elizabeth was gone. Logan was filled with a sense of awe as he watched this sacred event. Curiously, Elizabeth's aura didn't simply leave her body; it redistributed around the room. One of the other nurses Elizabeth was close to had gotten some. Both Kersti and Logan also received a little, but Everett got the most of her brilliant aura. For a few moments Logan wasn't certain what he was witnessing, but when it suddenly hit him he gasped. The first law of thermodynamics; energy cannot be destroyed and instead only changes states of matter, was in action before him! He had just seen it happen! He felt Kersti's hand find his, and her fingers squeezed in between his own. Though she could not see the auras, perhaps she too felt something change. He hoped that some day he could tell her what he just witnessed.

He was frozen in awe as he watched the transformation of energy. Usually, he had a hard time seeing his own aura unless he concentrated on it. Well, he certainly was concentrating now! As he looked at his forearm, he saw the layers of Elizabeth's aura had condensed into a thin band consisting of all her different colors. Elizabeth's outer layer—

the golden one with purple lingers—was not nearly as wide as when it was surrounding Elizabeth's body, but her aura was now layered on top of his aura. Normally the outer layer of his aura was a deep emerald green, and he too had purple lingers. Yet now he simply sat transfixed as he watched Elizabeth's aura coalesce and blend with his own.

Never had he seen anything as incredible as the two auras migrating and mixing in a glowing dance. As the colors passed, they separated into shafts of colored light. It reminded him of the way beams of light filter through clouds. As the emerald and gold beams of light passed each other, millions of small sparks of every color imaginable formed. It was the most amazing light show he'd ever seen. And when the migration was complete, the emerald-green layer of his aura had returned to the top. The layers of her aura had fully condensed beneath his original aura, and he could only see her outer golden layer. He suddenly became aware of an odd yet powerful scent and realized it was Elizabeth's perfume. Warmth inundated his body, and an infinite peace settled over his mind. It was as if he had crawled into a bed warmed by the heat of a lover on a cold winter night.

Soon enough his left brain took over and began to analyze the situation. What did all this mean? Years of experience in dealing with medical emergencies allowed him to develop the skill of remaining calm and being able to clearly reason in nearly any situation. This was way out of his realm of experience! He was far out of his comfort zone, though he wasn't exactly afraid . . . only overwhelmed. Absolutely overwhelmed. A flashback suddenly overtook him, transporting him back to his childhood.

His grandfather, whom he loved dearly, had recently died. He had been an island of sanity in an otherwise insane family. They were all at the funeral, though both his parents were drunk. Logan was standing, and the minister was praying. Dad passed out and fell over some chairs. Mom walked out of the room. Everyone looked at Logan. A question glowed in their eyes: *What do we do?* They were asking him, a ten-year-old boy. *What do we do?* He was overwhelmed and went up instead to look at Gramps. So overwhelmed. How could he leave? Just leave like that? And now for the first time in 40 years, he remembered looking at his grandfather and feeling comforted. Logan could smell his grandfather's musky odor and felt like someone had wrapped a warm blanket around him. He also had a realization and wondered if this is why he was so comfortable dealing with dying people.

A drink. Suddenly, Logan wanted nothing more than that. Yet what an odd thought to have. No drink had passed his lips in 24 years. He analyzed the thought in his mind as if it were a log drifting by in a rapidly flowing river. Observe it. Process it. Make a choice whether to act on it or not. He chose not to drink, but other thoughts took its place. The smell of his grandfather. The smell of Elizabeth. Feeling warm and comforted both by his grandfather and Elizabeth. She had just died. Gramps had been dead for three days at the time of the funeral. Could that mean that the aura wrapping was not temporary? Did the essence, the soul, and the energy of a person stay with you always? Permanently? The first law of thermodynamics . . . energy is not lost, it is just transmuted.

"No greater love..."

"The ultimate gift is to give your life for another."

Someone was whispering in Logan's ear even though no one was there. He thought, *If you die, does your aura add to others' auras?* Was the ultimate gift to release your energy and add it to their energy? People returning from the brink of death claimed to have seen their loved ones, which would make sense. As your aura, your energy leaves the physical body, you would enter the same energy state as those who had died and gone before you. You could interpret that experience as seeing your loved ones.

A closer and more imploring voice chiseled into his thoughts. "Are you all right?" Kersti asked gravely while shaking his shoulder.

"W-what? What? Oh, yes, I'm okay. I was just . . . just thinking," Logan said faintly.

"You had the strangest look on your face. I was talking to you and you were just staring at your arm. I was a little freaked out . . . I thought . . . well, I—"

"I know what you mean. But it's alright. I just had a tidal wave of thoughts and feelings come over me. Someday I'll tell you about it. Now, what were you asking me?"

"Do you want to go tell her family or should I?"

"Oh, thanks for asking; that's my responsibility. I'll go do it," Logan murmured, slowly standing and gliding wraith like across the room.

Chapter 9

The Sharing

Two long days had stretched by since Elizabeth died. The loss had been difficult for them all, but Logan reminded himself that before anything could begin something else must end. The end of a moment. Of a day. Of a lifetime. And now Elizabeth could begin a new journey beyond death.

And there was the matter of his renewed friendship with Kersti to take his mind off the memory. They were walking together to the cafeteria for lunch. "It really feels good to be having lunch with you again," Logan said. Kersti replied with a sweet smile. As they walked down the hall, she purposefully bounced alongside him, occasionally jostling elbows, just like she did when they were kids. Logan melted.

Ever since they shared the experience of Elizabeth's death, his apology in the cafeteria, and a few other small conversations, Kersti had been enjoying his company . . . maybe even too much! She had a sort of sexy dream about him and was worried about where this might all be heading.

"Do you remember when I was telling you about how people look different when they're dead?" Logan said suddenly. The question alone was interesting, but the force in his voice and the twinkle in his eye when he spoke captivated her.

"Aside from the fact that they're dead!" she teased. Remembering Elizabeth, she quietly added, "Yes, of course I remember."

"Well, I think I know why," he said in a rush. But even before she understood the words an intense tingle jolted up her spine. It was such an amazing tingle, yet what a strange reaction. What was happening to her?

"I know some of this may sound strange. I have only spoken to one other person about it and he's my own doctor and friend, so I would appreciate it if you kept what I'm about to tell you confidential."

"Of course," Kersti said reassuringly, intensely curious.

As they passed through the doors of the cafeteria, Kersti passed into a new realm of understanding. After collecting their trays and loading up on lunch, he told Kersti what her own aura looked like. She set her tray quietly on a table and sat down with a look of amazement plastered across her face. Logan told her about auras and what he witnessed when Elizabeth died. Silence followed as Kersti picked at her food without eating. After what seemed like an eternity, Logan asked, "You believe me, don't you?"

"Oh, absolutely," she blurted out. Then, realizing how insincere she might have sounded, she added, "I do, really. It's just that there's a lot of information to take in. I was thinking it makes perfect sense you would have that gift! Do you know what we used to call you back when we were teenagers?"

"A dip-wad," Logan grumbled.

"I only called you that after you disappeared from my life," Kersti said, lowering her head and giving him "the look."

"Ouch!"

"Uh, huh!" Kersti tried to force herself to frown, but it was just too hard to do anything but smile when Logan was so near and glancing up at her with wide, glowing eyes. "No, seriously," she added, "we called you the Wizard! The girls talked about how you had a wise, magical energy about you! It was very sexy. I remember talking to Allison one time— you remember Allison, right? Blonde and perky? Well anyway, I said you were an old soul trapped in the wrong century. And from what you just told me, I guess I was correct." There was a slight pause. "I really liked Elizabeth," she said slowly. "In the short time I knew her, I felt a bond with her. I feel honored that she is a part of me now." Her voice fluttered with emotion, and Logan reached across the table to give her hand a squeeze.

"I know how you feel. You said I had a strange look on my face when it was happening, and you can probably imagine how it felt to actually be watching all of that occurring. To see her aura expand and drift away from her body and then sweep over and enter all of ours . . . I'll never forget it! Aside from ending up a little freaked out, I'm grateful that I was allowed to see a sacred moment. I loved her dearly and to know that she's . . . that she is always with me is . . . comforting." It was Logan's turn to stammer slightly, and Kersti gave his hand a squeeze.

"It's overwhelming, really. The implications of it all," Kersti continued. "Is that what our guardian angels are? All of our loved ones who have died . . . could they still be with us? Have they always been with us and always will be with us? Do they love us, comfort us, and protect us? Some people say that part of building and maintaining healthy boundaries is visualizing a protective dome of light around your physical body. And what's really weird is that I intuitively visualized my aura just the way you described it: A deep indigo blue surrounded by an outer layer of emerald green. What did you call those, er, those *lingers*, was it? That's right, I think. I have purple lingers."

"Yes, lingers! They're like fingers of light," Logan

said. "What color is your aura?" Kersti asked thoughtfully.

Logan blushed. He knew that question would come up eventually, but he hadn't expected it right then. "It's like yours," he admitted. "Of course I have different layers underneath, but I also have indigo blue with the outer layer of emerald green."

"And the lingers?"

"Purple. Just like yours."

"Are you blushing?"

"Maybe . . ."

Kersti laughed musically. "I like that! We are the same," she said, smiling. But beneath her lazy grin, her mind was racing wildly. "Do you think that's what intuitive thought is? The ability to be quiet enough, introspective enough, to be able to "hear" what the energies supporting you have to say? You know, if this energy is additive and if people transfer their energy or soul to yours when they die, do you think we could conceivably gain their thoughts and memories?" Kersti paused in awe, almost unable to believe the incredible nature of it all.

"Now you're cooking," Logan encouraged. "I'll tell you, it's so nice to talk to you about this. I have been thinking a lot about these things and to be able to talk with you about them has been great. And *will* be great, since I feel we are only beginning to discover this new world together. You know what they say: "Two heads are better than one!"

Logan dipped a silvery spoon in a bowl of green chili chicken stew. Fishing out a chunk of chicken, he chewed on it for a few moments before adding, "You know"—he swallowed—"something you just said reminded me of another thing. You said we could "gain their thoughts and memories." I do sculpture. Bronze, mostly, but I also do gold and silver sculptures with gemstones and exotic wood. Ever since I was a little kid, I had an inherent skill at carving and making things with my hands. I started out carving blocks of soap when I was four or five. My latest piece has 60 oz. of sterling silver and 42 oz. of 22 karat gold. And that's not to mention the diamonds, emeralds and rubies. I've sculpted them all into a piece that has dragons and mermaids and various other sea creatures all in the disguise of a jewelry box. It's quite spectacular, if I do say so myself!"

"Which you do," Kersti teased.

"Indeed, I do," Logan agreed, smiling. "But the point is I only took one jewelry class and that was in high school. I had an intuitive sense and knowledge about what to do and how to make things. Then I saw a V.R. program on the holo-jector at home about the Habsburgs in the old Austro-Hungarian dynasty. For several generations the Habsburg family spent the empire's money on making gorgeous pieces of art. Of course, these were made from the best of the best materials. Gold, silver, gemstones—the biggest gem-quality emerald in the world, which is about the size of both your fists put together! Breathtakingly beautiful, all of it.

"To give you an idea, I remember one was an automaton, which were all the rage in the courts of Europe. It was a king's carriage drawn by horses, all carved by an impeccable hand. I can barely begin to describe it, but try to visualize a horse drawn carriage made from gold and gemstones. That's how spectacular it was! An archer sat on top and, when you wound up the spring, the carriage would slowly move down the length of the table. But wait until you hear this: at random times the archer would shoot a golden arrow. Whoever the arrow landed closest to would have to drink a full glass of wine! It was a royal drinking game!

"Anyway, I had never even heard of the Habsburg dynasty or seen any of its incredible artwork before watching the show. I had only seen the first few minutes of it, and I knew what the pieces were going to look like. But then, all of a sudden, I realized I had been there before! In other words, I just *knew* I had once been a jeweler in the Habsburg's dynasty.

75

I used to think it was a past life or reincarnation or something like that I was remembering, but this sheds a different light on the subject. Help me think about this. How would that work? Our physical bodies—"

"Are here to carry our soul or energy," Kersti murmured faintly, eyes wide with excitement and understanding.

"If that's true, then each physical body is brand new while the soul continues on and retains thoughts from past lives."

"Just like getting a new pair of shoes," Kersti blurted out. "On the outside the feet look different, but on the inside the feet are the same!"

Logan just stared at her for a few moments. "Umm . . . well, I wouldn't ever have thought of that myself but I guess that is a fair analogy. Thanks for sharing," he added with a laugh. *God, I love you*, he thought to himself.

"I guess that's what reincarnation is," Logan continued. "I don't know why I thought before that somehow the physical body came back. After all, it's the soul that gives us our thoughts and feelings and makes us who we are."

Kersti mulled over the words in her mind. "Not really comes *back*," she mused. "Our souls never truly leave."

"You're right; they never leave," he agreed. "If what I saw with Elizabeth is true, our energy passes on to our loved ones."

"So I guess we're spiritual creatures having a physical existence," Kersti reminded him, beaming at Logan. Another intense chill spiked along her spine when he smiled at her.

Nor was Logan immune to Kersti's beauty. He simply gaped at her glowing face and flushed cheeks until his brain neurons finally fired again. "Exactly," he said quickly. After a pause, he added, "Although I do wonder why we don't have all the memories from our past lives."

"Maybe it would be too much information. I mean,

can you imagine starting out in life with all of those memories?"

"That makes sense. We would have an information overload—"

Logan's tel-chip cut him off with a single beep, alerting him to an incoming call. "Excuse me, Kersti. I have a call." He momentarily debated whether to verbally activate the tel-chip or give it two rapid taps. Deciding to go with the taps, he let the call come through. After talking for a few minutes, Logan explained, "Well, my dog leash is tugging me to the ER."

"Is that a new model of leash?" Kersti asked, craning her neck to glance behind Logan's ear at the tel-chip. "It's so small, I didn't even see it!"

"Small and solar powered. Just a few hours of indoor room light is enough to charge it. I really like it! No need to worry about charging the battery or anything. But it's still a dog leash, and you can't get away from it."

"Anything serious in the ER?" Kersti asked. She was playing with her fork again and paused to glance down at her untouched lunch. Dropping the fork, she sighed. She had lost her appetite.

"I'm afraid so. It's another patient dying of Vertig's syndrome. I am so tired of this disease," Logan said wearily. He had only eaten a few nibbles of his lunch, but he suddenly wasn't hungry at all. Not for the food, at any rate.

"Remind me to tell you something about Vertig's syndrome later," Kersti said, smiling radiantly.

"Good news?"

"Interesting news."

With a wave of his hand, Logan was off. As he walked to the ER, his mind was racing.

Chapter 10

Rat Brain

It wasn't a long walk to the ER, but each resonant footfall jarred Logan's mind. The reverberation of each step reflecting from the hallway walls bounced back at him. Amplified a thousand times over, the sounds crowded into his thoughts. Overwhelming, overpowering, overpopulated.

And he pondered.

Human beings dominated the earth. There were fourteen billion of them living on the only blue planet in the solar system. When Logan thought of the overcrowding he was reminded of a rat study in med school. Experiments showed if ten rats were placed together in an environment that was neither crowded nor lacking in food and water, they would show tolerance towards the old and injured. They would bring food to those unable to forage for themselves. But when 10,000 rats are crowded in the same space and have to fight for food and water, they become intolerant. Violent scuffles break out frequently and the old, young and sick die through starvation or physical violence until the population reaches homeostasis with the environment. Similarly, when fourteen billion humans are crowded together on a single planet the primitive rat brain within each man's mind predominates. Mayhem and violence ensues. When it comes down to overcrowding and insufficient supplies of food and water, humans are in no way superior to rats in their behavior towards others.

Homo sapiens are the only mammals that never learned to live within the boundaries defined by their environment. More people means using mankind's intellect to produce more food, which gives men the ability to have more children. So we harvest more food. And have more kids.

More food.

More kids.

Ad infinitum . . . like the fading echo of Logan's footsteps in an endless corridor.

Chapter 11

Vertig's Syndrome

Logan ran his fingers through his fine hair, trying to comb the tangled thoughts from his mind. Rat brain or otherwise, he was a doctor and there was a patient in the E.R. that needed his help. Time to concentrate, not think of overpopulation. A patient was waiting. A patient with Vertig's syndrome. Vertig's. What could he do? Go through the motions? It was all useless, all senseless, and there was no hope, no hope . . .

He was suddenly overwhelmed with grief. And tired. *So* tired of this disease.

Vertig's syndrome. This century's "Black Death." There had always been diseases and war around to keep the human population in check. Like malaria. And smallpox. Bubonic plague, AIDS, H1N4 and Sartin flu.

Now, there was Vertig's syndrome.

It was a miserable way to die. Dr. Kellen Vertig's research determined the pathophysiology of the disease and so the condition was subsequently named after him. A dubious honor. Dr. Vertig described it as "a syndrome of severe depression, accompanied by catatonic apathy, anorexia, severe malnutrition, muscle wasting with rhabdomyolysis, weight loss, electrolyte imbalance, and renal failure." The above symptoms progressed and intensified over the course of three to six months and resulted in death. More than anything else, the disease resembled the mixed organic and inorganic "failure to thrive syndrome" seen in children. But "failure to thrive syndrome," while commonly seen in children, rarely resulted in death. Meanwhile, Vertig's syndrome had a single inevitable outcome: death.

Charming, Logan thought.

The first cases appeared within three months of the first series of nuclear detonations in the Middle East. It was believed to be an unusual reaction to nuclear radiation at first because the disease was confined to the Middle East. As the wars expanded into Africa, so too did the spread of Vertig's syndrome. After five years and thirteen nuclear detonations, there were over 73 million deaths. Pakistan and India combined had 40 million deaths while Africa had 20 million deaths. The remainder was concentrated in Israel and the Palestinian states and surrounded those areas in other countries subject to terrorist acts. The United States, Russia, China and what was left of the United Nations eventually aggressively stepped in and demanded that the hostilities stop. Nuclear detonations ceased, but countries remained unwilling to surrender their nuclear arsenals. Hostilities with conventional weapons continued, and there was always the threat that they would escalate into another nuclear war.

Every nuclear weapon has a specific "fingerprint." Each batch of weapon-grade nuclear material was so unique that it was easy to determine which reactor the material came from. Moreover, the radioactive fallout pattern could be traced to the specific weapon that was detonated. So it was easy to make a worldwide map of the nuclear fallout pattern and identify the weapon that was responsible for that specific area.

While the lawyers had a field day over it, the doctors

at the Center of Disease Control who were tracing the outbreak of Vertig's syndrome noticed that the disease pattern did not correspond to the fallout pattern. Initially, the deaths were isolated in the areas of fallout. But they soon began to spread to large, overcrowded urban centers outside of the fallout areas. Ultimately, people began to die in rural areas around the entire world. That's when the doctors concluded it was not due to radiation. Nor were bio-weapons or viral vectors responsible; each known vector was in turn excluded through extensive studies.

Seventeen years following the first nuclear detonations, there had been nearly 6 billion deaths. Nearly half of the world's population was dead from Vertig's syndrome and war, yet to this day they still didn't understand the etiology of Vertig's!

Logan had a realization about the syndrome. He had only begun to see auras in the last two years, well into the die-off of mankind. Once again, "First Law of Thermodynamics" flashed across the movie screen of his mind. He had learned to accept these flashes within his mind's eye long ago, believing the saying that, "We will intuitively know things that used to baffle us." The first law states that energy is not lost; it is only changed into different states of matter. As people died, was their energy channeled into the auras of the living until it built up to the point where auras became visible? Or could it be that auras had always been there and something simply happened that allowed him to see them now? The latter certainly seemed to be the more likely of the two considering all the changes in his physical body as he aged.

Getting older was a strange experience. As his 107-year-old grandmother used to say, "Getting old is not for wimps!"

Chapter 12

The Emergency Room

Logan turned a corner and kneaded his forehead with a thumb. Strange thoughts had been plaguing him as of late; perhaps he had been overworking. Or maybe there was another layer to the aura gift, something yet to be discovered. Either way, now was the time to think about the patients at hand. Including the one that now called for his attention.

The ER patient was Paul Martin, a 42-year-old male with end-stage Vertig's syndrome. Like many others he had collapsed on the street and, by law, had been brought in by ambulance. The centralized computer record showed that he had a D.N.R. order. That was the first documentation checked when someone was picked up by ambulance or admitted with Vertig's syndrome. For years the healthcare system had been losing billions of dollars by running full codes on terminal cases of Vertig's syndrome. In many countries and some states in the United States, the law had now changed to account for such cases; if you had Vertig's, you were automatically a D.N.R. And after 6 billion deaths worldwide, there were simply not enough resources available to run full codes on a disease process that was inevitably terminal. If a dead body was recovered from the street, a bio-waste team would immediately take the body to the cemetery for cremation. No autopsy, a fast police report and get them in the ground! There was nothing quite like a body dead from Vertig's. It was an empty shell. A dry husk. Withered, unseeing eyes sagged in loose folds of skin. There was no reason to suspect or check for foul play. And either way, the system was fully overloaded.

When Logan strode through the doors of the ER, Paul was already in exam room three and hooked up to an assortment of monitors. Grabbing Paul's chart, he watched the device's holographic emitter glow to life. He had just scrolled down to the lab results when he heard the all too familiar tone of the monitor going flatline. Logan did not know this patient well; he had only met him once before. Yet now as he glanced at the dying man, he was for an instant certain he had known Paul all his life.

The intensity of their eye contact in those final seconds of his life made Logan's breath stop. Fear did not lie behind that tremulous gaze. Instead, utter disbelief colored his dark pupils. "I never made a million dollars," those eyes seemed to say. "I never raised a family. I'm not sure I was ever in love. And now . . . " As Paul let out his last breath, Logan caught his own breath and slowly inhaled.

The nursing staff was quick to respond to the tone of a monitor going flatline and anxiously awaited the doctor's orders. For a moment Logan was silent, lost in a thousand jumbled thoughts.

"Vertig's," he murmured quietly at last.

They nodded in solemn understanding and returned to their prior duties. Logan was meanwhile engulfed by a deep wave of sadness for this patient. Dying here all alone with no family, no friends, no apparent connections to keep him interested in and bonded to life. When Logan did the history and physical in his office, he knew that the patient was an accountant with no outside interests, hobbies, friends or family. This man also did not have any religious or spiritual beliefs. They had spoken at length about developing friendships and interests and how beneficial they can be for our physical, emotional and spiritual health. Six months earlier, Logan made a diagnosis of dysthymic disorder and depression, rule out Vertig's syndrome. Now he realized those symptoms had merely been the beginning of Vertig's.

Logan remembered Paul's first visit. Even then his aura had noticeably lacked both usual color and intensity. As Logan's ability to see auras strengthened over the past year, he had routinely begun to notice this same trend in other patients with Vertig's. Their auras seemed as dull and lifeless as their depression made their existence.

Through his peripheral vision, Logan glanced at his own forearm to see if he could notice any change in his aura as Paul released his spirit. He waited awhile, but nothing happened. Which made sense, after all, since he was not close with this patient. Logan's sadness turned to melancholy. He wished he could have done more for this man. He knew it was not his fault. He had done all he could. Yet somewhere deep inside, he felt he could have done more. As he sat with this freshly departed patient he whispered a prayer for him and all people with Vertig's, and the world.

He remembered something Hippocrates had said . . . or was it Galen? That each physician has his own personal graveyard to walk through. It is filled with patients who were too far gone beyond the realm of the physician's knowledge. Or perhaps the physician's thought process was flawed or he was unable to do enough fast enough. If an insecure physician visits the graveyard too often and obsesses about his mistakes, he is certain to drive himself crazy because every doctor makes mistakes. Only the grandiose, narcissistic physician never visits this graveyard because he believes he has never made a mistake. The humble physician knows that all healing is channeled through him, for the true source of healing comes from a higher power than the physician himself. So the humble physician will visit this graveyard when necessary to learn from a mistake. To stay in touch with his own humanity. To revisit and say a prayer for those who have gone ahead.

Logan finished his prayer with a soft exhale. He closed the massive, wrought-iron gates and left the graveyard behind.

Chapter 13

A Ride to Remember

Logan's hover was a little harder to fix than Marc thought.

"So I replaced the main chip in the mag-drive system easy enough, but balancing the pole reciprocators was trickier than usual," he told Logan over the tel-chip one evening.

"*Was* trickier?"

"Am I the best mechanic or ain't I? She's ready to be picked up when you're ready."

"You are the best, Marc. No doubt about it."

A pause. "Although, if you don't want to pick her up so quick that would be fine. I've, uh . . . well, I've got a few places to get to next week and showing up in a ride like that —"

Logan chuckled. "Have her ready for me tomorrow, pal."

"You sure? Well alright, you got it doc!"

And so the hover was finally done. Kersti offered to give Logan a ride to pick up his hov, and he happily accepted. He relished being in her presence. What an understatement that was! He had loved her since the fifth grade and had thought of her all his life! Yes, he enjoyed being in her presence. Loved it even.

"What a week," Logan said with a sigh. He'd already told her about Paul's death in the ER. "Talk about extremes! On one end of the spectrum you have Elizabeth, who was well loved and loved well. She was surrounded by friends and family all her life and especially in her final hours and experienced the most serene, loving, peaceful death you could imagine. Then you have Paul. Lonely, unloved, abandoned Paul. The emptiness that clouded his face was frightening. Honestly, sometimes I get so mad at this fucking disease I can hardly stand it! I always feel so hopeless and helpless because there's nothing I can do. I wish . . . well, I wish someone could find a cure or at least the causes behind Vertig's syndrome." Logan slumped back against the passenger seat.

Kersti reached over and squeezed his hand. A smile flickered over his face and a familiar chill snaked up his spine when she touched him.

"Funny you should say that," Kersti said with a smile. "Remember I had something to tell you about Vertig's?" Logan nodded, tracing and memorizing the smooth contours of her face as she continued. "Well, my husband works out at Sandia labs and has top secret clearance—"

Always willing to be a smart ass, Logan was quick to interrupt. "If you tell me, are you going to have to kill me?"

Kersti rolled her eyes. "Yes, of course," she said quite solemnly. Then she broke out laughing. "But you'll want to know this before you die! Besides, you won't be a great loss to society."

"Ouch," he groaned. Yet this was just another thing he loved about Kersti: her ability to hold her own in the smart-ass department.

"A-n-y-w-a-y," she said, glaring at him with a *Before I was interrupted!* look, "he has top secret clearance and they've been working on this thing for the military. The reports will be published next week, so he didn't see the harm in telling me early."

"What does he do out there?" Logan asked.

"You've probably heard the joke about what our educational degrees really mean. You know . . . a Bachelor of Science or B.S. degree stands for "Bull Shit," a Master's or M.S. stands for "More Shit" and a Ph.D. stands for "Piled Higher and Deeper!"

Logan chuckled. "Yes, I have heard that. But it's still funny, especially coming from you."

Kersti glanced over, a question glowing in her bright eyes.

"What?" Logan asked.

"*Especially* from me?"

"Well, yes, you tell a good joke."

"Do I?"

"You do." He paused, beaming. "You always have."

A faint blush painted her already-rosy cheeks. "Oh. Thanks. Um . . . anyway," she mumbled quickly, "my husband's a *double deeper*. He has two Ph.D.'s. One's in biochemistry and the other is in bio-mechanical engineering."

"Wow, that's impressive!" Logan feigned a pout and scrunched up his eyebrows. His next words dripped with jealously. "Is *that* what attracted you to him?"

Though somewhat surprised by the sudden change of tone, Kersti was quick to respond. "For your information, Scott—that's my husband's name—isn't just brilliant. He's also physically attractive. Plus, he has a big . . . well . . ." She pulled her hands off the steering wheel long enough to spread her hands about ten inches apart. Hesitating a few seconds for effect, she added, "brain!"

They broke into laughter, and when Logan finally caught his breath he said, "You're funny. Shallow, but funny. Please keep your hands on the wheel, will you? My brain may not be so big, but I still don't want to lose it."

Kersti blushed, "Logan!"

"What?" he whispered.

"Stoppit . . ." She said playfully slurring the words together like a little girl learning to speak for the first time.

"Stop what?"

"Being so . . . interrupting me!" she said quickly, cutting herself off. "Now let me get back to that top-secret thing. Like so much technology in the private sector, this started as military research that didn't pan out in having a military application. But, medically, it could be amazing!"

"Alright, I get it. Enough of the proemial antics! What have they discovered?"

"Impatient, aren't we? They call the thing a Scrivner Scanner after the main inventor, Dr. David Scrivner," Kersti explained. "It's like a holoscan, PET scan and EEG all rolled into one. We can use it to see the brain's physical anatomy and to pinpoint areas of cellular activity. The Scanner measures all brain waves, including sub-alpha and sub-beta wave. This is amazing, it even found a new brain wave they call sub-zeta. They were able to correlate these new brain waves to various emotional conditions. Observing the combination of these brain waves and tracking what area of the brain each comes from allows them to accurately predict the emotional state a person is in. They were looking for a foolproof lie detector test at first, but then it morphed into mind control. That's when the goal became total behavioral control, although thankfully they failed at that element."

"Thank God, definitely," Logan agreed.

"They've been playing with this thing for about five years and have found out a lot of interesting stuff about the human brain. Evidently, way back in the 1990s some scientists were using scanning electron microscopes to count the spin of subatomic particles. While these researchers were using those antiquated microscopes, they noted their thoughts could change the spin of the particles. So if the particles were spinning to the left, they could think that they should spin to the right and they would. I think Scott said something about

Heisenberg's theory of uncertainty. At any rate, they concluded that our thoughts and prayers can influence and manifest change in the physical world. So basically, the energy of our thoughts changes the physical world. That's quantum physics for you!"

Logan leaned forward in his seat. "Incredible." he murmured, thoughts racing to absorb Kersti's words.

"It gets more interesting. At the turn of the century, a Dr. Jamin made a hypothesis about Alzheimer's disease. It sounds like he practiced intuitive medicine, something we don't see much of anymore. Anyway, he hypothesized that Alzheimer's was a disease of emotional disconnection. His prime example was President Reagan, who developed Alzheimer's. Reagan . . . now here was a person who had to act as if he was in control all the time! In reality, though, he often wasn't in control. He had to put on a facade that was quite different from his internal emotional reality. So for example, imagine that there's a terrible terrorist act. During the press release Reagan feels like crying but can't because there's a billion people hanging on his every word. He's their leader and has to be strong for his people, so his face is stone while his heart bleeds in pain. That is emotional disconnection.

"Dr. Jamin said he saw it in a dream that goes something like this: He is standing inside a brain, looking at a neural synapses. A normal electric impulse passes smoothly through the synapses. The truth is the truth, and the synapse works normally. So he's standing there in the dream and watching the synapse when suddenly there's an emotional disconnect. That conflict causes a short-circuit in the brain. It sparks at the nerve synapses, causing scarring. Eventually, this scarring leads to the neurofibril tangle that is pathognomonic for Alzheimer's disease. For people who routinely separate their emotions from their outward presentation, the scarring eventually becomes permanent and causes the neurofibril tangles, thus nerve synapses to not function optimally. This leads to dementia. The doctor reached this hypothesis after observing many patients over years of practice . . . and, of course, following his dream. He concluded that patients who were emotionally disconnected often develop Alzheimer's disease."

A pause. A long one. Kersti glanced over at Logan and nodded, hoping to prompt a response. She wondered if he was stunned by the magnitude of the realization or by the dream or by her words. Smiling, she pretended it was the simple fact of her speaking to him that left him speechless.

Logan was meanwhile impressed and deeply awed. He loved how Kersti could remember and explain things that she heard. He knew doctors who couldn't have explained that idea as well as she just did. Yet instead of saying, "I love you" like he wanted to, he took the intellectual and restrained route —and then realized he was doing precisely what she had just talked about. He could feel his synapses scarring!

"Wow," he breathed. "Now that I hear that hypothesis, I can remember some patients of my own who were the same way. But I don't think I could have correlated the symptoms with the disease; Dr. Jamin did have good observational powers! Or, as you said, he practiced intuitive medicine." Not wanting to scar any more brain tissue, he added with a huge smile, "And you amaze me with how well you explained all that. I'm impressed!"

A bright blush dyed Kersti's cheeks red. "Really?" she questioned, pretending to be fully absorbed in the suddenly fascinating hover controls to avoid glancing over at Logan.

His smile widened. "Are you blushing?"

"No, of course not!" She declared, finally looking at Logan.

"You are, don't deny it. I think it's cute."

"Stoppit," she murmured again, "And quit grinning at me like that," she snapped. Careful to keep one hand on the wheel, she pressed one palm against his cheek and turned his head forward. "Watch the road, will you?"

"I thought *you* were driving."

"Yes, well, I'm terribly clumsy and need help sometimes. So you warn me if anything's coming my way."

"Alright, alright . . . *watch out!*"

"What?" she shrieked, wrenching the wheel so hard they nearly hovered into the opposing stream of traffic.

"Joking, joking," Logan said quickly.

"That wasn't funny; you are mean!" She playfully snarled.

"I know. I'm sorry," he said softly, reaching out to take hold of her hand and give it a quick squeeze. His fingers intertwined with hers.

"Well . . . just don't do that again, okay? That's dangerous."

"I know, I know, but you are too cute!"

"Hey."

"What?" Logan asked.

She looked down, and he followed her gaze. His hand was still clutching hers tightly. Grinning, Logan pulled away and tucked his hands in his lap. Kersti glanced over briefly, and there was something between longing and sadness radiating from her eyes. "That's okay," she said softly. "It was nice."

"What?"

"Your hand on mine . . ."

They lapsed into silence, and Kersti chastised herself for feeling this way. Yet how could she deny her own heart? She had been having so many loving feelings towards Logan. Each time he complimented her, she remembered that her husband never praised her or even seemed to appreciate all that she was . . . not to mention all that she did for their family.

Kersti powered down the hover car and swerved to

land at the entrance of the ground level interstate. "*So,*" she continued, trying to dig back into her head and out of her heart, "getting back to our earlier conversation, the researchers had empirical evidence that our thoughts are a type of energy that can influence the physical world. They failed at implementing the Scrivner Scanner for military purposes, brainwashing and behavioral control, but the Scanner is so good at differentiating and categorizing different brain wavelengths that they were able to predict who would come down with certain emotionally-caused diseases. These include depression, anxiety, all the different stress and lifestyle cancers, and . . . guess what else?"

"Vertig's syndrome?" Logan chimed in.

"Yup, Vertig's! They have a 99.3% accuracy rate. Most of this is new territory and I'm not even sure it's legal, but you know the military! They've installed Scrivner Scanners in some of the metal detectors at hover ports and sporting arenas under the guise that they can predict who has bad intentions. Anyway, they offered free air travel for people who were willing to go through an interview process. What they found in people who have Vertig brain wavelengths was that they were essentially spiritually bankrupt. For the most part they either didn't have any spiritual beliefs or had adolescent spiritual beliefs that didn't work for them. You know . . . big guy, white beard and hair, white robe, up in sky, keeping score, etc. What they didn't have was a spiritual lifestyle in their day-to-day existence. They thought money would make them happy, and their life was basically working to make money. They didn't know how to play. And they rarely, if ever, had fun." Kersti paused thoughtfully and rubbed the steering wheel with one thumb. "Just the opposite was true for people without Vertig's," she added. "They lived a spiritual lifestyle and still had a childlike innocence that allowed them to play and have fun. But again, you know the military. They had to go and try to figure out which was the better spiritual lifestyle. They separated out all the major religions: Christian, Jewish, Hindu, Islamic. There was even a category for what they considered "new age" spirituality, which included people like Christian Scientists and"—Kersti nodded at Logan—"the spirituality of the 12-step programs. They didn't find any difference between the varying religious or spiritual beliefs. What seemed to matter was they had spiritual beliefs they could live by."

Kersti waited for the light to change to allow entrance onto the interstate. She found herself acutely aware of how close Logan's body was to hers. How terribly, wonderfully close. "Oh, I almost forgot," she said suddenly, more to distract herself than anything else. "They found that people without Vertig's made room in their hearts to love pets. Especially dogs. Especially Samoyeds. Especially Samoyeds named Zeus and Loki!" Kersti teased, referring to Logan's beloved dogs.

"I knew it!" Logan cried out, beaming with excitement. "I knew they were a blessing, but I didn't know they were saving my life, too."

"Seriously, the thing about pets is true. People who love a pet have better health."

"Isn't it funny how people are always trying to find out which is better in any kind of group? They probably tried to figure out which was 'better,' dogs or cats. The concept of 'different but equal' seems to allude most humans." Logan paused, then added, "It reminds me of a historic fact. Back in 14th century Europe, the intellectual question of the day was deciding which is the 'true' language? Was it English, German, Spanish, Italian, French—you get the idea. Well, one day a French king had the bright idea of taking a bunch of newborn babies and isolating them in a nursery. The nursemaids were not allowed to speak to the babies, and the idea was that the babies would eventually grow up and start to speak the 'true' language. The nursemaids were instructed to have minimal contact with the babies so that nothing would influence the infants. Just basic contact for feeding, cleaning and changing diapers was allowed. Even cuddling was forbidden because there is a natural tendency to speak to the child in the process. Guess what the 'true' language was? Nothing! All of the babies died before they reached one year of age! The king repeated the experiment while changing a couple of the variables, but they all died again."

"I guess the 'true' language was love," Kersti said.

"Exactly! Without physical contact and nurturing, all of the babies died." Logan shook his head in exasperation. "The whole notion is ridiculous, though. It was hard enough to survive infancy back then without being thrown into some half-assed experiment set up by a narcissistic king."

"Would you let me finish this?" Kersti said, frustrated from all the interruptions.

"I'm sorry," he said sincerely, knowing he tended to get tangential in conversations.

Kersti smiled and, unable to suppress the urge, reached over and squeezed his hand. "So in the time it takes people to walk through a metal detector, the computer in the Scrivner Scan can classify people's risk factors for cancer, M.I., Vertig's . . . it's pretty amazing stuff!"

"Damn, you bet I'd say so! But it's kind of scary, too! Like Big Brother is really watching."

"That's what I meant when I said I'm not sure it's legal. Scanning people without their knowledge—I would feel violated," Kersti admitted, shuddering. "But anyway, let me get to the conclusions. The brain trust at Sandia labs concluded that at this time on earth, we're going through the most complex culmination of evolutionary factors ever! The earth is damaged from the greenhouse effect, the poorest air and water quality in history, ozone depletion and melting icecaps. More species are going extinct now than at any other time since we've kept records. War, multiple nuclear

98

detonations—we're killing ourselves and the earth! Simple as that. And if our life force is connected with the earth's life force, then whatever we do to the earth we do to ourselves. If you think about what we have done to the earth, it's depressing. What we do to ourselves, it's depressing. And depression is the main initial symptom of Vertig's syndrome. Anorexia, malnutrition, muscle wasting, rhabdomyolysis, electrolyte imbalance, renal failure—all of those are secondary to depression and apathy that cause people to stop eating. So they think it's a big snowball effect.

"At first, consciously or unconsciously, a person gets depressed by what is happening in the world. People have died by the millions due to nuclear explosions, and even more people continue to die—by the billions, really—due to this spooky disease. People are not finding any joy in anything, and everything's even more hopeless if a person doesn't have any spiritual beliefs." Kersti paused, looking at Logan. "That's when the person gives up. And that's what the brain trust says the bottom line is. People are simply giving up the will to live, and Vertig's is endgame."

They were both quiet as this simple truth to a complex problem finally became clear. Life had become so difficult that people were giving up. Endgame apathy. Losing the will to go on. And when the spirit dies, the body dies. As they contemplated this, Logan reached over and took hold of Kersti's hand.

She gladly held on.

Chapter 14

A Soul Honored

The wooden bench was worn from many years of standing in the sun. From waiting. From letting travelers rest upon its gnarled surface while their legs throbbed and their hearts sang. It was almost like something from his grandfather's stories. Like a place a frog would rest decades ago.

Logan calculated the distance between himself and Kersti on the bench. They were sitting together in front of the service station, waiting to pick up Logan's hov. Both were happy to be in each others company after sharing the amazing information about Vertig's. Still, the few inches between them seemed like a mile-wide chasm.

With a sigh, Logan leaned back against the bench. The solid support pressed firmly into his back. His eyes flickered over towards Kersti and he smiled, for he believed that when two people could be quiet in one another's company their intimacy had reached a new level. When the mind was constantly busy with incessant small talk, there was no room for a relationship to deepen. Logan believed when a couple could be quiet together the relationship took on a meditative state in which God could teach, be heard, heal and strengthen the relationship. For him, intimacy was feeling safe enough with someone he could share his true inner thoughts and feelings. Because of course, intimacy was not all physical.

Such a shame the physical was killing him. He *ached* for her!

Meanwhile, Kersti's mind was swimming in its own soup. She certainly tried to ignore the sensual spasms of emotions she had for him, but too often while at work she'd have fantasies of him just "taking her" on her desktop. And then there were those dreams. She had always thought guys were the only ones who were supposed to have *those* sorts of dreams. But here she was. Not even a teenage girl, but a proper woman. Dreaming of . . . Logan. She felt conflicted. Her body *wanted* him! Then her damn intellect would barge in and break up the party with a grumpy reminder that she was married with kids.

They were quiet for a few more minutes, and for a while Logan simply listened to the rustle of wind all around them. That faint whisper, swelling and fading in turn.

"Hey . . ."

"Yes?" Her response more excited than she wanted.

Logan glanced over, her eyes wide and glittering, danced expectantly across his face.

"Kersti, I was just thinking . . ." he began mischievously, with an adorable smile.

"Sex?" She whispered.

"I was . . . what?"

"Sex," she repeated with a grin.

"Y-yes . . ." he said slowly, a little baffled. Now she was staring at him with those doe eyes, twin orbs lush with promise. "Yes, yes!" he repeated, and they exploded into belly aching laughter. Logan grabbed Kersti's hands and turned to face her, still laughing. It was a long while until silence washed over them once more.

Logan confessed, "Back when we were teenagers, I wanted to make love with you but was too afraid. I was a scared, dumb kid," He rolled one thumb over her slender fingers. "Now, a part of me feels like I have something to prove to you. That the only way I can show you how much I love you"— Logan's voice quavered with emotion—"is to physically make love to you. But you are emotionally and spiritually bound to Scott in your wedding vows. I-I . . . I do not want to disrupt your marriage. That was never my intention, and still isn't. I'm not so supercilious as to believe that you would leave him for me. And what I do believe is that if we have sex, it would disrupt and possibly destroy our friendship because of the guilt we would feel. Eating away at us, asking us why, *why?* So I have come to a conclusion, but I wanted to talk to you about it so we both come to terms with a certain truth. There is *nothing* I would rather do than to make love to you! For the rest of my life! I love you *so* much! I-I've never felt this way before. About anyone." His eyes welling with tears, his eyelids the dam holding back years of flood waters. "Seeing your face, hearing your voice, listening to your amazing intellect and humor, smelling that subtle perfume you wear—you have *no* idea how much self control it takes for me to not grab you and start kissing you all over! But I have to control myself and fight those urges, because if I ever got started I could never quit. Yet how could I start, when you are married and have kids. I do not want to be a problem in your marriage. So . . . I want you to know"— his voice quivered, and tears leaked down his cheeks—"I would rather know *you* spiritually, than your body intimately!"

The dam broke, flood waters held since he was a kid released. Tears erupting, flowing wet and warm down his cheeks, healing.

"I love you!" she burst out, lunging forward to hug him. Tears cascaded down her cheeks as she kissed his wet face, and soon their tears were intermixed on one another's cheeks. They hugged rubbing wet cheeks back and forth. "I was thinking something similar, although I'm not sure I would— or even could—have said it so eloquently." A gentle laugh

echoed musically through the air, and she added, "I know in my past when I've loved someone like I love you, the only way I knew how to show my love was to have sex! What we're doing right now feels like a sacred act, beyond sex." Her arms tightened around him and she buried her face in his shoulder, sobbing loudly. She stammered, "We're honoring my previous vows... with Scott and honoring your desire to not be... a stumbling stone between my husband and I." Tears still streaking her face, she took each one of Logan's hands in hers and gently kissed the back of his hands several times over. "I want you to know that there is *nothing* I would love more than to make love with you! But know this too: the way you are honoring me right now means more than you know. No one has ever loved me this way—this is sacred! Really and truly. I have never felt so loved as I do right now. That you are willing to love and honor all of me, including my past commitments, rather than just manipulate me for my body . . . which, by the way, I feel I would easily give up to you right now . . ."

Logan cut her off by pulling back. "Well, maybe we should reconsider this while we still can?" he said quite seriously, face wet with tears.

She smiled and shook her head. "Doesn't matter. I know your heart now. I love you no matter what."

"And I . . . love you *always*."

They gazed lovingly at one another. Then, eyes brimming and spilling over with tears again, began to sob as they leaned together and enveloped each other in a tight embrace.

When words finally came to him, Logan whispered in her ear, "Besides, what we know about auras and the first law is that death is not the end. I will get a chance to know you physically one day. And baby, I will hunt you down! I swear it." His voice glazed over with a dominate, sexy tone. "Like a mighty hunter stalking his prey, I will find you."

A warm, wet feeling oozed up Kersti's spine.

"You better," she moaned seductively, still holding his warm, strong body flush against her own.

"I will. I promise."

Chapter 15

A Spiritual Solution

Spring faded into the summer months, and fresh blossoms were replaced by bright green foliage. But more than the season had changed. Just as the newly planted seed spreads its roots beneath the ground and secures a hold, so too did the seed of love, so small in the beginning, take firm root.

In that time, Kersti and Logan had co-authored a couple of articles. They had been careful to publish only after Sandia labs released its scientific data, whose findings seemed to only interest research-based scientific journals. But Kersti and Logan's articles were published in medical holograms, distributed in news reports to pocket computers around the world, and even featured on several holoshows. They were surprised by the universal appeal their articles seemed to hold. Soon they were invited to appear on talk shows and lecture circuits. It seemed that the public did not trust what a government-sponsored laboratory had to say. People were more interested in Logan and Kersti's interpretation of the data and especially in their spiritual approach to the treatment of Vertig's syndrome. Based on the suggestions in Kersti and Logan's articles, support groups for treatment began to pop up around the world.

In parts of the world where free speech had been

condemned for so long by the government, hoping for a spiritual awakening was too much of a leap of faith. But even these groups began to see some success. For these people, who for generations had lived in fear about talking to their neighbors and possibly being turned into the government for their beliefs, the simple act of fellowship and the ability to talk about their feelings had a healing effect.

Logan's favorite by far was V.A., which stood for Vertig's Anonymous, a twelve-step group for people with Vertig's. Those patients who began attending in the early stages of the syndrome—before depression and apathy got so bad that they stopped going to meetings—were actually cured through the spiritual solution.

Even in light of the progress, death rates remained atrocious. Estimates of the current morbidity and mortality rates predicted that only three billion people would be left on earth in a decade. Yet at least now there was some hope because there was a solution.

Logan found it interesting to observe human nature in the middle of such a devastating worldwide crisis. Attendance at churches spiked dramatically. But even then there were those who would live a morally bankrupt lifestyle all week, attend church on Sunday and think they would be saved from the ravages of the disease. They couldn't grasp that it was an *internal* spiritual awakening that needed to occur. And even though there was now a treatment for Vertig's, some people were so resistant to any suggestion of a spiritual solution or lifestyle change that their denial had become complete. It would always be those same people who would scream at the government in violent protests, demanding more money to be funneled into finding a medical treatment for the disease. Vast amounts of money were thrown away on research and failed medical treatment.

It seemed unfair to many in the world that there did not appear to be any cosmic judgment regarding the type of spiritual belief a given person had. Some religious fanatics appeared to be immune to Vertig's syndrome but had strong religious convictions; namely, that all infidels must die! So terrorism went on, albeit at a reduced rate, but only less so because there were fewer people on earth. Logan pondered this confusing discrepancy. How could God allow religious fanatics who killed millions with atomic weapons escape the ravages of Vertig's and allow seemingly innocent but spiritually naive people to die of the disease?

His conclusion: it was not up to God. It was a consequence of the individual's beliefs and choices. Once while his body and mind were folded in meditation, a quiet voice spoke in Logan's head. "Your body is a temple," it breathed softly, which made sense. Each individual makes choices to believe or not believe. The very act of *believing* in a spiritual cause strengthened the aura that protects from Vertig's. He thought about the outer space movies he loved as a kid and visualized the force fields that defended spaceships from onslaught. But if a spaceship was low on energy, the force field weakened and the ship became vulnerable. Maybe having a spiritual belief created a force field, and prayer, meditation and especially taking action to live a spiritual lifestyle could channel energy into and strengthen the force field.

No one religion was better than another—that had always been Logan's personal belief. These recent events seemed to point that out. Simply having a spiritual belief was most important. As an adult, Logan knew he was a Christian because he had a personal friendship with Jesus. He also believed that Jesus, Abraham and Mohamed were great teachers for the people in the Middle East. Buddha was the teacher for the Far East. The Great Spirit was the teacher for Native Americans in North America. It made sense that there would be different teachers for different areas. Different areas meant different languages, different cultures, that was elementary. In medical school, Logan learned there are actual physiological differences in the brains of Western and Eastern humans. The two groups are unlike in how they process information, and in how memory is stored and retrieved. So medical science proved that people in different areas learned differently. A great teacher would, in turn, speak and give information in a format that would make sense for the people in that part of the world. All the great teachers basically held the same core belief. Love God. Love others as you love yourself. Help others. After all, the truth is the truth, regardless of which spiritual teacher it comes from. The human tendency to need to determine which religion is better than another has nothing to do with spiritual teaching. Trying to prove whose religion triumphs is simply a smokescreen for the actual goal—the acquisition of power! Which, unfortunately, was the focus of many organized religions. Ultimately, the struggle for power could corrupt the spiritual teachings of the religion.

It appeared that having a spiritual belief, any spiritual belief, was enough for the human "force field" to provide some protection from Vertig's. The choice to not believe in a spiritual lifestyle led to death. Logan knew that was just the way it was, but sometimes it didn't seem fair.

*****

A couple of weeks after he had contemplated these differences, he decided to do some research on the matter. His friend Dr. Warren Cloud was the medical director for one of the state prisons. With permission, he shadowed Dr. Cloud as he did his rounds. Here, there were prisoners in all stages of Vertig's. As the syndrome progressed, the aura of the patient gradually grew dimmer, weaker, and more constricted, like a frail membrane unable to protect an infant. The depth of his aura and that of most of the people he knew was eighteen to thirty inches deep, and the auras changed in intensity and amplitude as their owners met other people. When meeting a loved one or friend, lingers would stretch out and greet one another. Usually. With these prisoners, it was a different story entirely. He noticed that most of the prisoner's auras were dull in color and had a low intensity. Many of the prisoners had auras that were only one or two inches deep, and they were rigid and lacked activity. These auras were compressed like protective shells.

Then there were the black layers enveloping many of the prisoners. Logan himself had a single black layer, an inky shadow, lurking in his aura and he often wondered what it meant. After interviewing a few of the prisoners, he could only conclude that the black layers were manifestations of major character defects. Not flaws like 'I have a bad habit of interrupting people when they talk' but rather defects like 'I like to rape women,' or 'I like to torture and kill animals and people.'

One interview left a deeper impression than most. The prisoner was in for domestic violence and rape. After the man settled down and realized he wasn't being threatened, he became willing to talk about his past and crimes. Logan sat across from him, noting with calculating eyes that this prisoner's aura was little more than two inches deep and dense like a shell. The surface layer was the only one where color was distinct, it was red and denoted anger. The remaining layers were compacted to the point of becoming color indistinct. All except the shadow layers, that is. The black layers were quite apparent as they migrated between the surface of the aura and the physical body.

As the prisoner started to speak of a rape, Logan followed a black layer that initially hovered about an inch from the surface of the man's skin as it migrated through the other layers of his aura. When the dark layer emerged to the surface and fully encased him, the man's demeanor changed.

111

His words held threatening promises, but a distant look glazed over his eyes. It was in this distant, dreamy condition that he relived the rape in detail. As he did so, his loose prison jumpsuit began to tent as he got an erection. That was enough for Logan, and he changed the subject.

Not surprisingly, this prisoner also had a history of physically abusing his wife. Logan asked him to talk about this segment of his past, and as the man began his tale another black layer rapidly migrated and assumed its dominant place at the surface of his aura. The previous black layer, which corresponded to the rape, migrated back down to its original position. Logan was amazed at how quickly this happened. As this new black layer encased him, his dreamy condition evaporated and was replaced by anger and aggression. Whereas he was staring off into space as if daydreaming of some event just a little earlier, he now made piercing, rigid eye contact as if trying to provoke a conflict. When he spoke, every other word was "bitch" this and "bitch" that. He verbally assaulted everyone with the intensity of his anger. When he pounded the desk with clenched fists and started to get up out of his seat, the guard gave him a glancing blow to the back of his head with a club. He immediately sat down, and faster than Logan could blink the prisoner's aura was once again the way it was when they first met. The red layer floated on top and both black layers were submerged below the surface layer. The prisoner's mood had changed just as rapidly. He was apologetic, but a steel edge glittered behind his words.

It was amazing and spooky how quickly the prisoner's mood and appearance changed as the different layers of the aura cycled to the surface and below it in turn. But what came first? Did a person's mood control his aura, or did the top layer of the aura initiate the mood? Could it be a combination of both? With this individual, it seemed that having the initial thought was enough to cause the aura to shift. Once the aura shifted, the man seemed obsessed. Or possessed.

At least jails were no longer overcrowded, but it was only because prisoners were dropping like flies from Vertig's. A guard told Dr. Cloud that the guards placed bets on who would die and who would survive their jail term. The smart money was on those who died. Currently, 92 percent died within five years of being sentenced. Most had little long-term hope, and apathy and depression ran rampant. Yet even here, the few who truly had a spiritual awakening as a result of their jail term seemed immune to Vertig's. Their auras were a dramatic contrast to those of the rest of the prisoners. When Logan observed the full assortment of men walking in the courtyard, they looked like a string of Christmas lights with only a few bulbs lit. A few bright lights in a string of dead bulbs. What would Darwin say? Was this natural selection of the human species on a planetary scale? Where would it end?

Were humans becoming extinct?

*****

Later that evening at home, Logan eased into a comfortable leather armchair in his office to ponder those questions and wonder about the meaning of the black layer in his own aura. Was there some way to access it? Could it be a relic of . . . a past life? A person he knew? All he knew for certain was he hoped that, whatever it was, it would not seize him the way it seemed to possess that prisoner.

Chapter 16

Research

Autumn leaves curled into smoky red shadows of their former selves and littered the earth with fire. Winter swept pale blankets of snow over seeds snuggling warm beneath the soil, and in the spring fresh flowers poked their heads, crowned with rainbow blossoms, towards the sky. Twice over the cycle passed as two years raced by.

For their part, Logan and Scott became social. But their interactions were always strained. Scott knew Kersti loved him and their children. He knew she also loved Logan. Once, Kersti and Logan both spoke with Scott and tried to reassure him that yes, they cared for each other, but it was platonic affection and would always remain that way. Scott nodded and grumbled in understanding and left the discussion even more certain of the hidden currents of his wife's heart. Because of course Logan and Kersti's love for one another had grown. Though still platonic, they could finish each others sentences, ate the same foods and even had the same dreams at times.

Their business was booming. When determining a company name, Logan pointed out that they were even side by side in the alphabet. Since K comes before L, K+L Inc. was born The company had developed a research program at Sandia labs.

Once Kersti pulled Logan aside and told him, "Don't think I haven't noticed that whenever we write an article or book, you always put my name first—even if the original idea was yours!"

"That's because I love you," Logan replied, "and you will *always* come first in my mind and heart."

"Oh, baby! You melt my heart," she whispered and enveloped him in her arms. As she pulled away, her lips brushed his cheek and pressed a kiss to it.

*****

Money to finance the experiment was easy to come by. The government was still investing heavily into any research that had to do with treatment of Vertig's. The difficulty was getting access to either of the two Scrivner scanners at the lab.

Kersti quit her job at the hospital and was now CEO of K+L Inc. After drafting several ideas, she presented a proposal to a philanthropic group in Denver, Colorado. The group focused on delivering health care to the medically indigent in North America. They had deep, deep pockets and old money! Though they had been around for 400 years, their philanthropic focus changed as the world had changed. The group's investment strategy had been to observe new technology and invest early. And they had some *big* investments. They placed their money in Standard Oil back in 1865 when the availability of whale oil was declining and the demand for oil for lighting, heating and automobiles was increasing. Then there was General Electric when alternating current was standardized. Microsoft, when computer technology was in its infancy. And Hyper-Fluxx, when the tri-aniline magnets and computer system was developed for hover cars and sub-stratosphere spaceflight. The group was worth more than some countries, and Kersti proposed that the group buy a new Scrivner scanner for K+L Inc. The group would benefit because they would receive major credit from any new medical discoveries as a result of the experiments. After the experiments were done, the scanner would belong to the philanthropic group and could be used by them for diagnosis and treatment of medically indigent patients. Besides, the group needed a doctor to operate the scanner and interpret the results. Logan and Kersti agreed to take on that role, and the deal signed. Soon after, the experiments began.

K+L Inc. was proud of the experiment it had designed. As with many in science, Kersti and Logan stood on the shoulders of the giants who preceded them. They collated the results of previous studies done with the Scrivner scanner and developed several hypotheses. They had a central premise: If the Scrivner scanner was able to predict emotional states of mind, could a scanner be altered to selectively bring about a desired emotional state? By isolating the particular combination of brain waves that correspond to that emotion, then stimulate it with the amplification mode, bring the chosen auric layer to the surface on demand?

They began the experiment using prisoners and other volunteers. Kersti would operate the scanner, input data and print images. Since Logan had the ability to read auras, he would observe which colored layer of the aura was on the surface and, at a separate computer terminal, would input the data into the mainframe. The Scrivner scanner would collate the color observed with the different brain waves. After inputting several hundred individuals, the mainframe became pretty good at reading brain waves and predicting what the emotion and color would be. For the sake of accuracy and safety, Logan was always present during a reading to verify.

Soon he started to get help with this duty!

The morning things changed began quite ordinarily. For Logan, at any rate. He checked the calibrations of a scanner while guzzling down the last sips of a tepid green tea. The first prisoner of the day, twiddled his thumbs and raked dirty, chewed fingernails through his ragged black hair.

"Ready?" Logan called to Kersti.

Her fingers danced over a touch panel. "Whenever you are."

"Then let's get started."

Kersti inputted a series of commands and the scanner hummed to life. The prisoner's eyes darted from her to the machine and back again. "It's safe, don't worry," she assured the man. "Just relax and you'll be out of here in no time."

The prisoner's aura flickered as the layers began to shift. A faint orange glow concealed beneath clouds of black poked towards the surface. "Easy, now," Logan murmured to himself. "Kersti, check the scanner and be sure the color reading is . . . Kersti?"

Though her fingers remained stiffly poised above the panel, her face was bleached white and she was shaking. Her whole body fluttered like a leaf caught in a sudden breeze. Her eyes were locked on the prisoner.

"Kersti, what's the matter?" Logan yelled.

"O-orange . . ." she choked out.

"What?"

"Orange. The aura, it's . . . orange."

Logan followed her gaze. "You can see—"

"The aura. Logan, I . . . Logan, I see it, I see the aura! It's faint, just a blur, but . . . I can see it now."

Soon after, one of the radiology technicians reported the same transformation. He, too, was beginning to see auras. Meanwhile, Logan's own ability intensified. He was able to distinguish more subtleties of color and intensity. Research revealed that there were increasing reports from around the world of people seeing auras and developing other spiritual gifts.

After about eighteen months, they had fine-tuned the scanner and rebuilt the amplification mode several times. A patient would lie down, and the initial scan would collate the colors of his or her aura with the different brain waves and sub-waves. The vibratory rate of each color would be isolated. The amplification mode utilized an elaborate feedback loop where the vibratory rate of a chosen emotion and color would be amplified, and then the feedback loop would be engaged. The end result was that the amplified color and emotion would be brought to the surface. Extensive trials revealed that the layer of the aura that was on the surface was responsible for the emotional reality the person then experienced.

And what results! They soon realized they were totally unprepared to therapeutically treat the emotional states brought about by this technique. Because of the incredible potential this new form of treatment held, extra funding was easily obtained. Soon they had additional psychiatrists and mental-health therapists on the staff. Many different therapeutic modalities were tried. A combination of cognitive behavioral therapy with rapid eye movement and meridian tapping seemed best at integrating the most disruptive character defects and traumatic events. Attempts were made at erasing the disruptive layers of the aura. Once that layer of the aura was brought to the surface, the vibratory rate was altered and the amplification turned down in order to dampen its overall effect on the person. But this left patients complaining of feeling 'incomplete.' Almost as if 'a piece was left behind.' This was so disruptive to their sense of well-being that the majority preferred to have the character defects or trauma back rather than feel emotional emptiness.

Dr. Jamin had developed the theory that Alzheimer's was a disease of emotional disconnectedness. He also had a famous quote: "The shadow self is still self." Even though a dark part of our character—"the shadow self"—may be a part we no longer want, it is still a part of us. Logan believed this statement best summed up what was going on with his patients. If you take a piece of the "shadow self" and erase it from a person there will be a sense of loss, a void, in the person. After all, most character defects are the result of some type of trauma inflicted on the growing child. As a survival tactic, a wall forms and hiding behind that wall is the shadow self. And so the "shadow self is still self," and if you just remove the shadow self you lose that part of you that creatively, as a child, learned survival techniques.

When someone who had been sexually abused was scanned and that layer of the aura was brought to the surface, it was not simply an intellectual process like saying, "I was sexually abused." It encompassed the entire being: spiritual, emotional, physical and intellectual. While being scanned you intellectually understand you were sexually abused, you also physically feel pain, emotionally feel shame, guilt and fear, and spiritually sense the violation. Logan once heard a Zen Master claim you carry the energy – sexual, emotional, physical or intellectual energy – of every person you've ever had contact with, whether the contact was willing or not. Consequently, while being scanned you're connected to how *you* felt as a child being violated, but you're also feeling the emotional, physical, spiritual and intellectual energies of the *perpetrator*.

When the victim of sexual abuse again experienced what it felt like to be abused, combined with the aura of the perpetrator of the abuse, it was overwhelming! The Scrivner scanner combined the reality of the victim and the perpetrator. Cause and effect. The trauma and the survival tactic. Only then could a person heal. The victim could integrate the shadow self back into the self, resulting in a whole self. This healing process seemed to work best by having the victim feel the shame they carried from the molestation and understand that they, the victim, was not at fault in any way.

After discovering that part of the perpetrator's energy was combined with that of the victim, Logan at first attempted to isolate the perpetrator's energy and then erase it. But it was discovered that it was important for the victim to feel the perpetrator's energy. The victim of abuse often feels that he or she was somehow responsible. If he had acted differently, or done something differently, the abuse would not have happened. This is not true, and so it was important for the patient to experience the perpetrator's energy and understand that he was the victim. Because the most important lesson for the victim to feel was— *victims were looked upon as objects*. Not humans . . . mere objects.

There wasn't anything they had done wrong to cause the abuse. Most child survivors of abuse feel guilty as adults. They feel they somehow caused the abuse to happen. As if they were not "good" enough to avoid the abuse or even that they earned it. During the process of integration on the scanner, the victim felt the perpetrator's illness. Then, when the victims saw on all levels that it was the perpetrators fault, not theirs, all guilt was swept away. That allowed victims to reach acceptance and know they did not cause the abuse. This gave them freedom from the shame that they carried inside for many years. When a person was able to feel that experience at the core of his being, he or she was truly healed.

After this process, the victims realized that the perpetrators had been ill themselves. Most of the time, the perpetrators had also been abused and were re-enacting their own pain. The treated victims felt empathy for the perpetrator. Common sentiments became, "I saw and felt him as a man dying of a disease he didn't cause, like someone dying of cancer. Even if you don't like the person, it's hard not to feel the same empathy you would feel towards any sick or dying person." Feeling empathy is often the first step towards acceptance.

People with this level of acceptance and these types of feelings healed faster. There was soon a therapeutic goal to replace the pain, shame and guilt with a healthier emotion. Empathy, acceptance or, ultimately, forgiveness.

Many therapists had difficulty with this approach. They thought it unreasonable for someone who had been sexually molested as a child to heal by accepting and forgiving the sick perpetrator. Debates erupted, but finally someone wrote an article using Albert Einstein's statement that "A problem cannot be solved using the same mindset that created the problem."

The solution given in the article was that shame, guilt and rage were the emotional roots of the problem of abuse! Whether it was sexual, emotional, spiritual or physical abuse did not matter. Trying to use the same mindset to solve a problem is ineffective. Love, acceptance and forgiveness are a different mindset than rage, guilt and shame.

This article facilitated a paradigm shift. Therapists became supportive of the integration process, which allowed victims to see and feel how sick the perpetrator was. It also allowed the victim to replace his or her own negative feelings of blame, guilt and shame with positive feelings of acceptance, empathy and forgiveness.

The results were amazing! People who had life-long diseases, including alcoholism, drug or sex addiction, codependency, were cured after several treatments. However, there was one big *if.* The therapy could work only if the victims continued living and learning a lifestyle based on spiritual progress.

Chapter 17

Scanner Death

Logan was excited about observing people on the scanner during the death process. From observing Elizabeth's death and witnessing several others, he knew there was an energy transfer. The first law was at play, so no one really died! Now, if only he could study it in a clinical setting with proper scientific techniques and equipment.

With his new company he could do just that, and it was easy to get volunteers to be studied. There were still one million people dying every year from Vertig's. The laws limiting medical experiments on humans had become obsolete long ago. Mainstream society was doing everything it could to find a medical cure for Vertig's syndrome. There was fear that Vertig's was contagious, and society was less concerned about those with the disease than finding a cure so *they* didn't get it as well. Society was intolerant of Vertig's. There were the "normals," those without Vertig's, and those with Vertig's, who were "the bad" in the slang of the day.

They gathered volunteers from the general populace and from the prison population. All volunteers went through an educational process. They were taught "The First Law of Thermodynamics." They didn't use the word "dying" or "death" out of denial, but rather out of the belief and scientific evidence that it is a "transition." A transition from one form of energy to another. Volunteers watched others on the scanner and were allowed to do their own scanner work so they knew the process and would not be afraid when their time came to transition. The team decided to test "normals" first, then people with Vertig's.

The first patient to be observed on the scanner was a male named Stever. No last name, just Stever. He had developed lung cancer after years of nicotine addiction. It had metastasized to his liver and bones. Despite his addiction, his aura was bright and active.

"Will it hurt?" he wheezed, unable to breathe easily.

"No, Stever, you know from trial runs the scanner doesn't hurt. And what I've seen is that transition is not painful, either. If you have pain from the cancer, we will give you an opiate to help decrease the pain," Logan said.

"I . . . I don't want to mess up your experiment by taking drugs!"

Logan smiled, reached over and rubbed Stever's shoulder. "Thank you for your concern, but don't worry about that. Don't worry about anything. It won't interfere with the experiment, and the most important thing is your comfort. We will give you as much medicine as you need. As far as that goes, if at any time during the scanning process you want to stop, you just say the word and we will. I want to remind you again what it said in the contract. That your comfort and dignity during the transition is the top priority. You're giving science a wonderful thing, and we will not jeopardize your trust in any way. You have my word, not only as your doctor but also as your friend!"

"Thanks, doc, I do trust you," Stever said, then shook his head. "But doesn't the medicine affect the outcome of the scan?"

"It does to some degree. Opiates and other drugs seem to decrease the brightness of the color and the amplitude of the aura, but it does not change the underlying nature of the aura itself."

"What do you mean when you say 'amplitude'?"

"Amplitude . . . well, that is the movement, or activity, of the aura. Remember during the training when you were watching Frank's scan? When he was getting in touch with his feelings about being beaten as a child? Remember when he got angry, how his aura flared outward and red lightning bolts flashed out? Then, when he got sad, how his aura contracted like a shell around his body? That's what we mean by amplitude—the activity of the aura."

Stever bobbed his head. "Okay, I under . . . " he trailed off into a bout of choked breathing, barely managing to draw fresh air each time. Logan stood by his side, keeping his hand firm on the man's shoulder in support. When his breathing returned to a rough norm, Stever wheezed, "Logan, you're not . . .going to ask me any . . . embarrassing questions, are you? Because you know, hopefully . . . my family will be here... if they arrive on time." The question, lush with concern, was punctuated with labored breathing.

"No, Stever, no embarrassing questions. Nothing like during the therapy sessions. Remember, the whole point of this scan is to observe what happens to the aura at the time of transition. In fact, we won't ask you any questions. We will only answer questions that you have, or that your family may have."

After being hooked up to the scanner for less than an hour, Stever grumbled, "Doc, I don't think I can sit here any longer! I'm having"—his face contorted into a strangled grimace—"a lot of pain in my chest and back."

"Okay," Logan acknowledge, nodding his head. "Okay, let's give you fifteen milligrams of morphine."

Stever managed a hoarse chuckle. "Doc, I'm an ex-junkie. That ain't even going to faze me."

Logan shook his head. "We need to go low and slow.

Wait about five minutes; if you're still having a lot of pain, we'll give you some more. Remember how we talked about opiates decreasing your respiration? If we give you too much, it could cause your death."

Half croaking, half wheezing a laugh, Stever mumbled, "Hell, doc, ain't that why we're here?"

Somewhat embarrassed, Logan said, "But, Stever, your family's not here yet."

"But, doc"—he gasped, struggling for breath—"I'm really having a lot of pain!"

Logan nodded and swiveled his head to search for Kersti. She wasn't far—she never was—and when she saw him searching she glided across the room. Her footsteps, soft and silent, seemed like something eerie and ethereal. Yet her hand, so very warm and real, felt welcome on Logan's shoulder.

"Let's give him the dose," he said.

"You have to give the order verbally for the medical record," she whispered back.

"Thank you. Let's get him fifteen milligrams of morphine, slow IVP."

Then, as often happens in medicine, everything happened at once. Stever's ex-wife and mother arrived at about the same time Stever went into Cheyne-Stokes respirations—the kind of breathing that often marks a terminal event. Thankfully, the family members knew what to do from an earlier recital of sorts and, joining Stever by his side, each grabbed a hand and let the fading man know they were there for him. They repeated what they had told him in previous therapy sessions, and despite everything they loved him. Stever squeezed their hands, croaked some inaudible sounds and, after a few more minutes, drew a final gasping breath that was never exhaled.

Meanwhile, Logan's eyes were intent on the dying man while Kersti's fingers danced over the computer's touch-panel. He saw each layer of Stever's aura expand, intensify in brightness and rapidly cycle to the surface, one color layer after the other. What the scanner recorded were all the different brain waves associated with different emotions, rapidly cycling, until death.

What the scanner didn't record was equally important. Logan noticed Kersti pause and simply stare, awed as always, as Stever's aura brightened in intensity, the layers cycled to the surface and the amplitude increased until it filled the room. As the aura subsided, it washed across the room. After transition, there was no aura around Stever's body. Most of his aura was with his mother and his ex-wife, a little with Logan and Kersti, and none at all with the technician. The technician was the only person in the room who Stever did not know.

There would be a lot of statistical data to go through. For a moment, though, it was easy to forget that. A deep grief suddenly seized Logan. A thick lump swelled in his throat, threatening to choke him. In his mind, he knew his friend and patient had just transitioned somewhere else. He knew Stever was not dead. He and Stever had grieved and cried together, knowing this day would come. And right there, as his mother and former wife wept hot tears over their departed loved one, the physician and scientist inside Logan reminded him he had a lot of intellectual data to sort through. The quote, 'Every physician has his own personal graveyard he must walk through' occurred in his mind. He knew he would later emotionally walk through the graveyard and visit Stever.

It bothered Logan to hear people talk about how cold their doctor was. Of course, there is a balance to everything. He had cried with many of his patients. But when a patient is in a life or death crisis, the best doctor is one who is able to turn off emotions and deal with the emergency at hand. Unfortunately, some doctors found it easier to keep the emotions turned off permanently! And that was not the kind of man Logan was or ever wanted to be.

Logan, Kersti and Stever's family met with the grief counselor to talk over their experience. After 30 minutes Kersti and Logan thanked them for participating, gave each a hug and told them to call if they had any questions. Leaving them with the counselor, the pair wandered off into the hallway outside.

When they were alone, Logan gently took Kersti's hand in his own. "Thank you," he said softly.

Her wide, confused eyes roamed his face. "For what?"

"Helping me back there."

"Helping you? It's you who's always helped me—"

He wrapped his arms around her in a big hug and whispered, "But wasn't that amazing?"

"Incredible," she assured him, beaming back and returning the intensity of his hug. "I see what you mean about the amount of aura left with each person being in direct proportion to the importance of the relationship with Stever. His mother got the most and the tech didn't get any because Stever didn't know him."

"Exactly! Oh, baby . . . I'm so glad you are able to share this with me! I don't . . . I . . ."

"Yes?"

"I don't know what I'd do without you. That's the truth. If I ever had to be alone again, I don't—"

"Logan," she said softly.

"Yes?"

"A day at a time, right? I mean, no matter what's coming"—she squeezed him into a tighter hug—"we'll always have this to remember. And somehow, I feel it's going to be okay. You'll see."

Logan continued to hug Kersti. It felt wonderful to hold her in his arms. God, she felt good! At times, he had such difficulty honoring their platonic relationship. As they

130

separated, Kersti looked up at him, gave him a sweet smile and a couple gentle nods of her head as if to say, "I know, I know, it's hard for me also!" He knew exactly what her body language said.

They continued testing "normals" on the scanner. The results were similar in all cases. The largest quantity of the dying person's aura was channeled to the people they felt closest to. Spouses and close family members all received a larger share of the aura than casual acquaintances. An interesting observation was the colors among family members were sometimes similar. Was this a product of nature or nurture? Were the auras similar because of their genetics or because they lived around each other and were taught similar ideas and philosophies from a young age.

One discovery among the prison population that was a bit disconcerting was the tendency for one or both of the parents of the prisoner to have a very dark aura. "Stormy," the techs called them. Sometimes the parents would have a darker, more intensely disrupted aura than the inmate did. In those cases, the research team wondered who the real criminal was. Was the child abused so they had no choice of becoming anything but a criminal? Logan, Kersti and the team saw this so often they spoke among themselves of mandatory sterilization of those with such stormy auras. Would those with "stormy" auras just pass it on to their children? If so, should it be stopped before it spread?

Soon enough, the time had come to begin testing people with Vertig's syndrome. Again, there was no shortage of volunteers. So many dying, so many trying to find a cure. Before long, Logan and Kersti's team was in its fourth week of working with Vertig's patients.

"Paulette, this is Dr. Rainell," Kersti said, introducing them.

"Nice to meet you, Paulette." Logan extended his hand in greeting, but the woman standing before him did not raise her hand. Thin, emaciated and utterly disheveled, she looked to be in her late 40s at the youngest. She lazily looked down at the ground and had minimal responses, all symptoms typical of advanced Vertig's syndrome.

"Paulette," Kersti continued, "is a 28-year-old woman brought to us by the public housing projects. She signed the medical release forms and appears to know why she is here." Logan bent down to try to make eye contact. "Paulette, do you understand that this is an experiment to see what happens when you die?"

"Yes," she murmured, almost inaudibly.

"You will not feel any pain, but we need to hook you up to the scanner. Okay?"

"Okay."

Logan leaned over and whispered into Kersti's ear, "I have to wonder if this is even legal. Is she medically competent to make decisions?"

"She filled out the forms herself and was much more conversant three days ago. I think she's slipping fast," Kersti quietly replied.

"Okay, baby, I trust your judgment," he replied quietly so no one else could hear.

Kersti's eyes locked with Logan's. She winked and smiled; she liked it when he called her "baby."

"Her BUN and creatinine are elevated," Logan said, checking a scrolling list of data on a computer screen. He nodded to Kersti and she returned the nod, each realizing it wouldn't be much longer now. And it wasn't. Normal protocol was for a scanner technician and nurse to always be present while the patient was hooked up. They would then call the doctor into the room to monitor the dying process when they saw the vitals become erratic. This time, that was unnecessary.

"Is her family here yet?" Logan asked.

"There is only one, her brother, and he just got here!"

132

"Good. And . . ."

"Yes, he's already been through the trial run and knows what to do," Kersti replied, even before Logan had finished asking the question. She did that often now. Seemingly read his mind, that is.

"Thank you," Logan said with sincere appreciation.

They had about five minutes to spare. Everyone had just gotten into their monitoring stations when Paulette began to gasp for breath. A moment later she was choking on a final inhalation and the monitors showed flatline. Oddly, Logan saw the little aura Paulette had left simply vanish! Kersti was also carefully watching and did not see any visual change in the brother's bright aura. Later on, they interpreted the data of the scanner the brother was hooked up to. There was no recorded increase in energy transferred to the brother's aura at the time of Paulette's death.

The brother was with the counselor already when Logan groaned in frustration. "Same as the others all month! How can that be?"

Fred, a smart ass of a technician, said, "I don't know, you're the doc."

"The first law . . ." Logan whispered, puzzled.

"What?"

"Nothing. Now then, remind me, how many transitions did we have?"

"She was number four today, and we have five scheduled for tomorrow. But you know how that goes. We had one no-show today. Freddie's family – you know, Freddie Williams – called to tell us he died on the ride over here. They didn't drive fast enough, I guess," Fred concluded.

Once Vertig's was in its final stages, the progression of the syndrome was fairly predictable. Rhabdomyolysis is the breakdown of skeletal muscle. It releases myoglobin into the blood, which in turn clogs the kidneys and initiates renal failure. The amount of dying people allowed researchers to come up with an algorithm to determine when death would occur. Scheduling people to transition . . . who would have guessed?

"Okay, thanks everybody. Good job today! Is everyone okay?" Logan waited for nods and small smiles before adding, "I'll be in my office later today if anyone wants to talk. Remember, everyone in this room is more important than the science! If you're having difficulty, you know I'm always available for you. And I saw the shrink affectionately lurking around in the hallway a minute ago; remember, you can always talk to her, too. By the way, that reminds me . . . everyone's mandatory weekly therapy is coming up, so don't forget about it! It's not worth doing all this work if we come down with the disease ourselves. Now, goodnight. Everyone have a good evening!"

Leaving his team, Logan entered his office. After another day of valuable statistics, it was time to sort out the day's discoveries. Minutes later, however, there was a soft knock at the door. "Yes, come in," he said, glancing up from the data he had been considering.

The door swung softly open and Kersti stepped inside.

"Oh, hello sweetness," he said with a warm smile.

"Hello, doctor," she murmured seductively.

Logan looked back at his paper. "I thought we'd gone through this."

"Through what?"

"Knocking."

She rolled her eyes. "Oh, God, not the knocking thing again. It's polite to knock, so don't try to wean me off of it."

"Yes," he said, letting the paper he was holding flutter down to his desk, "but you're always welcome here. No matter what I'm doing. So next time you knock I'm not letting you in, got it?"

Kersti sidled over and sat on the corner of his desk.

"Whatever you say, baby."

They loved their playful flirtation together. It was fun being playful and to know they loved one another dearly. Besides, being flirtatious meant while they never actually sampled the goods, they could both have a wonderfully active fantasy life. Maybe here, maybe there, then this, then that. They both knew this was an emotional affair and probably not the healthiest thing to do, but they loved each other and it was fun for both of them. Plus, it was a great stress reducer at work. They both always tried to look their best for the other person and constantly did little things to make each other happy. For instance, they learned that they both gave great back rubs. Sometimes, they did big things for each other. For Kersti's 50th birthday party Logan bought 50 dozen red roses! She broke into tears and gave Logan a hug that onlookers thought would never end . . . and that her husband, Scott, didn't appreciate one bit. Logan did his best not to overstep the boundary of their platonic relationship, but he longed for her!

Logan knew all about her less-than-passionate marriage to Scott. Scott was safe. Scott was secure. Scott, with two Ph.D.'s was often critical of Kersti and their children. He would often get angry and blame things on Kersti, even though she was not at fault. Since he was the one with two Ph.D.'s, he knew everything and refused to go to therapy with her. Once, she went so far as to threaten to divorce him. Scott called her bluff and still refused therapy. She reneged. Logan thought she was nuts to stay with someone unappreciative. He even loved her loyalty – just wished it was with him.

"Interesting results today, huh?" Logan said affectionately.

"What was so interesting about them? Weren't they the same as all the others all month?" Kersti said, looking goofy and cross-eyed. "Yes," he acquiesced, grinning at her. "*You* are just so interesting to me!"

"Oh, doctor, I bet you say that to all the nurses."

"Only the one I love."

"I know," Kersti said, getting serious. "It's hard for me, too. Are you okay? Is this work arrangement getting too difficult?"

"No, no!" he assured her quickly. "Like I told you months ago, I love you so much I'm willing to honor that love for you by respecting your previous commitment. But . . . I still wish you were mine."

"Oh, baby! You're so wonderful."

"Besides," Logan grinned, "if we're not working together, how will I know when you become available?"

She sighed. "Always thinking, aren't you?"

"Only about you."

A wonderful daydream danced across her mind, but then she had to change the subject. "You were saying earlier . . . what was interesting about the results?"

"Well, I'm perplexed as to where the energy goes. I mean, on all of them? All month? You know—"

"Don't say it! I'm tired of you saying it." Kersti interrupted. "I know, I know—*The First Law of Thermodynamics.*"

"Well, Kersti, if you're so clever then where did the energy go?"

"It *is* odd, isn't it? When normals die, we can see and measure the energy transfer of their aura to their family members. But people with Vertig's, we can't see it and the Scrivner scanner can't measure it. It's very strange. Could the disease change the energy somehow? Change it so that the scanner can't detect it and we can't see the energy transfer to family members?"

"It's possible, I suppose. But our sensitivities can measure a flea farting! And that still doesn't explain why you and I can see their aura, weak as it may be, and the scanner can detect their aura before they die, but then they die and the energy is gone. Just gone! It doesn't make sense. It can't just disappear!"

"I know . . . the first law."

"Well?"

"I know, I know! Don't lose sleep over it. We'll figure it out. Like you always say, "Things happen in God's time, not ours," Kersti said lovingly.

"What would I do without you," Logan said, blowing her a kiss. She jumped to catch it on her cheek and drifted out the door.

Chapter 18

Breakthrough

Kersti burst into Logan's office the following morning in a flurry of excitement. "Last night I was reading *The Prophet*, Kahlil Gibran's classic," she explained before Logan had a chance to ask what the fervor was all about. "When he's talking about prayer, he says, 'When you pray, you rise to meet in the air those who are praying at that very hour, and whom except in prayer you may not meet.' It inspired me with two ideas. First, let's do an experiment where we hook up more than one person while they are praying and see what happens. Plus, we could expand on that idea and scan people who are praying for a patient with Vertig's while the ill person is dying!"

It took Logan, who had been busy scribbling in a notebook, a few seconds to process her suggestions. "I like that," he said, stifling a yawn.

She feigned a pout. "Well, you don't sound too excited."

"No, no, I am!" he said, more enthusiastically. "I am just . . . a little tired."

Kersti narrowed her eyes. "You went to sleep on time last night like you promised me you would, right? No more pouring over research journals until five in the morning . . .

right?"

Ignoring her question, Logan started to consider the technical aspects. "Each scanner has five channels, so we could scan five people at a time," he reasoned. "Fred will need to hook up the laser-halo detectors for the brain waves, one for each person." For a moment, Logan's excitement waned. "We'll have to represent a new proposal to the board, that could take time . . . what?"

"You didn't answer my question," Kersti grumbled accusingly.

He sighed. "Yes, I went to bed on time."

"And didn't get up early?"

"No . . . well . . ."

"Logan!"

"Alright, alright," he said, dismissing the matter with a wave of his hand. "So I got up a little early and came in to read up on a few things, but I'm fine."

She sighed. "How early, Logan?"

"Well . . . definitely not earlier than four—"

"Logan!" Kersti interrupted, stalking over to stand before his desk. Her hands flew to her hips as she poised herself to lecture. "We've been through this so many times! Your health is important, too, and you need to be getting sleep and taking care of yourself above all. These experiments can wait an extra hour while you . . . are you even paying attention?"

Logan's eyes leapt up to roam her face. "Of course, baby. Always. I'll sleep extra tonight, I promise. Meanwhile, tell me about that second idea of yours."

"Well . . . okay. So I was praying and in a meditative state last night. Remember we both believe that when Jesus said no one gets to the Father except through him, he said that when he was in his Christ consciousness? Since everyone has a Christ consciousness, he wasn't making a derogatory statement about any religion. Not the way radical Christians

140

abuse the statement and use it as a weapon to say people of other faiths will not get to God unless they believe only in Jesus. Energetically, we now know there is our physical body and also our spiritual body or Christ consciousness—whatever you want to call it—and then God. Physical body, Christ body and God. All that got me to thinking about how most religions have some version of the statement that there is no eternal life except through God. So when people with Vertig's die—I mean, transition," she said, quickly correcting herself, "the reason we cannot see their spiritual energy add to their family . . ."—she paused for effect—". . . is because they truly die! What if God gives us many reincarnations but if, because of free will, we repeatedly chose a life without God then eventually our free will wins and we truly die!"

"Spiritual death," Kersti heard a voice whisper.

"What?" She asked, quickly looking behind her. "I thought I heard a voice?"

"I didn't say anything," Logan said, glancing at her curiously before adding, "But, wow, I think you may be on to something. *And*, I think you are brilliant!" he said excitedly. "I'm impressed! I mean, that could be it. That would explain why we cannot see or measure any change in people with Vertig's. So, it seems like we have an interesting theory to investigate. Good thinking, baby! B*ut*, before we do that," Logan asked inquisitively, "how many voices are you hearing?"

"*Just one*, and that's my inner, intuitive voice. We highly evolved spiritual creatures all have one," Kersti said in a mocking tone, flipping her hair back over her shoulder.

"Okay, just making sure we weren't dealing with schizophrenia or multiple personality disorder."

"*Oh*, you're being funny? Glad you explained it; I would have missed it myself," she said sarcastically.

He laughed. "Let's get to work and do what we do best—teamwork! If you could get the technicians started on the scanners and laser sets, I'll get started on the new proposals."

"Yes, sir!" she exclaimed, snapping to attention. Giving a sharp salute, she did an about-face and started to exit the room.

"At ease, trooper," Logan said. "You are not dismissed yet."

Kersti froze in her tracks and turned to face him. He was already up from behind his desk and was slowly, with a broad smile, walking towards her. He wrapped his arms around her, squeezed her into a big hug and lovingly whispered in her ear, "You are amazing! This is brilliant spiritual intuition. I'm so proud of you and feel honored to be able to work with you."

She melted into his body, feeling loved, honored and respected. Usually she was taken for granted, but to be told these things with such love and respect. She hugged him tighter, and Logan felt his shirt dampen with her silent tears. "Oh, baby, did I say something your heart needed to hear?"

Kersti hugged tighter and adamantly nodded her head. *Yes!* she cried out in her secret heart. Because she loved him, always him, and needed him so much. "I love you, Kersti Craddock!" Logan whispered into her ear, using her maiden name. Kersti trembled as she cried in his arms.

*****

Like everything in research, what they thought would take a couple days took a couple weeks. The technical aspects were more difficult than plugging in five laser sets. Logan could not follow everything the technical crew said. Something about thermocouples overheating with all five channels running simultaneously. Although he was usually technically savvy, it was nice to say, "Make it happen!" And they did.

Logan's proposal to the board went well. After he

142

presented it, he was asked to leave the room while the executives conferred in private. When he returned, he was told that the proposal was acceptable and they were giving him more time and money. Logan wondered if the military was partially funding this project, since the government only threw money at the military! The physician in him wondered how different it could be if only half the money spent on defense were to be spent on health, education or simply putting everyone through a Scrivner scanner to treat their emotional and spiritual problems. It would be a different world. As a physician and a person in recovery, he saw abused and neglected children grow up to be adult perpetrators, sometimes even on a global scale. Stalin, Hitler, Mao, Hussein, Rossini and Tso were just a few examples he marked off in his mind.

*****

The first family to be scanned simultaneously was that of a convicted mass murderer. They were perfect test subjects. The inmate, John Wilson, had developed Vertig's while in jail. His parents were normals. They were devout Christians and very willing to participate in the experiment. Whether they were hooked up to a scanner or not, they said that praying for John's soul was what they would be doing anyway while he was dying. They participated in the intake therapy and were signed up for aftercare, which accomplished two things. It gave participants the chance to go over the test results, to feel that they had truly participated in the advancement of science. It also gave them access to counseling and therapy after the transition of their loved one.

Logan was appreciative of the fact that they had a group of gifted techs and counselors who were all indispensable at making the clinic operate. He was cognizant of the fact that every person had a vital role. No one was more important than another. He always tried to make everyone feel important and valued, both individually and as a part of the team. From his days in private practice, he remembered reading a study that pointed out how important every single person was in a medical office. When a person is sick and not feeling well, does the person who schedules the appointment sound helpful and concerned? When that patient comes in the office, do the front office personnel seem empathetic and compassionate? Is the nurse who does their vital signs helpful and conversant about why the patient is there today? All of these contacts are equally important in the health of the patient because the mind is the single most important factor in overall health. If any of the office staff are rude or uncaring, the speed of the patient's healing process could be affected. The very fact that other people cared about a patient's day-to-day existence was essential for overall health. Without it, people lose hope. When they lose hope, they lose interest in life. And as the whole world was now experiencing, if you lose hope you can develop Vertig's and Vertig's is a death sentence.

Chapter 19

A Sacred Event

The scanner clinic had its own six-bed hospice to care for patients just prior to their transition. John had been brought here from the jail two days earlier. There was no need for security, and the transfer was as simple as signing a piece of paper. End-stage Vertig's patients were depressed, apathetic and hadn't eaten for days, so the last thing on their minds was escape! They were hopeless and had no desire for anything . . . not even life itself.

"Logan, we're starting soon," grumbled a frustrated Kersti. Her fist hurt from pounding the door of his office, which was usually never locked, for the past ten minutes. She hoped he was alright; what if he'd accidentally locked the door and then something happened? He hadn't been listening to her advice and was getting barely an hour or two of sleep each day for a week now. She tensed; what if his body finally gave out? What if he needed her but here she was, trapped on this side of the door?

"Logan!" she cried, mashing her fist against the door again.

"Kersti?" called a voice from somewhere behind her.

She whirled around. "Logan?"

There he stood across the room, the picture of

puzzlement. He cocked his head uncertainly, and his eyes darted from Kersti to the door and back. "What are you doing?" he asked.

"Oh, nothing too important," she drawled. "Just almost having a heart attack after scouring this building for the past hour, looking for you, and finally finding your stupid office door locked and getting no answer! I thought you never locked it."

He scratched his head. "I don't." Wandering over, he wiggled the doorknob. Stuck, indeed. Retreating a few steps, he adjusted himself into an athletic position. "Maybe it's just . . . *jammed!*" he yelled, running and slamming himself into the door. It burst open and swung with a crash into the wall; Logan, meanwhile, lost his balance and ended up sprawled across the floor.

"Logan!" Kersti called out, kneeling to help him stand. "Are you okay?"

"'Course," he said softly, brushing off his clothes. "Now, enough of this silliness. We have an experiment to run per your brilliant plan, baby." He swung the door away from the wall to survey the damage. "Though we'll need a repair crew in here later."

Kersti walked with him into the new room. For this new phase of the experiment, the room was clinical out of necessity, comforting out of respect. The walls were painted white, which helped the aura reader, or 'visualist', see the colors of the auras more easily. A subdued back lighting also helped enhance the colors. The transition chair was a comfortable, oversized recliner that was adjustable to any position the patient wanted. Smaller chairs were brought in for family to sit in. There were even pillows scattered around the floor if someone wanted to meditate. Knee pads were available for those who wanted to pray on their knees. There was a pond in the corner of the room that was shaped like an abstract heart. It was about fifteen feet across and had large, beautifully-colored koi, easily seen from the monitoring chair. On the other side of the room was a cascading waterfall, flowing over rocks, with a stream wandering through the middle of the room. Numerous plants and mosses grew along the stream bed, around the pond and all over the nooks and crevices of the waterfall. It was long known that watching fish swim, being around plants and the oxygen they produce, the sound of running water, and the positive ions produced by splashing water all had calming effects on the human psyche. The staff had even started to use the room as a rest area. The room had a peaceful feel while being scientifically practical.

The room was divided lengthwise by a Carin force field. Developed by Dr. Carin Renee, this was an application of the mag-lev hovercraft technology. Two high density tri-aniline magnets were used, one in the ceiling and one in the floor. Regular alternating current was 60 Hz, or 60,000 cycles per second, but the current for the mag-lev system was computer modulated to cycle at 240 million cycles per second. Run between the two magnets, it created a dense electromagnetic field. It was so dense that no other electromagnetic wavelengths, including light, could pass through. The effect was that people on both sides of the force field got light and sound reflected back to them. On the participant's side of the field, the patient and his or her family could see a reflection of themselves and their side of the room. The same was true on the observer's side where Logan and Kersti sat. The observers watched a holo-projection of the participants. The beauty of the system was that while the patient and family had their privacy, if there was a problem they were in reality all in the same room. Logan and Kersti could walk right through the electromagnetic field and deal with whatever emergency might be occurring.

The actual equipment for the scanner was in a separate room, which was well insulated for sound. The lasers that scanned each person were marvels of modern medicine. They were tiny, only about two by three centimeters, and mounted in the ceiling. Yet they would follow wherever the patient moved. Two beams were emitted, one in the sagittal direction and another in the coronal direction. The beams oscillated back and forth, scanning the entire head so no brain wave could be missed. Initially, the information was relayed from the laser to the scanner by telemetry. But solar flares and cosmic radiation caused interference, so each ceiling laser was connected to the scanner by a thin fiber optic cable. This gave the ultimate in clarity of signal.

Kersti and Logan arrived just in time. The hospice nurses were just about to call to say they thought it was time for John and his parents to be brought into the room. The parents had been through the recital training, and everyone was seated. John was zombie-like in the chair. He was emotionless and appeared dead, except for his breathing. Even though John had abandoned them years earlier both parents were tearful, knowing this was the last time they would see their son. It rarely mattered how big a disappointment a family member might have been during his or her life. When it came down to the last time a family would see the person alive it was usually an emotional experience, all except for the patient with Vertig's. John drooped like a rag doll in his chair. His parents sat by his side, each holding one of his limp hand in theirs, and holding each others hand, completing the circle. Their eyes were closed, and they appeared to be praying.

Both Logan and Kersti were in awe of the beauty and magnitude of the parents' auras. These two were obviously loving human beings. Their colors were similar to each other and magnificent! Each had many smaller layers of color fluttering beneath their dominate layers. Logan and Kersti's experience so far led them to believe this meant there were many people who loved these two and the previously

148

departed left some of their energy behind with these two kindred spirits. Their dominant colors were a very pleasing forest green, with bright flashes of sapphire blue, surrounded with a golden-white layer. The husband had a few lingers of red. Both had large auras that stood out almost 32 inches from the physical body. They were stunningly beautiful.

Having assumed their places on the observers' side, Logan whispered to Kersti, "If everyone could see what a magnificent creation of light we are . . ." His voice quavered, and trailed off. Kersti wrapped his hand in her own and gave it a gentle squeeze. She knew from his voice he would have tears in his eyes. This was one of the things she had grown to love about Logan. He was not only able, but also willing to express his feelings when they came up.

Kersti and Logan had just gotten accustomed to the beauty of these two auras when they both gasped. Kersti reflexively reached for Logan's hand, and he grabbed her and encompassed her in a full body hug. The room had filled with a clear, golden-white light of blinding intensity. John was in the center chair with a barely visible, dark, constricted aura. One parent was kneeling on either side of him, praying, with their own beautiful aura shinning. Then surrounding all three, a bright, golden-white sphere enveloped them in its brilliance. It looked like a miniature sun glowing with the three of them in the center.

Kersti and Logan were captivated. Logan always felt honored to be a part of someone's transition, but this was truly blessed. They stared in awe for what seemed like only seconds but later discovered it was almost twelve minutes. It was a timeless beauty.

When John's heart finally stopped, a monitor emitted a single faint chime that marked physical death had occurred. The parents prayed a while longer, and the beautiful golden globe lessened in brightness and seemed to evaporate into the air. The parents tearfully hugged and consoled one another.

149

With the force field still on, the parents could not hear Logan and Kersti talking.

"That was . . . incredible," Kersti whispered almost breathlessly.

"Amazing!" Logan agreed.

"I thought you were going to crush me in that bear hug."

"I-I'm sorry, baby. I was excited!" he stammered.

"When the light first entered the room . . . well . . ." Kersti held her hands up in wonderment.

"Oh my God . . . no pun intended!" They both burst out laughing.

"It was *so* beautiful," Kersti said.

"There are no words, *no* words, to describe it."

"It was so intense . . . so vibrant!"

"Could you even see what happened to John's aura when he died?" Logan asked.

Kersti shook her head. "Not a bit."

"Neither could I."

After an awe-inspired silence in which each reminisced about what they'd seen, Kersti asked, "Did you hear the voice?"

"Didn't you feel me jump?"

"Well, yes, of course, but I wasn't sure. I thought maybe you jumped because I jumped."

Logan repeated the voice's words. "Where two or more of you are gathered . . ."

". . . in my name, so too am I!" Kersti finished. "What do you think it was?"

"I think . . . well, it's a bit out there, but I think that was the Holy Spirit. Is it possible?" Logan asked astounded.

"How is any of this possible? I'm a little freaked out right now. I feel simultaneously blessed, confused and sort of scared!" Kersti confessed.

Logan wrapped his arms around her again, pulled her

close and gave her a loving hug. Then he said, "I know, baby . . . me too, me too."

"I think we just saw the Holy Spirit," Kersti said quietly, her head pressed against Logan's chest.

They turned off the force field and walked over to the parents and gave each a hug. "We are sorry for your loss," Logan said. "We both saw the two of you are very loving people. If there's anything we can do for you, just ask."

"Thank you."

*****

While the first time was most dramatic, seeing the Holy Spirit was always exciting. They continued to monitor people with Vertig's while other people prayed for them. The results were very similar whether the family in question was Christian, Muslim, Hindu, Native American, or even one aboriginal family. The Holy Spirit—or "Casper" as Fred, one of the more sacrilegious technicians, named it—would always show up and fully encompass those who were praying. The Holy Spirit's energy field was so bright it was hard to see what was going on inside its blindingly powerful aura. Logan and Kersti could not determine what happened to the Vertig's patient's soul at the time of death. The visualists could not see any noticeable change, and the information from the scanner was inconclusive. The Holy Spirit was such an immense energy pattern that the very idea of measuring its energy with the scanner or visually comparing changes with one's eyes was laughable.

"How do we scan the Holy Spirit?" Logan pondered aloud. "How can we possibly quantify a change of energy from something so small to an energy pattern so immense?"

"Maybe if we pray real hard, God will send Jesus so we can have a physical body to put the laser on," suggested Fred.

151

"You are going to need Jesus if you keep making those kinds of suggestions," Kersti grumbled, slightly offended.

"Sorry," Fred apologized timidly.

"There has to be a solution," Logan said.

"Doc," Fred offered, "this may be a problem with no solution."

"He's right," Kersti admitted. "Or, maybe a solution will become evident later on. We could just state the facts we've discovered and have people reach their own conclusions. I think that may be the most powerful solution. People will see and believe what they want to. Spiritual believers will see that normals pass on their energy to their loved ones when they die whereas people with no spiritual belief—that is, Vertig's patients—cannot have their energy measured when they die. They have a spiritual death . . . that is a powerful statement."

"You're right. Thank you. Just the way you phrased that was perfect," Logan said quietly. "It gave me chills."

"Well," Fred interrupted. "For my part, I won't be satisfied until I put a laser on Jesus!"

"Fred, you're terrible!" Kersti chastised, smiling.

"I know. I try," he said proudly.

Chapter 20

Pain

Zeus, Logan's beloved thirteen-year-old Samoyed, the dog that taught him unconditional love, was dying. He had a brain tumor and was having seizures. It was painful watching Zeus have seizures, but knowing he would soon die was excruciating. Logan promised his friend he would not let him suffer.

The medicines helped some. But when Zeus had an episode of seizures that couldn't be stopped after giving him multiple trans-sonic injections of the medicine, Logan knew it was time. He got his beloved Zeus to the vet in ten minutes in his hover and in another ten minutes was telling Zeus how much he loved him. Zeus heard and wagged his tail, thump, thump, thump, as Logan lay with him on the floor. Logan didn't move as he held his best friend in his arms. The veterinarian working around him used a trans-sonic injector and gave sweet Zeus the last shot, behind the nape of his neck.

Laying with his head on Zeus's chest, Logan heard the thumping of his tail stop, felt his friend's breathing stop and, through tear-glazed eyes, saw Zeus's beautiful golden aura brighten, then separate from his body. Tears poured out of Logan's eyes, blurring his vision. He watched his arm, which was embraced under Zeus's head, but didn't see any of Zeus's golden aura add to his own. Did he miss it through the tears? Was it different with animals? He dissolved into a sobbing child, clutching his friend and crying, thinking Zeus's energy was not with him. God, this was painful. He felt completely alone.

*****

He would bury Zeus on his favorite spot, the hill overlooking the pond. But before that could be done, there was one more painful thing to do. Many times he had watched Zeus, Loki, and other dogs greet each other. First they'd see each other, and as they got within six feet of one another, he'd see each one's golden lingers stretch out to make auric contact with the other. Only then came the ultimate smell and sniff time.

After arriving home, he simply stood by the front door of his house. The doorknob was so close, yet to reach out and gently turn it and step inside seemed like an unthinkable act. When he finally went in the house to tell Loki the bad news, he wasn't aware of being inside until he saw her standing across the room. She knew something was wrong because Logan was crying. Loki had always been very sensitive to Logan's emotions.

Zeus's body was still in the hov outside. Loki was apprehensive and refused to get within twenty feet of the vehicle. She paced from side to side, wondering why her best friend didn't get up to greet her. Logan talked her into coming closer. When Loki got within ten feet, Logan saw her golden lingers stretch out in greeting towards Zeus. Logan, and evidently Loki, witnessed Zeus's lifeless body being unresponsive. She jumped backward like she'd been struck at by a rattlesnake! She knew her friend was dead.

It wasn't until Logan was digging the hole to bury Zeus that Loki came up to actually smell his body. Her nose

154

worked along his legs, his body, and finally paused by his head. Her tongue, small and pink and uncertain, brushed Zeus's nose. Receiving no response, she lay down beside her friend and placed her head over his.

For three weeks Loki would wander from room to room, looking for her companion. She also sat on his spot on the hill and howled the softest, most sorrowful howl Logan ever heard. His grief was increased by the thought that Zeus's aura was not with him. It was different with animals, and that made him sad. The being that taught him about love was not a part of his aura. But he always would have the memories of Zeus and the experience of feeling unconditional love.

Chapter 21

Pain Unendurable

One month later, Logan's life changed forever. It was the end of the week, and Logan was busy sorting through data from the previous day. A soft tap sounded at his door.

"Yes, come in," Logan said.

The door slowly swung open. Silhouetted in the doorway stood a familiar figure.

"You're still knocking..." Logan smiled, then saw an unfamiliar frown.

"You're upset?" he asked, dropping the data emitter and crossing the room to wrap Kersti in a gentle hug.

Her lips briefly flickered into a small smile. "Hello, Logan. It's good to see you."

Logan could feel in the hug something was wrong. Coupled with the distress on her face—she was shivering ever so slightly, like a frail leaf in a breeze, in his arms.

"Baby, you're trembling. Are you sick?"

"No, I'm sad."

"What happened to you?"

"Logan," she said sorrowfully, "it's not about me. It's about . . . us."

"Us?"

"In a way. Actually, it's about the end of . . ." Kersti broke into tears. Sobbing she said, "Logan, I have to leave!"

"What do you mean?" Logan said, breaking their embrace.

"I can't work with you anymore."

"WHAT DO YOU MEAN?" Logan repeated loudly, fear overwhelming him.

Kersti paused a moment and caught her breath, "Scott is jealous of our relationship and the time the job takes away from my family."

Logan went numb, then stumbled around for words. "Well, he knows there's . . . there's no physical relationship, right? That y-you and I have a platonic relationship that we never . . . well, we've never even had an intimate kiss! Not one! I know there were multiple times early in our relationship when you reassured him we were just good friends, and t-then there was that time the two of us together approached him to make sure he was okay with the working arrangement when we first started this program!" His throat was beginning to tighten and he was stuttering, stammering, and praying that, somehow, his words would make a difference.

"He knows," Kersti said solemnly.

"B-but what changed?"

"People change."

"What does that mean? What happened? What does he want? And there's a way, there's got to be a way, why . . . we could cut back on your hours, have him watch you here for a while, prove to him that—"

"It won't matter. Logan, he wants me to quit entirely."

"OH MY GOD! Kersti, I-I can't do this without you! Oh God, please no!" Logan pleaded.

"Yes, you can," Kersti said quietly, reaching out to touch his hand. Logan stumbled backwards.

"WELL I DON'T WANT TO DO THIS

WITHOUT YOU!" he shrieked, fear turning to panic. He began pacing, murmuring to himself. "I-I . . . oh, God, Kersti," Logan cried, breaking into tears. "I LOVE YOU!" he sobbed. "I do this job to be around you! I do it to see your face every day, to hear your voice, to watch you laugh, see you smile, smell your breath, that tiny hint of perfume. I do it to see your brilliance every day! Every day you think of something I don't think of. You have a solution I don't see. YOU COMPLETE ME, BABY! We are a team! I-I don't want to do this by myself. I can't!" Tears streamed down his face as he gazed at Kersti.

"You see," she whispered. This is what Scott is picking up on. We love each other!"

"Well, of course we do! We've loved one another since we were kids. We told him we haven't done anything, and we've acted completely honorably—when most damn people would NOT have!" he added defensively.

"We have, and we can be proud of ourselves for it. But we are having an *emotional* love affair!" Kersti brushed a sleeve over her cheeks to mop up her tears. "Everything you said," she murmured, her voice dripping with agony, "is true. *Everything*, Logan . . . I agree with everything you said. I look forward to getting to work to see you. I want to be here to be with YOU! I love working with you! You are kind and patient with everyone on the team. I love watching you work. You think of something and then physically get it together so it works. Your voice, your humor, your hugs, your back rubs, the smell of your breath! After a long day, the smell of your body pheromones drives me nuts! More times than I can count, I'd get a whiff of your body odor or breath and wanted to grab you and kiss you and . . . damn it! I even dream of you." Then, laughing back a sob, she added, "And when you're not looking . . " She paused, then mumbled, "I look at your butt as you walk across the room."

Stifling a laugh, he said, "Well, of course! I'm always

watching your butt. I just didn't want to sound so crass at such a sensitive moment!" Both laughed and cried at the same time.

Kersti lunged to hug him. She'd never felt so *good* just being hugged. She melted into him, and they became one. His strong arms and broad chest physically comforted her, and his falling tears were emotional proof of his love. Their tears mingled together on her rosy cheeks, and she thought about how her husband had never cried with her. She loved Logan so much!

Logan had never seen a woman he thought was more beautiful. He loved everything about her—physically, mentally, emotionally and spiritually. God, she felt good in his arms! He held her tightly against his body, feeling the sleek curves of her body fold against his, her head rubbing against his chest. Her arms, tight around his body, held on like he would slip away. Her sweet, soft breasts pushing against his chest. Her body warmth healed his soul! He could feel it healing him!

One of his hands carved a smooth path from her shoulders down to the small of her back, tracing every fine muscle and mapping those places that made her gasp softly. Pausing where that sweet curve of her bottom started, he traced small circles on her pants and wished he could bury his hand inside them. Kersti moaned and snuggled closer to him. Logan turned his head towards hers and kissed the side of her hair, her face, her neck. She smelled so good, though the soft perfume together with the unique scent of her skin always made him wonder what she tasted like. He was getting aroused, and so was she. At the same moment, they became aware of something else.

"Baby, look at our auras," Logan whispered.

They did not break the hug but half turned, loosening one side of their arms and looking down at their bodies. The intensity of their auras together had geometrically increased

160

to four times its usual flare. The colors were brighter, and the activity was more intense. Bright lingers flashed back and forth in the narrow space between their bodies. Their own personal lightening. This was not dangerous lightening; this was love lightening! They stood in awe, looking at themselves. Their auras curled, twisted and caressed one another, energetically doing what they both wanted to do physically!

"See, baby, my energy likes your energy," Logan said in a playfully sexy voice. "Look! We are glowing together."

Kersti dipped her head in agreement. "And, see, mine likes yours." But there was a hint of grief in her voice, which Logan picked up on.

"We can't do this, can we?" Logan asked sadly.

"You know we can't."

They continued to hug, savoring every second, drowning in one another's arms. "After coming this far and being so honorable for so long," Kersti said sadly, "we can't."

After a couple minutes of tearful hugging and watching the light show, Kersti said, "It's strange how you noticed we are glowing. That's how this started. A couple months ago, Scott came by to pick me up and saw us standing together. We both had data emitters in our hands, for God's sake! But, later, he said we glow when we stand together . . . and he doesn't even have the gift of seeing auras!"

They were still hugging, neither wanting to break this intimate moment. It felt so good, just holding each other, sharing their energy that belonged together.

"So," Logan murmured, "just because he saw us standing together, 'glowing', you can't work here anymore?"

She paused. "Well, sort of . . ."

"What do you mean? Talk to me! What happened?"

Still hugging, Kersti opened her mouth and closed it wordlessly. Logan caught the smell of her breath, and he loved it. When she finally spoke, the delicate scent wafted to him with each word. "Well, it's sort of embarrassing, but

161

Scott and I were having sex and I said your name."

"Oh, God," he gasped.

"Exactly. It wasn't good."

"I can imagine."

"I apologized, of course. I tried to reassure him that we had never had sex, but of course he doesn't believe me. He's obsessed with the idea now. I say your name during sex, and we 'glow together!' We finally went to therapy. We've had several sessions, but he still won't let go of it."

"Leave him!" Logan pleaded. "I know you love me!"

"I do! I love you more than anything! But . . . Logan, it's not that easy. Scott is the father of my children. He's not a great husband, which is why I said we were having sex instead of making love, like . . . you and I would," she added, smiling, longingly at Logan. "But he *is* a good father. Maybe . . . maybe when the kids are grown," she said, hopefully, trying to give encouragement. "Logan, you told me that raising kids was a sacred duty. That the damage or trauma done to a child stays with them into adulthood. I need to do as good for them as I can. I already feel guilty for the amount of time I've put into this project . . . time spent away from them!"

"Oh, they'll be fine," Logan said.

She slapped his butt.

"Oooh! Do that again," he moaned.

"YOU were thinking more about yourself than my children!" she snarled.

"Yes, I was," he whispered, brushing his thumb slowly along her cheek and savoring its delicate lines and texture. "I love you."

"And . . . oh, Logan, I will always love you!" She hugged him again and held on tight like their lives depended on never letting go.

"Kersti?"

She looked up at him, their faces mere inches apart. "You know I love you more than anything. I've loved you since the fifth grade!"

Tears swelled in Logan's eyes again, and seeing his tears drove Kersti into a sobbing mass clutching to his chest. Her tears strengthened his embrace as he struggled to get his words out coherently. "I love you more than anything. I would do anything for you! I've respected your wishes and not made sexual advances at you, even though I wanted to. I've fantasized about it and dreamed about it, but I love you so much and respect you so much that I honored your request and did my best to keep our relationship platonic."

"And I love you for treating me with honor and respect. I've never known a man who's done that before!" She burst into fresh tears, pulled him tighter and buried her face in his shirt, crying.

After they stopped crying, Logan said, "Kersti, my goal in this life is that, when I die, you can look back and say, 'Yes, he truly loved me with all his heart!"

"I know that already," she sobbed.

"That could happen in one of two ways. Either we will get some time in this lifetime to share our lives together, or you will stay with Scott and later look back and say, 'Logan loved me so much he respect my wishes and let me go.'"

Dissolved by the tears, they became one. In the end, their words didn't matter. Not their yells or their whispers. All that mattered was that deep embrace and the tears. Dissolved by the tears, they were one.

And their auras, dancing and singing.

Glowing.

*****

That was it. In another two weeks, she was gone. In those two weeks he tried to talk to her, but her motherly instincts were stronger than her love for him. On his less selfish and self-centered days, he respected the strength and courage it

163

took for her to follow through with her commitment. But most days he wanted to die.

She was not just gone from work. She was gone from the continent! Scott accepted a job at a research lab in Australia and within two months they had moved. She did not want to talk – too painful! Logan felt like he was dying. His heart was broken. Shattered. The crumbled pieces splintering beneath the heavy feet of time like shards of glass.

Kersti never called him, which was a dagger in his heart. So all communications ceased. He did not understand. He couldn't. How could this love they had together just . . . end? A love of such magnitude, and it was gone! Boom! Done! Over! No, he would never understand. Logan, with daggers in his heart, still loved her. Yet he would honor her wishes, despite the fact that they were the opposite of what he personally wanted. So he didn't call her.

Logan descended into a spiraling state of grief he had never experienced. Zeus was gone. Kersti was gone. He wanted to die, hoped to die so the pain would end. He thought about her constantly. He prayed for her happiness but was mostly ensnared in the worst two words of the English language: "What if?"

He was a zombie at work. He was useless. Utterly and absolutely helpless. His fellow workers consoled him the best they could and picked up the loose ends. The project was at a standstill for about three months.

During those months, Logan truly thought he was dying. The emotional pain was overwhelming. He lost twenty pounds because his appetite was gone. Vanished. Dead, like himself. Headaches ripped through him nearly every day, even though his head had never hurt before. He was less tolerant of his back pain. He started to get chest pain. One time it was so bad he thought he was having a heart attack. He rushed to the ER and had a full cardiac workup. The results

164

were normal. The diagnosis—separational anxiety! "No shit!" he snapped at the ER doc.

He did not sleep well at night. He would drift off around midnight, totally exhausted from thinking about "Her" all day. At three in the morning he would jolt awake, thinking of "Her." Desperately trying to calm himself, he would try to read or watch the holo-projector and would usually drift back to sleep at around 6:00 am. At 7:30 in the morning he would be on his feet to be at work by nine.

Every day and night was the same. He thought about every waking moment he had ever had with her. From the time they were kids until the day she left, over and over and over! It felt like his own personal version of hell, thinking about the *only* girl he ever loved in his whole life and that she left him, that his love was not enough for her. He thought he was going crazy. He knew he was depressed. He began taking antidepressants, but they did not help. He started therapy, which was slow.

Then it happened. An old demon surged forth from the black depths of his mind. He thought about drinking. Intellectually, he knew drinking would not help anything. But the pain was overwhelming. The pain had to stop. It was getting worse, not better. The old saying about time healing all wounds was not true. Some pain is forever.

He had gotten so busy with the project and with Kersti that he had stopped going to AA meetings months ago. Early on in his recovery, he had a relapse. He felt horribly guilty. The wisdom of his sponsor shone through when he said, "All a relapse means is you didn't do what you need to do on a daily basis to maintain your spiritual health." In the AA big book, it says something like, "You must find a Higher Power who works in your personal life because, at some point in time, that will be the only thing between you and a drink." All the wisdom of AA suddenly came flooding back to him. He knew what he should do. He knew he should call his sponsor. He knew he should go to a meeting and talk about wanting a drink. He knew he should get on his knees and ask God to relieve him of the obsession of Kersti. These things Logan knew. But . . . the pain! He wanted to die so the pain would stop. He didn't care. He didn't care about himself or anyone else. Self-pity was a warm blanket, and he wrapped himself up tight. That's when he roared out the next two worse words in the English language, "Fuck it!" Hoping the whole world would hear, he savored the taste of those words on his lips and cried them again and again. He didn't care anymore.

On his way home from work he stopped by the liquor store. Decisions, decisions! In the 24 years since he'd quit drinking, all sorts of new brands of alcohol had appeared on the market. He decided on a new expensive brand of tequila. Only a couple hundred bottles were made per year! Tequila had never been his drink of choice, but it always put him down quick.

When he got home, he sat down at the kitchen table. Fuck the shot glass; he had a brandy snifter! He never liked the salt and lime, so he filled the snifter until it was half full and brought it up to his nose to inhale the wonderful aroma of alcohol. He was just about ready to drink when Loki, 70 pounds of Samoyed, came bounding into the room, jumped up and smacked her two front paws on the table—which she had never done before—and knocked over the bottle of tequila! "Fuck, Loki, what are you doing! You stupid fucking dog!" Logan snarled. She immediately jumped down and solemnly came over and laid her white, soft face in his lap. Her deep, dark, soul-penetrating eyes peered deeply into Logan's own. He set the untouched snifter of tequila down, wrapped both of his hands around her sweet face, kissed the top of her head and whispered, "I get it."

He started to cry. He cried until his shirt and Loki's head were wet with tears, and even then he sobbed on until he felt a warm tongue dance over his hand. Loki sat there with him, licking his hands and doing her best to comfort him. "My higher power works in mysterious ways, even through a dog." he murmured, kissing her nose gently.

Logan didn't drink that night. Instead, he called his sponsor. He called his therapist. Over the weeks that followed, he went to an AA meeting every day after work and called his sponsor each evening. He got his spiritual life back to where it had been before he became obsessed with Kersti and the project. He hit his knees every morning and night to thank God in gratitude for everything he had been given . . . and, especially, that he'd been given a second chance without having to drink.

When he prayed in the mornings and evenings, he would say loudly, "Do you want to go pray?" Wherever Loki was in the house, she'd run into the bedroom and jump up on the bed, paws hanging off the edge. When Logan knelt, they could hold "paws". His prayer life changed, and he felt more connected to his higher power. Previously when he prayed, it was just him and God. You would think that would be enough. Yet now he had more joy in his heart while praying *because* looking at a happy, smiling Samoyed face *has* to bring joy! It was like God smiling back at him! The reflection of God is doG! Some people are lucky enough to feel that.

Chapter 22

Guinea Pig

It was a while before Logan finally got his head back into his job. He had been on autopilot, but thankfully, most of what they had been doing was routine items the foundation wanted done. It required very little creative thought on his part.

He still missed Kersti, but the love he felt for her helped his creativity blossom again as time trickled on. Though he could never forget her, the very memory of seeing her, of holding her, of loving her, struck a chord in his soul. Sometimes, he could close his eyes and almost imagine she was beside him once more, locked tight in his embrace.

In the lab, they had become quite comfortable monitoring the different emotional conditions that occurred with different layers of the aura. The team was able to bring up specific layers of the aura for any given person to experience. After experimenting on many volunteers and getting predictable results, Logan was determined to try the procedure on himself next.

"We don't think it's a good idea," the entire team told him as soon as he presented his proposal.

"There are always risks in science!" Logan argued. "Dr. Salk tried the polio vaccine on himself, and think how much we could learn if I was the guinea pig!"

"And think how much we will lose if something happens to you," Carrie, the new technician, chimed in.

"The foundation already agreed," Logan said nonchalantly.

"You're fucking kidding? No way!" Fred cried out.

"My contract is almost up for renewal, and I might have mentioned there might be a problem if . . ."

"Is this some death wish since Kersti left?" Fred accused.

"Of course not! Well, maybe a little . . . no, no, I'm kidding! It will be okay, guys! I'll be fine," Logan said emphatically.

The team shuffled around a bit, exchanging glances. Finally, Fred said, "We've already done it safely with others. What's the big deal? Plus, you know he's going to do it anyway. So let's not make it a hassle!"

"Thank you, Fred. You're wise beyond your years! We have the scanner reversed, so instead of monitoring the different aura layers we will amplify the bands and bring them to the surface."

"Which bands will that be?" Carrie asked.

Wishing the room could be dark for effect, Logan murmured, "Oooohh . . . the dark, black, scary ones!"

"I knew it! I knew it!" Carrie sounded scared.

"And so what? We already know what they mean in other patients. I just need to . . . I want to see what mine are. It's about being a first-hand witness regarding what some of the dark bands in my aura mean This is what we do as research scientists right? Research!"

"It just seems like an unnecessary risk," Carrie stated.

"Duly noted. Now, let's get on with it! I trust all of you with my life!" Logan said, raising his hands in an exaggerated silent prayer. Fred glanced at Carrie and rolled his eyes.

Logan wasn't the only one who missed Kersti's brilliant mind. The project missed her because she and Logan were the only two good "visualists." Others in the group had started to glimpse auras, but to them the folds and layers of brilliant light were mere flickers and faded glows. Not one could match or even come close to the specificity of Kersti and Logan. And now that Logan was in the scanner, it left the group feeling like an important safety net was missing. The group would depend on Logan's ability to stay intellectually present enough to hit the emergency powers shutoff if necessary. The concern was if he was overwhelmed with emotional trauma, he may not be able to recognize he was in trouble and shut down the system. Fortunately, the group was very experienced by now, and most of the technicians were certain they could tell if a volunteer—in this case, Logan— was in trouble. Even if he couldn't.

The next day, Logan awoke feeling hopeful, loved and happy. He rolled over and slid his feet over the edge of the mattress, poking his toes around to find his slippers. Keeping his eyes closed, he thought back to the dream he had. He had been in a large, beautiful home filled with love and gratitude. There was a knock at the door, and when he answered it, he saw Kersti and Zeus had come to visit! Kersti swept him into a long, wonderful hug and a passionate kiss-- she did taste good! He started to kneel to hug Zeus, but instead Zeus stood up on his back paws and hugged him like a human. The three of them took a walk in silence around a gorgeous mountain lake that spread from just outside the house. Then, disconnected as dreams can be, the three of them were suddenly swimming underwater as if it was a normal part of their physiology, pulling oxygen from water. They swam to a golden-white light dome burning underwater. Zeus led the way with the two humans following as they swam inside the light dome. It was safe and loving. Logan awoke feeling comforted, knowing this was a hopeful dream and he had the love of Zeus and Kersti for support.

A few hours later in the lab, they adjusted the laser to scan Logan. "Now, Doc," Fred explained, "I've hooked this up like a dead man's switch. As long as you hold it in your hand, the power stays on. If you drop it or release it on purpose, it will shut down the system, easy enough?"

"A no-brainer, Fred. Thank you!" Logan paused, debating the thought, but finally added, "I know I have never asked this of the group before, but I have also never been the one under the scanner. Can I ask you guys to give me a moment of silence or pray along if you know the Serenity Prayer?"

The three present in the room fell silent. Logan was happy when Carrie repeated the words of the prayer with him. "God, Grant me the serenity to accept the things I can not change; Courage to change the things I can; and the wisdom to know the difference."

When they finished, Logan smiled at Carrie. She said, "Al-Anon."

He chuckled. "It's well known how much the Al-Anon loves the alcoholic. Should I be worried?"

"No, not you! Now, if you were my ex-husband, I'd have to recuse myself!"

"Well, thank you for being here," Logan said, smiling. "I feel better because of it. Now . . . let's get started!"

The team knew what to do. They were to scan through the different layers of his aura, keeping each layer at the surface so Logan could experience the emotional reality of it for about a minute. Then, they would move to the next layer. When they got to the black layer, they were instructed to leave it for about five minutes unless Logan dropped the dead man's switch or the team saw something disconcerting.

Logan got comfortable in the recliner and began to watch his aura. He could see his legs, arms and torso fairly well. Carrie had the idea of bringing in two full-sized mirrors and angling them so he could see the side view of his head and torso. Of course, the whole session was being recorded so he could talk about the entire experience in real time if he wanted.

"Ready?" Carrie called out.

For a moment, Logan simply watched the colors of his aura lazily drift around him. "Ready," he murmured at last.

They got started. The aura layers from his parents, Elizabeth, all the other people who left him some energy-- these were closest to his body. His predominant surface layers were indigo blue, a thick layer of emerald green, and purple lingers. In this layer, Logan felt the way he normally did. "My thought process seems normal," he said. "Nothing feels out of place yet."

The next layer was thin and golden yellow. When brought to the surface of his aura, he immediately had a vision of Elizabeth, who had such a touching death experience he would never forget it. In an almost overwhelming wave, all of her love flooded over him. He was back in the ICU watching Elizabeth put the wedding ring in Everett's hand, saying she would always love him, thanking him for a wonderful life together, closing her eyes and peacefully releasing her energy. His heart fluttered sadly when her aura layer was cycled away and replaced by a fresh one. Hers was so loving.

The next one he knew all too well. He recognized it immediately! The color was mostly red, which he knew represented energy and/or anger. He knew the feeling, the energy, even recognized the smell! Logan could feel the powerful intellect and a weak, atrophied emotional capability. It was his father! This was incredible! It was as if he sensed their entire relationship within a matter of moments. There was no time or space. He felt his father's love for him as a baby, his disappointment with him as a teenager, feeling proud of Logan when he graduated from medical school. It

173

was an immediate sensation of their entire relationship, all at once. Interestingly, Logan could feel his dad's entire emotional record. Yet these were not only emotions where Logan was a part of the incident and therefore aware of how his father might have felt. He could also feel things he never knew about his father. Like the time when, in an alcoholic depression, his father stuck a shotgun in his mouth. The gun was icy in his mouth, the trigger hot, his tears hotter. But he did not pull the trigger because of guilt he felt regarding a thought that was repeating in his head, over and over—"If I do this, what will it do to my son? What will it do to my son?" Logan could sense this thought echo again and again in his father's head. Then the depression his father felt, the grief, the despair of feeling utterly alone and hopeless about his alcoholism, slammed into Logan's mind. For Logan, it was painful and educational. He had an immediate sense of what his father was like emotionally, mentally and spiritually. Logan sensed the overwhelming pain, despair and loneliness his father lived and drowned in.

"Are you okay?" he heard Fred's voice dimly inquire in the background.

"Just . . . sadness," Logan whispered. "It's amazing what people put themselves through before they ask for help."

Then he recognized his mother's energy pattern. Like with his dad, Logan's sense of smell recognized her first. He sensed all of their interactions, both good and bad. Most interesting for Logan, he sensed all of her loneliness, pain and grief regarding her marriage. His father was not emotionally available for her. He neglected her emotionally, mentally, physically and spiritually. All the areas where the emotional needs of a spouse should be shared, discussed and worked on were abandoned. Neglected. Covered by the dust of time and forgotten. His father was intoxicated most of the time and was unable to even try to interact with his mother on those levels. It was no wonder Logan felt like his mother consumed and overwhelmed him on an emotional level. He was a child. Her emotional needs should have been met through her husband. Since her husband was unavailable, she came to Logan for all of her emotional male support. As a physician, Logan knew about the surrogate spouse syndrome, but he felt it on an internal level instantaneously from her energy. To say he intellectually understood why was piffle! But feeling his family dynamics from all perspectives at once was somehow healing. By feeling the pain, isolation and despair of his father's alcoholism, he understood why his father was unable to provide emotional support to his mother. Feeling his mother's fear, confusion and loneliness and realizing she did not know any other healthy way of dealing with her emotional pain, he understood why, of course, she would come to Logan. Because Logan was a child, he was intellectually and emotionally incapable of giving what she needed, and it was only a matter of time before she started drinking to kill her own internal pain.

He saw in an instant the damage this did to him as a child. To be placed in that position of power, to be responsible for the emotional security of his mother! He intensely resented and was fearful of the responsibility. He was a child and should have been loved and nurtured to become what he and God wanted him to become, not be forced to become the emotional support system for two sick alcoholic parents. It was intensely damaging for a small child. He also realized how he continued to live out this family dysfunction in his own adult relationships. It was an amazing experience. He understood how you could eliminate ten years of therapy by having clients experience, on every level possible, their family dynamic from the personal vantage point of their mother and father. The parents would have to be dead so you would have part of their aura, but for those patients it could be miraculous!

175

Then it all changed. No one had to tell him this was his black layer. It was as he suspected. The energy of his chemical dependency roared over him like a tidal wave in a violent storm. It was like a black cloud dropped across his life. At once, he felt every drink and drug he ever took. If that didn't feel creepy enough, he also felt all of the emotions he ever had as an alcoholic and addict. Instantaneously! The obsession that he wanted more. And more. And more. The lying it took to get away with being an alcoholic. The manipulation in order to get what he wanted. Sensing all of the selfishness that never brought any true pleasure. He again felt trapped, ensnared, suffocating in the obsessive thinking of living his entire life while trying to get more and more without any positive outcome. Just the isolation, the loneliness, the fear of everything, the same negative feelings day in and day out, over and over. He was in hell!

Then it changed. The darkness, obsessions, lying, loneliness, fears—they were all the same feelings. But the characters in the play were . . . different? He was intoxicated and was . . . was . . . beating up a woman? Logan had an instant of confusion. The woman was familiar, terribly so, she was . . . no. It couldn't be. His mother? Was he beating his mother? Then Logan "smelled" the truth. He was his father and experiencing his father's alcoholism. All the other feelings were still present, but now he also felt self-righteous and entitled. Logan experienced his father raping his mother while intoxicated. His father was with hookers, too, as he fueled his sex addiction. Just when Logan thought he could not stand any more, the vision changed again.

Logan had known his grandfather and once again, even after all these years, recognized his grandfather's smell. All the alcoholic feelings were there—obsession, lying, cheating, manipulation, isolation, loneliness, fear. If his father's "flavor" of alcoholism was linked to entitlement, self-righteousness and sex addiction, his grandfather's "flavor" was low self-esteem. Logan bristled to feel how his grandfather, whom he loved so dearly, came home every night thinking he was not good enough. Thinking he didn't do his job well enough, didn't say the right thing to one person, should have stood up for himself with some other person. He didn't make enough money for his wife and family. He felt useless, so he tried to people please everybody —maybe if everybody liked him he would feel better about himself. He drank to kill the internal pain, over and over!

Another change. Was this his great-grandfather? Same feelings, same disease, different flavor. Then it changed again. He went back five generations! Pain. Suffering. Misery. Pain again. Deeper and darker and so much pain! He couldn't do this anymore. He was stuck in hell! All the same feelings and fears. The obsession of needing to get alcohol but receiving no pleasure from it—over and over! The cycle repeated, different actors stuck in the same play, passed down from father to son, father to son. He was dying. Logan felt all of his forefathers dying, it was over, there was no sense in going on. It was over and he was hopeless. He was dying. No, he was dead!

He became aware of someone shaking him. Someone was in his face. He slowly realized everyone in the group was circled around him. Trembling, he felt cold, and his shirt was wet. Then he became aware of voices.

"Doc, Doc, are you okay? Doc!"

He allowed the voice to simply wash over him for a few moments, delusional, thinking Kersti was beside him once more. Then he felt embarrassed. "WHAT? YES! WHAT? Stop talking so loud!"

"Are you okay?" Logan didn't recognize the voice, but the tone was terrified.

"Yes, I'm okay!" Logan responded groggily.

"What's your name?"

"What? Don't be stupid!" he growled defensively.

"Then what is your name?" The tone was calmer this time.

"Logan Rainell . . . I'm Logan."

"Do you know what day it is?"

"Oh, for God sakes, don't play those psych games with me!"

"Then what day is it?"

To his horror, Logan realized he did not know what day it was. Embarrassed, he acquiesced, "Well, I guess . . . I guess I don't remember what day it is."

"What about the year?"

Logan thought for a second. "No," he said sheepishly.

"Do you know where we are?"

"Yes, yes . . . this is the lab, and we're in a scanner on the base."

"Good, that's right! Good! Now, who am I?"

Logan angled his head towards the voice. Though he still did not recognize the voice, he did recognize the face.

"Carrie. You are Carrie!"

"Good, Doc, good!" She rubbed his shoulders. "You had us worried."

"Why? What happened?" Logan murmured, sitting up properly and rubbing his head.

"Why don't you tell us what happened," Fred suggested.

Logan asked for a glass of water and tried to relax. But it was a struggle to do so; his mother's scream seemed to be etched into his eardrums, and each time he closed his eyes he would see his father beat her as if the image was tattooed into his eyelids.

"Okay, I remember the set up," he said slowly. "I remember feeling my mom and dad's energy and was fascinated at how much I learned about them. I suddenly knew more than ever before, instantaneously, and it was incredible! The possibilities for therapeutic use in treating depression and other psychiatric problems resulting from dysfunctional families are unlimited! It was amazing!"

"Then . . ." Logan trailed off, drawing a deep breath. "Then," he continued solemnly, "it was my chemical dependency. I had forgotten how awful it was. I was depressed . . . no, suicidal. I felt paralyzed with apathy. I saw my whole family's disease and felt hopeless! So hopeless!"

"When it got bad," Fred interrupted, "were you able to think of dropping the dead man's switch?"

"How did you know it got bad?" Logan asked.

"Doc, you were trembling and crying!"

"That's why my shirt is wet?"

Fred nodded. "Yes."

"To answer your question, no, the dead man's switch is not feasible. When you experience that magnitude of negative energy, you're totally overwhelmed. I was in the moment, and it seemed as if I was getting a million bits of information a second. I didn't have a cognitive thought process of, "This is getting intense, let's get out!" It was all just flooding over me. Maybe with experience or after visiting the same energy pattern several times it may feel familiar enough that you could consciously leave. But the first time it's happening to you, it's . . . impossibly overwhelming. I not only experienced my own chemical dependency but also my father's, my grandfather's, and all the way back five generations!"

"My God," Carrie gasped. "No wonder you were overwhelmed."

"Are you sure?" asked Fred.

"Yes! I am sure! It was weird. I not only sensed I was experiencing my father's alcoholism but also saw him interacting with my mother. I even saw him interacting with me as a child, but the strangest thing is . . . well, you might find this hard to believe, but I could *smell* my father! If you would have asked me what my father smells like five minutes

179

before we got started, I would've thought you were nuts. But as soon as I smelled him, all the memories flooded back and I knew immediately it was my father. Same with my grandfather. I grew up in an alcoholic family, hated alcohol, swore I would never be an alcoholic. But I became one because that is what I saw and how I learned to deal with my problems. Probably just like all five generations I just visited. It was passed on whether we wanted it or not!"

Logan started to feel more grounded, and the team could sense when he switched from his heartfelt feelings to his intellect.

"What if . . . oh," Logan murmured, excitement building as his mind connected his experience to science. "What if all the energy of chemical dependency—the feelings, the memories, the trauma—doesn't exist in a linear fashion as we believe. *This* is my life. *That* was my father's life. That's how we see it. But I just experienced five generations of alcoholism, and each generation seemed so real I thought I was there and it was all basically the same, just different people. So what if, just like the energy of alcoholism passes on from one generation to the next, what if the fact that I am now 24 years sober heals the generational family disease!"

"Going backward? But . . . how can that be? You just experienced all of your family's alcoholism," Fred pointed out.

"No, not backwards. I'm talking about future generations!" Logan stated. "That my recovery from chemical dependency or any other family dysfunction doesn't operate in linear time and space. My recovery doesn't just heal me, it heals the energy of my family for future generations! We already know that alcoholism is caused both by environmental and genetic factors. What if, generation after generation, there is so much alcoholic energy built up that there's not only an environmental but also an auric effect in which the auric energy actually *changes* DNA. If that's true,

180

future generations will be genetically predisposed towards alcoholism! Scientifically, we know the neurochemistry of alcoholics is different than non-alcoholics. So what if the energy of recovery changes the DNA back to normal?"

"That," Carrie said slowly, eyes wide in shock, "would be an amazing discovery! Plus, knowing it could heal your children would give a new incentive for staying sober."

"Gives a whole new meaning to 'the sins of the father are visited upon the son!'" Fred added. "It's kind of spooky!"

"But, like Carrie said, what an incentive for staying sober! If we can prove this, we'll—"

"Well, that'll be a problem," Fred interrupted. "How would you prove that?" Before Logan could answer, he added, "Oh, and before you cure the world, do you know what day it is yet?"

"Yes, it's all coming back now. It's Thursday, April 26."

"Okay, you pass, Doc. Just looking after you."

"And I appreciate it, Fred, and all of you! That was a strange but educational process." After a moment, Logan thoughtfully added, "I just visited five generations of alcoholics in my family and realized the alcoholic energy pattern is passed on in the aura from generation to generation. I've been sober for 24 years, and if I had a son we could check his aura."

"But you don't have a son," Carrie said.

"So a study would need participants who have generations of alcoholism in their family and have good quality sobriety. By that I mean true emotional sobriety, not just white knuckle, not drinking sobriety. When that person dies, we would check his or her children to see if the disease is passed on."

"Makes sense to me," Fred agreed.

"Me, too. And what if not just the DNA changes," Carrie added, "but also emotional and spiritual sobriety is passed on. 'Love and tolerance of others,'" she quoted from AA's big book. "If the bad parts of the disease are passed on through the aura, why not the good stuff as well?"

Chapter 23

Healing Family Trees

The team easily came up with the requirements for a new study on generational alcoholism. They were as follows:

1. A history of alcoholism in the family for multiple generations.

2. The person in recovery had worked all twelve steps with a sponsor.

3. The person in recovery had quality, emotional sobriety. This is to be determined by talking to their family. There are many chameleons in AA. What matters is how the person in recovery treats his own family. This is where quality sobriety becomes evident.

4. The person in recovery died within the last five years.

5. The deceased recovered person had adult children who could be interviewed and scanned.

Finding families that met these requirements was not difficult, and within a short period of time the team had a list of candidates who fulfilled the criteria. After interviewing and scanning several children of deceased recovered alcoholics, the study was complete and the results were conclusive.

"Can we state in the conclusions that we've proven

spiritual evolution?" Logan asked, inputting data to the holo-jector.

"That's going to cause controversy if we state it that way," Fred said, leaning over Logan's shoulder to glance at the report so far.

"We're scientists!" Logan retorted. "We can conclude what we think the results indicate. Physically, the DNA no longer produces the abnormal neurochemistry causing alcoholism. Spiritually, the auras didn't pass on the black layer."

"Okay, men, estrogen to the rescue!" Carrie exclaimed, stretching her lanky body across the desk to peek at the front side of the holo-jector image. "I think if we release our results and let people reach their own conclusions, that will be more powerful than any conclusion we try to spoon-feed them. What's important is we show our results were entirely conclusive—that is, when children of emotionally and spiritually recovering alcoholics were scanned, they showed the healthy aura of the recovering parent, *not* the black layer of chemical dependency. Even though generations of chemical dependency energy were passed on from one generation to another via the aura, even though the DNA showed the genes for alcoholism, when someone finally has the courage to do the work for true recovery the entire bloodline is forgiven! After someone finally feels the guilt and shame the disease causes, not only in themselves but also the entire family tree, then the generational dysfunction is not passed on. And iso-genic mapping proves it changes DNA back to normal. It heals the entire family tree from the disease! *That* is a powerful conclusion!"

Logan acquiesced and added, "But I was wondering if we should make a conclusion that we have proven there is such a thing as emotional and spiritual evolution? That we have shown evolution in action!"

Fred scratched his head for effect. "Have we really proven that?"

"I think we could make an argument for it! We showed scientifically that the energy of alcoholism was passed on from generation to generation. When someone in the family heals, the disease is not passed on to the next generation," Logan concluded.

"*I*," Fred loudly suggested, "think it would be best if we stayed consistent. State our results, let people reach their own conclusions, and stay out of the debating society! Like we have done with our other research papers. And they've all been very successful!"

"Once again, three heads are better than one . . . especially when the one is me! Stuck in my ego and wanting recognition for all the work we've done!" Logan joked.

"Doc," Carrie said, shaking her head, "don't worry about that. We're going to get recognition; this is incredible stuff!"

"Of course you're right," Logan said, feeling the emotional healing that had resulted from his own scanning wash peacefully over his mind. "Have I told you guys you're the best research team and that I love each one of you?"

"Doc, I ain't gay!" Fred blurted out. "In fact, I'm kind of homophobic, so if you keep your "love" remarks to yourself, I'd be more comfortable."

"Fred, how about you shut up," Carrie kindly suggested.

"Thanks for sharing, Fred," Logan said smiling.

Chapter 24

God's Work

The research sparked controversy in the scientific and lay communities. AA and the whole twelve-step community enjoyed getting some scientific validation for their work but had no official statement since tradition ten states, "We have no opinion on outside issues."

A short while later, Logan was contacted by one Abraham Goldstein, an elderly Jewish man who had spent his life interpreting scrolls, clay tablets and the original Greek bible. He was an expert in Hebrew, Aramaic and all three types of Greek. They exchanged a long tel-chip conversation in which Logan felt he was being interviewed for his level of knowledge but mostly for his trustworthiness. He must have passed the test because, soon afterwards, Abraham asked if they could meet in person; he had an interesting scroll he wanted to show Logan. Abraham had always wanted to visit New Mexico, so Logan made reservations at the La Fonda Hotel in Santa Fe.

They met in the enclosed courtyard of the dining room. Logan knew Abraham at once; he had an incredible aura! Bright, vibrant and thick—at least three feet in radius, it glowed with numerous layers of color. This was a man obviously loved by many. And if the overall beauty of

Abraham's aura wasn't impressive enough, the thick golden surface layer with its golden lingers was entrancing. Breathtaking. Logan stopped walking, awe-struck, as he witnessed Abraham's golden lingers spreading out to *everyone* in the room, gently caressing and imparting love and calm to all. He looked like a sun with beams of golden light breaking through the clouds, touching all. Blessing all. Abraham sensed Logan and scooted around in his chair. As his golden lingers encompassed Logan, he felt love, peace and warmth envelope him. "Ohh . . . my . . ." involuntarily escaped from Logan's lips. They started to shake hands, but it morphed into a wonderful hug.

"Thank you for that," Logan said with a sigh, still in awe.

"For what, my son?" Abraham asked.

"The gift of your aura. Your lingers gave me such a greeting."

"Seeing auras is a gift I do not possess, my son. But I felt you enter the room and love occur."

"Indeed." Logan proceeded to describe Abraham's stunning aura and the gift he was to all in his presence.

Waitresses decorated in richly colored dresses offered them a traditional meal of blue corn chicken enchiladas with green chili, whole black beans, rice and pico de gallo. Desert was fresh sopapillas and local honey. Conversation during the shared dinner was social, but after dinner Abraham invited Logan to his room to see the scroll.

Abraham kneeled slowly beside the room safe and typed in a lengthy numerical code. Gently taking hold of the scroll with both hands to remove it, he clarified, "Of course this is a copy, my son. The original is in one of the most secure locations in the world."

"Where's that?"

"The security vaults beneath the Vatican."

"Really?"

"They put Fort Knox to shame, my son!"

"Interesting. I guess they have to spend their money somehow," Logan said quietly.

"Oh my son, you have no idea. Not only are there guards around the clock but also as soon as new technology is developed that would improve the security, it is immediately implemented. No amount of money is spared."

"Do they have many artifacts?" Logan asked, glancing at the scroll clutched tightly in his companion's hands.

"Yes, my son, they do. Many wondrous, wondrous artifacts! But that is not what they are guarding."

"Then what *are* they guarding?"

"Secrets!"

"Like what?"

"Like this scroll," Abraham murmured in a whisper. "I am convinced, my son, if they knew I had transcribed a copy of this we would not have had a wonderful dinner together."

The hairs on Logan's nape prickled uncertainly. "Are we in danger?"

"Probably," Abraham said calmly.

"Oh, God! Why did you pick me?"

"*God* is why I picked you, my son," he replied softly. His eyes locked onto Logan's eyes, penetrated Logan's soul and offered reassurance. If eyes are the window to the soul, Abraham's wise and trustworthy eyes, chocolate brown swirled with a hint of cinnamon, helped put Logan at ease.

"You and your team have made more of a spiritual impact on the people of the world than I think you are aware of. With the population decreasing as rapidly as it is due to Vertig's syndrome and war, more and more people are experiencing, first-hand, what your research has scientifically

189

proven. As you have stated, the first law of thermodynamics explains your results perfectly—energy is not destroyed, it just changes form! When I translated this scroll I decided that, at whatever cost—even my life, if it comes to that—this information must be made public," Abraham said softly.

"Oh my God!" gasped Logan.

"Indeed," Abraham said with a smile. "'My God' is what this is about!"

"How . . . how did you get the scroll?"

"I am old. I love God. And I love all people. Consequently, I have many friends, my son. One of them is the supervisor who works on the construction of the security systems at the Vatican. When putting in the newest system, which has a seismic holographic monitor, they dug lower beneath the existing vault than ever before. They found a small stone coffin that did not show up on ground penetrating radar or sonovision – it had the same signal as the surrounding soil, which he said was odd. In the coffin, they found several scrolls which I was asked to translate."

Logan's lips folded into an uneasy smile. "Is this something that, if I know about it, could jeopardize my survival?"

"My son," Abraham said with compassion, "I am sure there are very powerful people who would not want this information released. With power always comes danger. What's the old saying . . . ah, that's right: 'Absolute power, absolute corruption.' I am sure you have some confusion about the Vatican, as most people do. It is rational to think this is the Catholic Church and that it is a spiritual organization based on the teachings of Christ. It is easy to believe, then, that they would not hurt me or do anything evil. But the Vatican and the Catholic Church stopped being a spiritual organization hundreds of years ago." He lifted the scroll over his head and shook it in the air, crying out, "Probably about the time they consciously chose to suppress

190

information. They are a power structure, and not just any power structure. There are all types of power structures. Every government and political organization in the world, right down to every individual family, forms a type of power structure. Some of these structures are good and necessary. Some have lost their way. Power structures that choose to operate behind the guise of a spiritual organization and use their power to dictate, manipulate and suppress spiritual knowledge and beliefs . . . well, I do not believe in them, and the word that comes to my mind is *corruption*."

Logan's eyes narrowed, but he remained silent.

"Logan, my son. My feeling after reading all of your writings, seeing multiple lectures you've given, and now talking to you this day is that you are a man of God." When Logan remained speechless, Abraham added, "If I may ask you a question?" Logan nodded in the affirmative. "Would you die for the will of God?"

"Wow! You put it right out there on the table, don't you?" Logan exclaimed, though not unkindly. "It's not that easy." He paused to think. "How do I know this is the will of God?"

"You are correct to be skeptical, and it was unfair of me to ask that question. I apologize. *I believe* it is the will of God for this information to be made public, but all I can ask of you is whether you are willing to hear the translation and remember the perfect love of God is stronger than any fear. Listen and decide how you would answer that question. I will not force you to act against your soul. If you are feeling fear and your heart is telling you this is too dangerous, I will leave without saying a further word after you hear the translation."

Logan laughed. "After all of that build-up, how could I not hear what you have to say? Besides, I am not afraid. Just the opposite, in fact. As I walked down the hallway behind you on our way here, I clearly heard a voice say, *Trust this man!* Plus, after seeing your aura..."

191

"My son, it makes me happy to know that you trust me, but more importantly, I am glad you listen to your inner voice. As time goes on, it will become more important to listen to that voice!"

"Before you read the scroll," Logan said, "I must ask: Why do you think it is the will of God for this information to be known?"

"I do not believe any information should be concealed from the public. The fact that it was hidden and suppressed from people is in itself against the will of God who is about love, relationship and wisdom. The fact that it was suppressed to gain more power is disturbing. And there is a third aspect, which comes from the synchronicity of recent events. My friend finds the scroll. I translate it. It reminds me of the research you have been doing on Vertig's. There is an escalating death rate. Plus, never before in the history of mankind have the *energies*"—Abraham lifted his fingers and bracketed the word—"been culminating the way they are now."

"Okay, okay, tell me what the scrolls say. Any more of this and I'll die of suspense!" Logan said smiling.

"Very good. Let us begin, my son."

For the next two hours, Abraham read in Hebrew and translated the meaning. He reminded Logan how easy it was to mistranslate words from old texts. Though he provided several examples, the only one Logan remembered was 'BAD', which for hundreds of years meant 'wrongful action', 'worst' and 'opposite of what was morally acceptable'. Then, somewhere in the 1990s and early 2000s, 'BAD' took on a slang meaning that was just the opposite. If someone or something was 'BAD', it was good, hip, cool, popular. Then, about ten years after the deaths of the first Vertig's syndrome patients, 'BAD'" transformed into a noun. Saying that a patient had 'BAD' meant he had Vertig's. Abraham's point was obvious. If someone was reading a text 3,000 years from now and did not know how to interpret the contemporary meaning of the word, the translation of 'BAD' could be entirely wrong.

After the history lesson on the difficulty of translating the Bible, Abraham concluded there was some room for error. Yet they could deduce enough so that, when Abraham finally finished the translation of the scroll, they sat staring at one another in awed silence.

After a while, Logan asked, "So your point is there could be translational errors, but you and other experts believe this was part of one of the original scrolls that the Bible was eventually transcribed from and was purposefully hidden?"

"Absolutely, my son! The grammatical style matches several scrolls we have the provenance of."

"Abraham, it is obvious to me that your language skills far exceed my own. You are eloquent in Aramaic, Hebrew, Greek, Latin and English. I, on the other hand— and I mean this quite seriously, believe me—can barely speak English in comparison! May I recite what I heard so you can clarify the parts I did not understand correctly?"

"That would be fine. Better than fine, even," Abraham said, smiling. "That is healthy communication. You listen to what is said, repeat what you heard, and let the speaker state whether your interpretation is correct or needs clarification."

Logan smiled back. "Thank you." He opened his mouth to speak but closed it as quickly, suddenly feeling overwhelmed. A moment more of hesitation, and he finally began. "You and the other experts believe there was an explanation in the Old Testament that was purposely left out."

"Yes."

"God commands us to go forth, multiply and be fruitful! But there was also an explanation of the consequences of doing so that was purposefully omitted. According to your translation, when God said, 'Go forth and multiply and be fruitful,' He warned that we should be aware that the consequence of this increase in human numbers would mean a proportional decrease in the spiritual energy that will be available to mankind. With a large increase in numbers comes a decrease in spiritual energy and the ability to feel connected to God!"

"You see now why I contacted you, don't you, my son?" Abraham said softly.

"I think so. This correlates with my research and writings regarding the first law of thermodynamics—"

"Exactly!" Abraham interrupted. "Energy cannot be destroyed; it just changes form. You flip a light switch and the electric energy is not destroyed. It changes from electricity into light and heat. But the key lies in this: If there is enough energy to light 1,000 bulbs but you add 100,000 bulbs to the circuit, more energy does not appear. There's simply less energy to go around. You have been watching people at the time of death and have scientifically measured and visually witnessed the transfer of energy. When death occurs, the energy within a physical body transmutes into energy of a spiritual form. As a result of increased spiritual energy, many people can now see auras! It has been written and documented in thousands of cases that as the world's population decreases, the spiritual energy increases! An inverse relationship, if you will. That is an example of the explanation that was hidden from us. And as spiritual energy increases, it becomes more available to the physical bodies remaining on earth. With this increase, people are having all sorts of spiritual experiences. Seeing auras, telepathy, psychic healing, the power of attraction, remote viewing—all are occurring more frequently. People make things happen through quantum physics, prayer and the energy of thought."

"So," Logan finally asked, "you think they hid this

194

information for the acquisition of power?"

"Of course, my son!" Abraham paused, scratching his chin in thought. "At first, it was probably quite logical and with good intention. Think of life as it was back then. Very, very difficult! We probably cannot fully comprehend how difficult it was. Not enough food for your family. Backbreaking work to barely survive. There are many documented cases of infanticide due to lack of food to feed one more mouth. Infant girls were especially singled out because they couldn't work as hard in the fields as boys and, in most cultures, couldn't become warriors. The existing "power structure" probably had good intentions in concealing this truth. They may have believed we would go forth and multiply just long enough for life to get easier. We would develop enough infrastructure to produce adequate food and then slow down the population growth. Keeping our spiritual connection at that level."

"What spiritual level was that?" Logan asked.

"Who knows? Maybe there was a tipping point. At first they were aware of being connected to God, then at some point the human population tipped the scale and humans no longer could feel that connection to God. The connection to the spiritual energy decreased so much that mankind could not feel the spiritual power they had lost. That's when the acquisition of power became the primary goal. The only thing more seductive than power ... is more power! The only thing power wants? Not to lose power!"

Logan nodded thoughtfully. "Then," he added, "if you add into the equation tithing, where every good Catholic donates ten percent of their income to the church, that becomes a lot of power!"

"Precisely, Logan. Then the church had money to spread, make more churches, influence more people, make more money. Enough money to influence and change the entire course of history. The Crusades, the Inquisition, conquering the New World, the genocide of the Aztec and Mayan cultures, manifest destiny of America, the genocide of the Native American cultures—all are examples of a power system run rampant. We don't know where it started. It could have gone back further to ancient cultures like the Egyptians or Atlantis. Rome and the Vatican could have been relative latecomers." Abraham concluded.

Logan blinked slowly, trying to process all the new information. "You got excited, Abraham, and gave me a lot more to think about. So let me see if I have this right. The hidden information gives us the knowledge that we have two choices. The choice they hid was that we could keep the human population small and have increased spiritual energy and feel our contact with God. The other choice was to go forth and multiply, but in turn our spiritual power would decrease. The power structure at the time, be it Egypt or the Vatican or whatever other system, made this choice for all of us. As the human population increased, so did the belief in power structures. The downside was that spiritual energy thinned out so there was less of it available for people. Now, in modern times, the population has increased and the sense of God's presence decreased to the point we had nuclear war, developed Vertig's, and are killing ourselves off in record numbers. Is that basically what you're telling me?"

"Yes, my son! Before Vertig's syndrome and the nuclear explosions, our population on earth was fourteen billion people—the highest in history! Violence and crime were also at peak levels. They ran side-by-side. The higher the population, the more people to divide the finite amount of spiritual energy among. Now that the population is decreasing, there is still crime, war and death, but the levels are dropping exponentially. With the decrease in population, more and more people are developing spiritual skills and experiences. To me, this is very logical. More people, less spiritual energy. Less people, higher amounts of spiritual energy. As you have proven in your research, as people die their energy does not go away. That energy is added to the energy of those who remain behind. We are spiritually evolving! It is very exciting, my son! Think of it this way: What is the hardest job in the world?"

"Translating Greek?" Logan joked with a smile.

"Almost!" Abraham said, smiling back. "Raising children is by far the hardest job in the world, if done in a healthy fashion."

Logan suddenly felt like he was kicked in the stomach. He used to say that to Kersti when she would feel overwhelmed with the responsibility of raising her kids. He even remembered one evening in his office when he was relaxing in his chair and she approached, tired from the long day, and sat on the edge of his desk. She complained about wanting to stay in that office forever with Logan, or go anywhere in the world so long as they were together, because she did not want to face her children at home. It was so much, *so* much, and such an important duty, and what if she messed up, and—

Logan offered her words of encouragement and support. It was her 'sacred duty', he told her. And in the end, she chose her 'duty' over being with him. God, he missed her! He wished she was here right now to share this amazing information.

"Are you okay, my son?" Abraham asked solemnly. "You looked like you were going to cry."

"I-I was. Just . . . missing someone, that's all. I'm sorry, please continue."

"So, by the look on your face you would agree that raising kids is the hardest job in the world?"

"Yes, absolutely!"

"Very good. Because look at what happens in a family with a single child. That single child gets all the love, all the attention, all the energy from both parents. The Native

Americans used to say, 'It takes a village to raise a child.' I believe that is true. Each child takes a lot of energy! Now look at what happens in large families. There are so many kids that the parents don't have enough energy to meet the needs of all the children. I'm not being critical of parents; it is just a matter of time and energy. Even totally loving, dedicated parents simply do not have enough time to deal with large numbers of kids. So what happens is the older children start taking care of the younger children. Children raising children. No wonder members of modern society act like narcissistic, immature children. That's how many of us were raised – by other children!"

"So, back to numbers and energy," Logan interjected. "It sounds sacrilegious, but every known source of energy in the universe is a finite number. It can be an incredibly huge finite number, but no energy source is infinite."

"That we know of . . ." Abraham suggested.

"Yes, that we know of," Logan agreed. "They used to think fossil fuels were infinite, and now we're out of them. The Sun will eventually burn itself out. All the galaxies in the universe will eventually collapse back in on themselves. So, how can spiritual energy be an infinite resource? Imagine there is an incredibly large, humongous amount, but what happens to it when you add fourteen billion people all tapping into it. Seems to me there has to be a breaking point."

"Quantity of people, or quality of people, eh, my son?"

Logan glanced at the scroll again. "I'm beginning to understand why the Vatican's secrets are so closely guarded. Stating that God's spiritual energy is finite, instead of infinite will be very controversial for some people."

"Indeed it will be, my son! In the future, we may find out otherwise. For example, on the spiritual plane of existence, maybe God's spiritual energy is infinite. But when dealing with physical matter, humans, earth, galaxies, the universe, all energy sources are finite. Correct?" Abraham posed to the scientist.

"Yes, as far as we know they're finite." Logan paused, trying to recall how their conversation began. "So, Abraham," he asked at last, "what do you want to do? More to the point, what do you want me to do?"

"You and your research team have the ears and eyes of the world like no one has in a long time. People do not trust governments, for they are just more of the same power structure and all they care about is not losing power. My son, you personally speak in spiritual tones and use phrases that spiritual seekers all recognize and accept. Jewish, Christian, Muslim—it matters not what religion. Plus, the fact that you and your team are doing scientific research that has never been done before and are proving scientifically that this energy exists, places you in a unique position at this time in world history. The scientific community trusts your research. And spiritual and religious organizations trust your research."

"I think you're giving us a little *too* much credit."

"No, my son, I am not! I travel all over the world, and your research is known and discussed everywhere. Your papers and books have been translated into languages all over the world! I was in a cafe in Somalia a month ago. There were men sitting around chewing khat while speaking about your paper. You have a spiritual chord that has resonated with many throughout the world!"

"Well, that's all good, but my question stands. What do you want me to do?" Logan repeated.

For the first time, Abraham smiled brightly. "I would like you to write a paper or book regarding the hidden scroll and correlate it with the work you are doing with auras and the energy of people who are dying."

Logan groaned. "Why do I feel like you just set the hook and I'm swimming for deep water?"

Abraham laughed. "Because you were hooked, you are swimming . . . and God will guide you!"

"Could I just cut the fish line?"

"Doubtfully!"

Chapter 25

Logan: Healed Again

As requested, Abraham and Logan collaborated on a book. They were a good team and often worked late into the night, at first meeting in hotel lobbies and restaurants and later in Logan's mountain retreat. Logan often thought of Kersti and what she might add to this adventure. He still missed her. Would always miss her. He prayed for her and thought of her every day. He hoped she was happy and her life was fulfilling. It is what he had always wished for her. Throughout his adult life, he carried a childlike love for her. She was the girl he always thought about. Before he knew her as an adult, there was always the thought in his mind—a vague yet plausible possibility—that their teenage relationship was just "puppy love." Now that he knew her as an adult and knew he loved *everything* about her, being separated once more was much more difficult. He felt he was going through life with something missing. With the sparkle torn from his spirit. It was like smelling a rose with a stuffy nose. Watching a gorgeous sunset with dark sunglasses. There was a hole in his heart and soul. He spent hours thinking about all the times they had together. The sound of her voice. The way she smelled. How her lips smoothly folded when she smiled. How she stretched and swung her legs when she walked—no, glided! Her amazing intellect and how much she added to their team. The beauty mark engraved carefully upon her cheek. It was actually a scar from a dog bite, which she was embarrassed about. He thought it was beautiful. God, he loved her! And they'd never even made love!

"My son, are you gone again?" Abraham asked kindly.

"I-I'm sorry," Logan stuttered, inputting another sentence into the holo-jector. It was a particularly late evening, and the midnight hour coupled with the cozy comfort of the mountain home eased him into a calm surrender to his feelings. "Sometimes, it's so hard," he added, gazing into the dancing red embers of a glowing fire.

"You have nothing to apologize for. Love is a mystery. It is the most amazing, powerful force in the universe. It can also be the most painful, but, it is never something to be sorry for." Abraham paused. "May I ask you a question?"

"Of course, Abraham. Anything."

"Have you ever loved someone unconditionally?"

"Yes!" Logan cried without pause. "My sweet little Zeusy!"

"Zeusy?"

"His name was Zeus, and he was a Samoyed. Best dog there ever was. He died about . . . three years ago."

"God bless dogs," Abraham whispered, eyes glazed with distant memories. "God's love is in dogs like everything else, but since dogs don't have egos, dogs express God's love without ego! That is why they are here. To teach us unconditional love."

"Agreed. And Zeus absolutely taught me about unconditional love! I never knew what it felt like to love something unconditionally until he came into my life."

"How do you feel about Zeus today?"

"I love him as much as I ever did!"

"And the fact that he is dead does not lessen your

love for him?"

"No, of course not!"

"The fact that Kersti is no longer in your life does not lessen your love for her as well?"

"No, I guess not," Logan said slowly, tasting each sour word slowly on his lips before murmuring it aloud.

"So when you think of Kersti, can you feel the love in your heart just as with Zeus?"

Logan bristled with frustration. "Well, of course! It's just that . . . I WANT HER!"

Abraham laughed, though not unkindly. "Oh, I misunderstood! I thought this was about the unconditional love you had for Kersti. But it's about your ego not getting what it wants!"

Logan could hear the wisdom and laughed along with Abraham.

"Oh, yeah? Well . . . so what? It is hard not having her in my life."

"I know, my son. But this is reality. Dogs die, people die . . . or they move on. If it is unconditional love, you will always have that in your heart. You can access that feeling at any time by thinking of Zeus or Kersti. It is your love to keep forever. Love is something that comes from inside you. It is the closest people come to feel the love God has for us. That love is always yours. If the person goes away, of course you grieve the loss. But the love that was opened up . . . that, Logan, can never be taken away. It is always yours to keep!"

"Yes, but we were so . . . good together. We c-could have accomplished anything," Logan struggled to say.

"Those are conditions. Could have, should have, would have—that is not love. Are you in love with what could have been? Or are you in love with Kersti just the way she is, whatever she needs in her life, whatever path she chooses. You can choose to have the same love for her as you do for Zeus."

Logan was quick to defend himself. "I do!" he cried.

Abraham eyed him thoughtfully but said nothing.

"Most days, at least," Logan added, feeling the twinkle in Abraham's eyes seep through into his mind. "I have always wanted the best for her. That's why I didn't push myself on her. I did not want to add to the stress in her life. I do love her and want her to reach her highest good in this life, whatever that may be." Logan's eyes were suddenly swollen with tears. The next moment he was sobbing, and he buried his face in his arms. The dusky glow of firelight flickered over his hunched form.

"That's good, my son. Let your cheeks feel your tears running down your face. Don't wipe your tears away in shame. God gave us crying to cleanse our souls of pain, and when you cry you need to feel the tears flow down your skin and leave behind rivers!" Abraham hugged Logan as he cried.

It was better from that day on. Logan would think of Zeus and feel the warm, secure feeling of unconditional love. When he thought of Kersti, the calm feeling of warm, unconditional love would wash over his soul. When he needed a double-barreled blast of love, he thought of both of them! He felt incredibly grateful to have both of them in his life. The amount of time they were in his life did not matter. The gift of love was what mattered!

Chapter 26

"Energy Book"

When it was finally published, Logan and Abraham were astounded by the amount of attention their book received. It quickly transformed into a worldwide sensation and was translated into 38 languages. The actual title was, "*Spiritual Energy: Scientific Results from Scrivner Scanners and the Hidden Scroll.*" But it simply became known as the "Energy Book". It first reviewed the hidden scroll, which became known as Abraham's Scroll. Then the book covered how results from the Scrivner scanner scientifically correlated with the ideas of the scroll. Logan and Abraham traveled the world giving lectures.

Though his heart still pulsed harder when he thought of her, Logan continued to honor Kersti's request to be left alone. Once during the excitement of the new book, she wrote to congratulate them and wish Logan well. In the note, she said she did not have the courage to call. The thought of hearing Logan's voice was too painful for her. Logan's heart wrenched to hear this; she couldn't even talk to him! He trusted God's plan, but at times it sure was painful. At times he oscillated between anger and acceptance. He knew things happened in God's time and not his own, and he had been given the gift of loving unconditionally. An incredible gift!

But at times, his ego still wanted what all egos want—its own way! It wanted her! Kersti! His beloved always!

*****

Spiritual gifts on earth were growing exponentially. The more people transitioned, the more spiritual gifts bubbled up among those remaining. People's wrist holograms talked daily about seemingly regular people who had been given amazing spiritual gifts. People began spending more time helping others instead of being worried about their own selfish existence. For most people, the central concern and life goal had shifted. The goal was to help both yourself and others in spiritual progress.

The environmental condition of the world continued to degrade. Although humanity seemed to have finally shifted direction, the doomsayers said that it was already too late for the planet. That the current levels of pollution and nuclear fallout were already at such peaks that we were in a slow spiral to the end. Others thought that with the decrease in world population, which was now down to about three billion, it was possible to produce enough food in clean greenhouse environments.

There were other concerns. Along with the greenhouse effect, the magnetic pole shift had caused havoc in worldwide weather patterns. Agricultural land was at a premium, but with such unpredictable weather one could not depend on a crop. The majority of the world's food supply came from aquaponic greenhouses. Inside the greenhouses were tanks where fish were raised. Water containing fish waste was pumped through planters with different types of edible plants that pulled the nutrients they needed out of the water, leaving the water clean enough for the fish. This cycle was repeated until harvest. The end product was clean, edible fish and greenhouse plants. The science developed for the Moon and Mars colonies was now the industry of survival on earth.

Chapter 27

Paradigm shift

"For the last time: The Hundredth Monkey Phenomenon . . ..
Was proven . . . To be . . . A . . . *Hoax*," Fred emphasized
indignantly.

Logan and his team had just finished scanning a
patient and were now shutting down the scanners for the
evening. And by 'team', the term for once meant Logan alone
inputting data while Fred and Carrie bickered for what was
probably the tenth time that day.

"Are you sure? I always thought it was true," Carrie
replied, twirling a strand of hair around her finger.

"My Ph.D. thesis was on how urban myths contribute
to societal beliefs. So I researched the "H.M.P." as part of my
Ph.D.. I can tell you more about it than you would ever want
to know!"

Carrie rolled her eyes. "Hit me with the short
version."

"You want some? 'Kay, you've got it coming. In the
late 1950s and early 1960s, a group of Japanese researchers
were studying macaque monkeys off some of the islands in
southern Japan. Sweet potatoes were not an indigenous food
source, so the experiment consisted of dropping sweet
potatoes onto the sand and observing how the macaques

dealt with a new food source. Interestingly, it was a group of younger monkeys who learned that if you wash the potatoes off in the ocean you remove the annoying sand. The younger monkeys taught some of the older monkeys in the usual manner of observe and mimic. Over time, they started to wash off other foods before eating. In the original study, which took place over a time frame of five or six years, tribes of monkeys on other islands learned to wash their food. Which was plenty of time for monkeys who had learned this behavior to swim to other islands and teach other monkeys. In 1979, a Ph.D. named Lyle Watson wrote a book in which he talked about how amazing nature is. In this book, he inferred that it might be possible for societies to make an intellectual leap forward in knowledge. That 99 monkeys learned to wash food and when the "hundredth monkey" learned that bit of knowledge, it became ingrained in the society's psyche and telepathically transferred to all other macaque monkeys, including those on the surrounding islands. And so the "hundredth monkey phenomenon" was born."

"Well, that might be a stretch, but—"

"*Later,*" Fred interrupted, "Ron Amundson interviewed all of the original Japanese scientists and found that none of Watson's implications were based on the actual research. In 1985, Amundson wrote a critical paper of Watson and his findings. Watson's written reply fully agreed with Amundson, and he even confirmed his statements were based more on *intuition* than research. He stated that it was always meant to be a metaphor—what he believed was a good one! How knowledge might make psychic leaps amongst the same species once a certain amount of the species had learned the skill or belief."

Carrie released the strand of hair she had been toying with and twirled a fresh one. "True or not, I still like it as a story," she said. "It gives me hope that once a critical mass of people has learned to live in peace and harmony, others may finally get it!"

"I agree on that point," Fred relented. "It does give hope that humanity can make great strides forward in knowledge instead of inching along."

Logan glanced up from the scanner he had been examining. "Even though Watson's statement was not based on true research, there still may be some truth in it," he murmured.

"Don't tell me you're on *her* side," Fred groaned.

"Of course he's on my side," Carrie snapped. "That's the smart side."

"Well, I'm the smarter side."

"We're smartest!"

"I'm smarter . . . um . . . est?" Fred joked. Carrie giggled, and he grinned.

"Now that Fred's pleased with himself," Logan said with a chuckle, "might I add that many scientists and spiritual leaders believe that 'intuition' is the universe or God's way of telling us truth? Since I started to see auras, my intuitive voice has gotten much clearer and louder. When it says something, I listen!"

Carrie bobbed her head in agreement. "Who knows whether it's the instantaneous information network we have, our book, or the hundredth monkey phenomenon. Whatever the reason, you have to admit that more and more people are consciously making a choice to have fewer children."

Quite true, Logan noted to himself. It had been five years since the "Energy Book" had been printed. In that time, a steady stream of scientific studies and objective data was released to the public. Most all of it pointed in the same direction. As the world's population decreased, the remaining individuals not only felt better but also develop spiritual skills they previously did not possess. Aura reading was commonplace. You no longer had to wait to see someone's

211

face to identify them. You could see the color, size and complexity of any person's aura from a distance and tell who it was from there.

The art of healing had changed the most dramatically. Scrivner scanners, of course, helped immensely. People could experience entire generational dysfunction and have major life-changing therapy accomplished within several visits. Even more exciting was that certain healers learned to visually read auras and were now able to manipulate the bands in an individual's aura, just the way Scrivner scanners did. These people were called "scanoids," and they allowed patients to experience their generational dysfunction and receive the needed therapy without use of scanner technology. And this healing skill was rapidly spreading. As spiritual energy increased, more and more individuals received this gift and were able to help others.

The key finding lay in that people who had been healed through a Scrivner scanner often turned into scanoids themselves! The principal idea behind this skill was once a person's spiritual energy felt the healing and manipulation via scanner technology, then that person's innate spiritual energy "learned" this skill and was able to heal others and pass on the gift. Once a core of scanoids was established in a region, they would often set up classes and workshops in an outreach system so they could spread the gift to others in smaller communities. There were now several hundred Scrivner scanners and hundreds of thousands of human scanoids around the world, all helping people move through their emotional and spiritual traumas.

Then something happened that most doctors had always known. As emotional conditions improved, the vast majority of diseases resolved. Addictions, obesity, eating disorders, anxiety and depression, stomach ulcers, heart disease, high blood pressure—even many cancers had an emotional component. The incidence rate of all of these was dropping dramatically in a proportional relationship to human emotional improvement. Physicians who had now become scanoids were able to determine when subtle changes in the energy pattern occurred that might predispose a patient to a disease and thus work with the patient on an emotional level to prevent the disease from escalating. Pharmaceutical companies were becoming extinct. There were still cases when medicines were useful, but healing emotional energy patterns was much more effective. Energy healing had become a mainstay practice in medicine. And when two or more people prayed, "Casper" was certain to appear. Doctors, spiritual healers and family members would do "laying on of hands" therapy and consistently get results.

Not surprising, many people had a problem in the use of the term "Casper." The general public did not understand medical humor, which is often irreverent and usually crude. People in healthcare developed it as an emotional pressure release. In their case, Dr. Rainell and his team chose to continue to use Casper to avoid controversy. What started as a joke was now a problem. The Christians wanted to use "Holy Spirit", Native Americans preferred "Great Spirit", Muslims wanted "Allah", and all the rest jumped in and stirred up chaos. During an interview with the entire team, Fred best summarized the situation and solution.

"We figured if Casper was so sensitive to what he/she/it is called, Casper would stop showing up during our prayer sessions," he said. "Casper has shown up to each and every session we have done! If anyone has a problem with the name Casper, it appears to be a problem of your own making. Because Casper certainly doesn't seem to care!" Fred received a standing ovation, mixed with some "Boos", for his statement.

*****

After ten years of this paradigm shift in human consciousness, Vertig's syndrome was nearly extinguished. People still died of various causes, but overall there were fewer births than deaths and the hypothesis made in the "Energy Book" was accurate. Increased spiritual energy led to unprecedented advancements in intuitive medicine and healing. The mass consciousness had shifted away from self interest. No longer was getting ahead, making money, corporate greed, raping the earth, and other selfish acts the modus operandi. The new mass consciousness was focused on healing oneself and helping heal those around you. Though some still watched holovision, many were now able to link to the nightly telepathic news, which focused on topics of love and healing rather than typically newsworthy trauma and fear. Everyone could remember what it used to be like, but no one was interested in greed and self-centered pursuits anymore. Most people had an overwhelming feeling of love and compassion for their fellow humans, and all life on earth was seen as valuable and worth saving. Most people truly felt in their hearts the meaning of "We are all one" and behaved accordingly. For the first time in human history, most people truly "Loved their neighbor as themselves."

Chapter 28

Logan's shift

Logan was heading home in his hover. Hovering over the Sandia Mountains in a monsoon season rain storm was not the best of ideas, so he drove the old way along historic Route 66. His wipers zipped across the windshield but made almost no dent in the screen of rainwater. Squinting into the storm, Logan could barely make out that he was just entering "dead man's curve", made famous by an old rock 'n roll song in the early 1960s. The highway department had straightened out that curve substantially in the 1980s and again in 2054 when the heavy rains started. But there was still a minor twist at "dead man's curve". Not enough of a curve to slow down for under normal conditions, but the rain splattering down in sheets had almost reduced visibility to zero. Choosing the safer alternative, Logan slowed for the curve.

A sharp crack like a gunshot suddenly echoed through the darkness. An instant later Logan was . . . confused and sitting on the side of the road? He was aware it was raining hard. Quickly getting used to looking through the heavy rain he saw a distorted mass a few meters away. He tilted his head, trying to make it out. Then he realized he was looking at what was left of his car, crushed by a large granite boulder! He blinked, and knowledge came flooding to him. It coursed through his brain with a thrill more sizzling than an adrenaline rush. And it was instantaneous. No thought process required. The truth.

Heavy rain had loosened a gigantic boulder on the mountain. It had broken off and crushed his car. He emoted into hysterics, laughing at the chances of the event. He happened to be in his car, on that spot of the road, when the rain washed loose a boulder that had probably clung to the side of the mountain for a million years. Gravity finished the job off, smashing the boulder in the center of the roof of his car!

Part of the instantaneous knowledge was that he knew he was dead and in his astral body observing the event. He was almost surprised; it was totally painless. He was still laughing when a thought finally pierced his mind. *Well, if you gotta go . . . go out with some style!* He knew he no longer had a physical voice, but he said, "Thank you, God! Thank you, Jesus! When it's your time, it's your time!" It appealed to his ego, and it certainly was a memorable way to die. It was funny! He was still laughing! He always knew his Higher Power had a sense of humor, but this was priceless! If he could have picked his way to die, he could not have come up with a better scenario.

His heart sang out. *Thank you for this life!*

As his awareness of the situation grew, the physical environment changed. He was suddenly surrounded by other cars as they screeched to swerving stops amid torrents of rainfall. Everything was slowing down, and in another moment, his perception was that nothing was moving. People were standing still, and every individual raindrop was suspended. Motionless. Logan actually stood and drifted over to a droplet, stretching out to touch it. His finger passed through it. They were already on different planes of existence; his finger had no effect on the drop. Then he was aware of an intensely beautiful, clear light and turned to face

216

into it. Though he remained silent, laughter continued to bubble cheerfully in his chest. He remembered an old joke whose punch line was, "Stay away from the light!" As he moved towards the light, a distant thought drifted through his mind.

There's nothing to go back to.

An image of a massive boulder on top of his totally flattened car flickered into his memory. Different fluids oozed from underneath, one of them red. They mixed with rainwater and trickled in crimson rivers off the road. He wondered if the vision was some sort of test to see if he still had attachments to this physical life. Without looking back, he moved towards the light. Having spent the last 50 years of his life searching for his own spiritual recovery and finally achieving it, he was excited to see what the next phase of his adventure would hold. Now was his opportunity to experience his own "transition". This was exciting!

Time and space hovered at a standstill. All Logan was aware of as he entered the light was warmth, love and instantaneous knowledge. He saw the total experience of his entire life. Every event, every conversation, every action, every emotion—all one experience, not separated by time and space. Perhaps this was his *moment of clarity*, where the summation of life became clear. Some people have it at the moment of physical death. Since his death was so dramatic, it wasn't difficult to believe his occurred just after physical death?

Logan's moment of clarity was a lesson. Two lessons, in fact. The first was about his chemical dependency. He spiritually felt the damage he had done to himself and to others. He knew he no longer needed to learn that lesson. Now he understood that he did not need an external substance to make him feel better physically, emotionally or spiritually. Connected to this was a respect for his physical body. The knowledge washed over him, sinking into him, making him realize that our physical bodies truly are sacred temples that house our spirit. He felt this in his heart. Mind? He felt it somewhere! No longer would he need to desecrate his temple with substances, or work so hard as to break parts of his body. He was, finally, okay just the way he was.

The second lesson was Kersti. He instantaneously experienced their entire relationship. From the time they were kids to the last thoughts he had of her just moments before his physical body was crushed, each moment came flooding back. He had loved her! He would have died for her. He loved her, heart, mind and soul. Because she was in a committed relationship, he respected her needs. *He honored them*. The love he felt in his heart for Kersti was incredible. No words could describe love! Knowing her was a blessing! It was a feeling he knew he always had and always would have for her. During his entire life review, he only felt complete when he was with her.

At first, he did not know what was happening. He saw other lessons. Hundreds of them. Thousands of them! All collecting into his consciousness. Each life he had lived left a legacy of a lesson or two. They were all compiling into his consciousness and memory.

Logan was also aware of something else. His energy was splitting off and going to all of his loved ones and friends, just the way he had witnessed hundreds of times when he was with people who were dying. Much of his energy had gone to Kersti, his nephew and niece, all his friends and loved ones. His energy blending with theirs in the spiritual realm. It was an odd sensation. Though his energy was spread out amongst all of his loved ones, he was aware of still being a single, intact entity. He knew who he was. Where he ended, and where he began. He was aware at the same time that he was connected with all of them, he was connected with the single great source! God, Jesus, Buddha, Holy Spirit, Casper—there was no name that would do this

218

presence justice. It cascaded over him, cleansing him like the waves of the ocean, all with an overwhelming feeling of love and innocence. It was a wonderful feeling of being loved, nurtured and cared for.

He could sense all his loved ones. Zeus was first to connect with him, doing his full body wiggle and wagging his tail so fast it was a blur. The Samoyed kissed him as they rolled together in a soft, supportive mist. Logan was aware that Zeus was not a physical body, just energy. But it was an energy Logan loved, so his memories placed a "Zeus" body around the energy. *To make it familiar, safe?* he wondered. Then the spirits of his family warmed him like a sunny day on the beach. As he felt each one's energy, his memories surrounded the energy with a physical body.

His father was soon beside him. When his dad spoke, he did not communicate aloud. Instead, the familiar voice hummed softly in Logan's mind. *Your memories place a body on our energy pattern for now, but this will soon end. We think it happens to make the "transition" easier. I emphasize transition on purpose. We have been watching what you've been working on, Logan, and we are so proud of you!"*

We? Logan echoed.

Logan's grandfather was suddenly standing with them. There were three other energy patterns there as well, which Logan immediately knew were his great-grandfather and other ancestors. Since Logan had never met them, he had no memory of their looks.

Gramps beamed at Logan, his physical face glowing with light and happiness. *When you healed,* he said, radiating love and support that swept over Logan as if through spiritual osmosis, *we could feel the love and courage of what you did, and we were healed when you were!* Logan *felt* his Grandfather crying as if they were one and the same. Looking up, Logan saw tears flow down Gramp's cheeks.

It was such a wonderful feeling. He didn't feel love; he *was* love! He was complete.

At last, Logan was home.

*****

"And then—"

"Shh," Carrie shushed. "Listen. Hear that?"

Fred, disgruntled at being interrupted in the middle of a good joke, listened to the echo of the general phone as its ring reverberated throughout the lab.

"Think it's the one in Logan's office?"

"Dunno," Fred said. "Can I finish now?"

"Answer the phone first!" Carrie chided.

"Fine, fine! Don't know why we got that phone installed," he grumbled, stalking down the hall towards the faint ring. "Can't people just call our tel-chips?"

That was how, a minute later, Fred found himself spinning in Logan's chair and talking with a woman who was calling from Australia.

"Is Logan there?" she asked.

"No, he's not. Wait . . . is this Kersti?"

"Yes, it is!"

"Oh, hi! How are you?" Fred asked.

"Well, I . . . don't know how to answer that yet. It's about four in the morning here. I woke up startled and worried about Logan. I actually saw his face and, weird as this sounds, felt him hug me! I knew you would still be at work, so I thought I would call to make sure everything's okay."

"He left a few minutes ago," Fred explained. "We're having a bad storm, so he left early. You just missed him! Everything is fine here, though. He'll be so disappointed he missed you. Try calling his tel-chip!"

*****

Logan was home.

He was aware that, in this plane of existence, time and space were meaningless. There was no way to experience either. You were always present. No past, no future, just the present. And the present felt glorious! Being in spirit without a physical body was like freedom after confinement, health after illness, falling in love after loneliness. During this period of being home, he knew his energy was split amongst all of his friends and loved ones. He knew, too, that he had no control or influence over them because they all had free will. To him, it felt like his energy was a nurturing, comforting warm blanket. He could feel his loved ones periodically tap into his energy. A memory, what he meant to them, something he'd said or done. And although Logan had no direct influence over them, they could use his energy for support in making their own decisions. Simultaneously, he was always aware of being connected with the single, loving, great source. It was being constantly in love! Puppy love. Deep, knowing love. Playful, frolicking love. All love. All the time.

After an unknown period, Logan realized something was changing. Through his conscious contact with the one source, he was aware that he was asked and he accepted to come back into a physical body. It was his time to do something important. He implicitly trusted what he was asked to do.

His conscious contact intuited it was several generations later, and the human race had chosen to continue to decrease its population. Consequently, he would be born into a physical body with vast amounts of spiritual energy. He was excited! Another adventure!

Chapter 29

Leydon

Eyes closed, Leydon let a gust of wind catch his hair. Sea spray, ripped off the crests of broiling white waves, dampened his feet. The wooden pier was hot, baked by the summer sun. Toes sizzling, Leydon stretched up his arms and plunged like a spear into the ocean. Cold water heightened his senses. He peered around, blinking slowly, lungs swollen with air. A silver fish streaked past him, rolling its flaming red tail and it zipped away into the blue depths.

"Mother," he telepathically called, reaching out across continents.

"Leydon . . . you have arrived?"

"Yes. The transport was early, and I began by exploring the sea."

"Tell me tonight. Enjoy this moment for yourself. Love the ocean, Leydon, and the earth."

"Always, mother. Till tonight."

Leydon surfaced for a gasp of air and lay on his back to float on the water. He had wonderful parents. They had conscious contact with God. Though his parents knew they were the biologic pro-creators of Leydon, they were equally aware that their son's real parents were Mother, Father, God. They raised him with love, nurturing his ability to accept his

223

own power. They taught him at an early age that God was his Father/Mother and to listen to the inner voice that whispered softly in his mind and heart.

Throughout his childhood, Leydon could see auras. He had powerful intuitive senses because he listened to his inner voice. His dreams were prophetic, and he was a healer from an early age. He could cleanse pain, cure some illnesses, and heal disruptive energy patterns in the body with a simple laying on of hands. Animals, wild and domestic, followed him around. He could sense injured animals in the forest near their house and could sometimes heal them.

Every now and then, fragments from a distant past drifted to him. In time, Leydon came to sense that these were pieces of former lives. From childhood, he knew it was important to treat his body as a temple. The thought of using harmful substances or eating unhealthy foods seemed disrespectful to who he was. He loved who he was and the many gifts he had been given. Somewhere in his spirit, he knew he had a purpose. He was in constant contact with God; only these physical bodies sometimes scrambled the signal! His aura was exquisite, complete with a beautiful indigo blue layer, a bright emerald green layer, a thick golden layer, and bright purple lingers shooting out from the surface.

At 20 years of age, Leydon began traveling. He remained connected to his parents via telepathy. So whether sleeping at home or halfway around the world, he was never truly alone. There was never a time when he regretted his decision to explore the world. Traveling was easy for him. He could read auras, and even though all people could now see auras, his ability was different. He could trace the family tree of a person's energy. One man he met was particularly interesting; his shimmering aura carried the lineage of Socrates, Lincoln, Gandhi, Mother Theresa and Modessjabar. Yet also within his aura, hovering among the other layers, was an energy of Hitler.

"Now, don't worry," Leydon quickly explained when the man nearly dissolved into a hyperventilating mass. "Understand that the Hitler layer is just the shadow self energy trying to balance out the amazing, positive influence that is your energy. This is common energy balance. Even long families of positive, powerful energies will have a negative thrown in from time to time for balance." And Leydon's mesmerizing energy and wise words calmed the man.

Leydon could do more than heal and read auras. He had a strong body and was not afraid of physical labor. Many times after a healing or a reading, he would be invited to the person's home to enjoy a warm meal and rest. Sometimes he was asked to stay longer, even for weeks at a time. Many were drawn to Leydon. Leydon was drawn to one.

Many jobs were in food production, sustainable energy and healing of any or all of the four aspects of self: physical, mental, emotional, and spiritual. Entertainment and playing were also important industries since they helped people elevate their energy and happiness.

Leydon was born into a transformed earth. Money was nonexistent. Food, clothing and shelter were available for all who needed them. There was much work to be done and workers were treated fairly and with respect. Wealthy versus poor was a struggle no more. Humans finally understood that they were all in the process of evolution. If one of us suffered, the whole suffered. And suffering, above all, was no longer tolerated. The feelings of love, tolerance and acceptance were commonplace.

On the rare occasion that someone did commit a crime, everyone who knew that person would show up for the trial. Those who had in previous generations been called scanoids were now called seers. Seers would attend trials and find the disrupted energy pattern in the offenders' auras. Most often, the snags were fear or resentment. This allowed the offenders to recognize that it was their energy that was misaligned, not a moral, incurable flaw in their character. Those who relapsed in behavior were treated by seers to feel the hurt they had caused their victims.

Offenders generally acknowledged that the snag in their energy pattern was one they no longer wished to act on. Then everyone in the community would tell the offender one or two instances in which he or she did something good. This was an offering of love and forgiveness. Communities found that after offenders had gone through the process of recognizing their maladjusted energy and the harm they had done to their victims, it helped immensely for the offenders to hear all the positive ways in which the community still held them in high esteem. It was a way to accept them back into community.

Murder and violent crime were things of the past. Jails were nonexistent. Most people, however, could attest to attending at least several trials. Seeing others learn to alter their own behavior helped them improve their mental, emotional and spiritual lives within their families and their community. It allowed for continued spiritual progress.

One of the most important features of community trials was that children could take their parents to trial. It was recognized that children were not young and naive. *Because of their innocence*, they were some of the wisest souls in the community. The young had not been scarred by time, life and hormones. It was a community's *honor* to listen to and learn from what children had to say and teach.

Technologies were amazing. Most technological goals were based on helping other people and animals or healing the badly damaged earth. Teleportation was commonplace. One could travel anywhere in the world from certain locations, which were connected to other teleportation booths in a global network. Since everyone's mindset was focused on working for the benefit of humanity, keeping track of who was doing what was unnecessary. Everyone was doing what they could to help others or to play. Playfulness was seen as a necessary part of health. Most were balanced in work and play.

Yet as magnificent as this world was, Leydon could not help but feel a desire somewhere deep in his chest for something . . . else. Even now as the ocean waves lapped over his legs and arms and chest, his heart throbbed for a thing he did not have, that he did not understand, but that he knew he needed. He took to traveling to find it, and had been sojourning for about a year in Europe. But he only felt further from what he was looking for.

In a week, he planned to return to North America. Over the years, he had developed an internal auric compass. At least, that's how he thought about it. Just like birds could migrate vast distances by judging the earth's magnetic grid, he could tell when he was closer, or farther away from, what he was looking for. Leydon intuited he needed to be in Ouray, Colorado.

Leydon had heard of Ouray's natural beauty. There was also something very familiar about how the three waterfalls were said to come off the mountain and drain into the box canyon where the town was nestled. He consciously cycled through some of his aura layers until he found one where Logan was immersed deeply in a conversation with his grandfather. The elderly man told his grandson that they were originally from that area. A German immigrant married one of the native Ute women, and the Ouray area was considered sacred by the Ute Indians.

Chapter 30

Reunion

Leydon was feeling a curious excitement. His own aura swelled in amplitude and grew brighter when he went in one direction. He was being led by his aura. This was new! It stretched out in the direction it wanted him to go. He played with it and found that it played back. If it stretched in one direction and he went the opposite way, sadness and disappointment washed over him. When he followed his aura, joy and excitement bubbled inside him. He had been following this emotional compass for a long time to see the mysterious something he needed. Now his aura became the compass, an arrow pointed towards the promise of an even happier future.

He was tingling with excitement. Somehow, he knew this was it. The search for the unknown beacon ended at the natural hot springs in Ouray. Leydon's aura led him to the large pool area. He crossed the foot bridge stretching over the cold mountain stream, pausing for a moment to glance into the swift current as it rippled along on its endless journey to a distant sea. When he passed the buildings and saw the large pool, he froze.

Could it be?

After all this time, he still recognized the layers of

indigo blue, emerald green, and the purple lingers shooting out like lightning bolts. And there was more now. Over the generations, both of them had experienced spiritual growth. The purple lingers were now shooting out from a layer of golden white light, which meant a higher spiritual vibratory rate. Just like his aura!

She was bent over with her hands on her knees, talking to a little boy in the water. The boy giggled and splashed her before paddling away on his back. Laughing, she wrung a lock of soaked hair dry and twirled it around her finger, forming a soggy curl. Leydon was happy to see she was beautiful—at least from behind! She had a beautifully shaped bottom that curved up to a narrow waist before spreading to wide, strong shoulders. He walked up about fifteen feet behind her and stared down at her ass.

"I would recognize that a...a...a...aura anywhere!"

Even before he spoke, she sensed someone's eyes roving over her. Startled by the voice, she straightened up and whirled around, peering at Leydon. At first, she simply noted the obvious. He seemed to top the six-foot mark and was dressed in a tight T-shirt that revealed chiseled muscles. His eyes, cinnamon with a swirl of lime, glowed with pleasure. His gleaming teeth formed a broad smile that stretched from cheek to cheek. She smiled reflexively and, since he mentioned something about auras, let her peripheral vision absorb his aura. Deep indigo blue. Bright emerald green. Purple lingers shooting from a thick golden-white layer. So familiar. . . Suddenly, she understood.

"I knew you'd find me," she whispered, taking a few stunned steps towards him. Then she paused, shaking her head, fighting back tears of happiness. "For the last couple of years, I could sense you were looking for me. So I've been waiting and waiting. Waiting forever, if I had to. What took you so long?"

Leydon's mouth was dry. "T-thank you for waiting,"

was all he could manage to faintly stutter. She was beautiful to his eyes and took his breath away – still! He calculated her to be about five foot, five inches and just shy of 115 pounds. Dark brown hair, very slightly curled, cascaded down her shoulders. Her piercing blue eyes sequestered his soul! Her radiant smile showed perfect teeth and the cutest little dimples he had ever seen. He was still trying to catch his breath when she spoke.

"What's your name now?"

"Leydon."

"Ooh, I like that!"

A chill ripped up Leydon's spine, it was an exquisite feeling. He loved the sound of her voice. He stared at her, astounded by her beauty, her voice, her aura. After all these years, all the searching, all the travels, he had finally found her!

"My name is Derstinna," she said.

"Ooh, I like that," Leydon echoed in a low baritone. His voice, enticingly sexy, sent a sudden chill shooting up her spine.

They were in a visual, hypnotic trance. Both were speechless at one another's physical beauty. But, more than that, they were transfixed watching each others aura. Even though they stood ten feet apart, their auras pulled towards one another like two magnetic forces being drawn together. First, purple lingers crackled out like lightning bolts, crossing five feet and meeting in the middle. As if showing respect, the lingers gently touched and caressed. Then, getting excited, they started to spiral, swirl and intermingle.

Both Leydon and Derstinna had seen lingers meeting before, of course, but neither had ever seen anything like this! When their lingers met, they coiled around each other until they appeared like two single strands coiled into one double helix of DNA—equal energy strands that had met again at last. Each would follow the curve of its companion strand but not cross it or interfere with its destination, showing respect and honor. Multicolored sparks igniting between each coil as they glide past. When a hundred energy coils of DNA put on a light show, it was incredible!

Then the two separate golden-white layers coalesced into one large golden-white layer encompassing them both. This was now the backdrop for the dance of the purple DNA coil lingers. Purple light playing, dancing, sparkling in a layer of gold. It was beyond astounding.

Finally breaking their visual trance, Leydon stretched his arms toward her. "Should we help them get closer?" he called, his soft whisper amplified in the swirling aura dome around them.

Derstinna nodded, for a moment forgetting how to speak. "Yes, we should."

Locked together with intense eye contact, Leydon slowly walked closer to Derstinna. They could feel one another's energy. Derstinna's lungs were swollen with air she could not release, nearly suffocating, but she couldn't breathe. All this time she had been waiting, *waiting*, and at last he was here. Tears welled in her eyes.

While neither broke eye contact, through their peripheral vision they could see their auras. The next layer to make contact was emerald green. Each had a slightly different shade of green, and when the layers met they swirled, spiraled and danced but did not blend together. Indigo blue was next and had the same reaction. While the auras had similar colors and swirled together in the same shared space, they did not become one. They remained two entities simply sharing the same space, growing brighter and increasing in intensity the longer they clung together.

Leydon lovingly wrapped his arms around Derstinna and gently pulled her closer. She rested her head on his muscular chest. They could not believe these feelings! Heat radiated from their bodies, an intense boil of warmth they had never experienced before. Chills raced continually up and down their spines. Simply being together, cradled in one another's arms, felt so good. They could sense their auras synergistically weaving together and growing in power!

Being separated for so long, at last they felt complete. Alarmingly, the intensity continued to build and the only thing Leydon could relate this feeling to was orgasm. Yet he was aware he did not have an erection. This was beyond physical. It was a spiritual, holy feeling! As the sensation continued to grow, radiate and magnify, he was aware that she was holding him just as emphatically as he was her. The energy grew between them. The heat between their bodies intensified, amplifying the chills sizzling up and down their spines and stimulating them into ecstasy. An overwhelming anticipation was growing and building, and just when it felt that neither one could take any more, a calm sense of love, innocence and understanding washed over them both. They knew each other! It was a sense of bonding that neither had ever had with any other person. It was true, pure, unconditional love! She tilted her head to peer at his face and whispered, "Don't ever let go of me."

"Never," he lovingly promised.

Derstinna pulled away just slightly so they could look at each other. Tears sparkled in their eyes. Through their peripheral vision, now glazed with the mist of tears, they could still see their auras energetically dancing and swirling about with playfulness yet profound respect. And there was something new. They were encapsulated in a larger, wilder, brilliant golden-white aura of incredible intensity. Every cell was aware of the unconditional love they felt. Then the tears rained down, running in rivulets along their cheeks and cutting trails along the lines of their jaws.

As they continued to smile and weep, at the same time, an amazing transformation occurred. Derstinna and Leydon recognized one another's faces. The distant glow of the other's eyes, the way hair flowed and curled around ears and cheeks, every faint crinkle of a smile, each wrinkle, and every emotional nuance. It was as if they had always known that face.

As they watched, their faces changed. In another heartbeat, Logan was looking at Kersti! His eyes roved over her flawless skin, shining hazel green eyes, perfect teeth, the smile he could never forget, and the faint little beauty mark on her left cheek. She took his breath away!

Kersti was equally enchanted with Logan's piercing blue eyes, high cheekbones, distinctive nose, and the cleft in his chin that she always thought made him look like a movie star. He was just as she remembered. And he still made her dizzy!

As they both struggled to absorb the truth that Leydon was Logan and Derstinna was Kersti, their faces morphed into two other faces. These seemed familiar but were not faces either could put names on. Then another set of faces, and another, and another still. It took several cycles of transformations until they both realized that their spiritual energies had only been high enough when they were Logan and Kersti to remember that lifetime together. Apparently, they had been together many times before.

Yet, right here and now, the past didn't matter. Distant lives of love and loss were behind them. They were together in the same overwhelming feeling of love, unaware of time and fully immersed in the moment.

The next thing they became aware of was people clapping. Leydon and Derstinna emerged from their daze to see 50 or 60 people enjoying the moment, clapping and joyfully smiling at the two of them. They were so empowered by the moment that neither Leydon nor Derstinna broke the hug or felt embarrassed. They felt immersed in a sacred moment. Derstinna was quick to notice three people who were not smiling and clapping like everyone else but instead were bowing reverently with clasped hands in eastern fashion. As she made mental note of these three, Leydon noticed as well and turned towards them. Still embraced, Leydon and Derstinna nodded reverently in return. The trio slowly made their way over.

"Congratulations!" the oldest said kindly.

"Thank you!" Leydon and Derstinna said in unison, smiling at each other.

A pause. Then: "Congratulations for what?" Leydon added.

"For experiencing the completion! The completion is what happens when soul mates, essence partners, twin flames —whatever label you prefer—meet at this level of spiritual progress. It's an amazing, beautiful bond to witness. What we saw were the two of you hugging while your auras flamed like stars gone supernova! Then the Holy Spirit joined you and blessed your union. Everyone surrounding you experienced an intense, golden-white light and the wonderfully warm, radiant heat that is the energy of love. Blessed are those who are privileged to witness it. It is literally the vibration of love. While you were glowing, everyone present could feel God's love inside them! Notice how they were sending love back to you," finished the elder, bowing again.

Hear that, Ley?" Derstinna murmured, brushing her lips along his ear. "We were supernovas."

"You still are, baby. Always will be."

She buried her face in his shirt. "It was an incredible feeling," she added in awe.

"I don't think words can describe it," Leydon said quietly. He gently moved behind Derstinna and held her tightly against him. She wrapped her arms backwards around him.

The younger male of the trio beamed. "Think that's great? Just wait until you do the completion while you're having sex!"

The female standing beside the young man, who appeared no older than him, jabbed him in his ribs with her elbow. "MEN!" she snapped playfully. "Even as they become spiritually evolved, they are still men!"

"Well, that's reassuring!" Derstinna said, pulling Leydon tighter against her backside.

The young woman smiled. "We too are essence partners," she said softly, weaving her fingers through the young man's. "And, yes, you can experience the completion any time the two of you thank God in gratitude for each other and ask for God's presence to be with you." Then, leaning forward as if to be secretive, she whispered, "By the way, he's right. Wait until you do it during sex. It's breathtaking!"

The elder nodded thoughtfully towards some clouds flitting swiftly overhead. "No one knows what the completion is," he said slowly. "Some say it is two becoming one again. But who truly knows? Half of any adventure is the mystery. One thing's for certain, however. When two soul mates find each other, it does draw attention. It's hard not to notice the special nature of the reunion. Others feel the glow of love you emanate."

"No kidding!" Derstinna said, looking around.

The elder smiled. "Others," he continued, "say that completion is just another gift, just as God made sex pleasurable. And as you two will discover, when two people are very much in love, orgasm is even more intense. The completion is a type of spiritual orgasm for soul mates lest they forget they have something very special together."

"What do you mean?" Leydon asked.

"I have remembered my last four physical lifetimes," the elder said slowly, heaving a heavy breath, "and I have not yet found my soul mate. It is actually quite rare. We think that, most times, one has a physical existence while the other looks over them from the spiritual plane. These two"—he motions to the young couple beside him—"are the only other partners I have ever met. We know of several others around the world. I am a doctor of theology at the University of Colorado in Boulder. I spend time with these two trying to learn more about completion and bonding. I must say, to actually witness your first completion was an honor. Truly, truly an honor!" He bowed again. "And I highly doubt we were all here by coincidence," he added with a smile.

After introductions, they headed to a local restaurant, picked out a cozy booth, and ordered some lunch. The doctor took out an AV recorder chip and asked if it was alright to ask a few questions. He asked Derstinna and Leydon to go back through the experience so he could document as much as possible. The new couple did not want to let go of each other. While eating, their thighs rubbed together, making full contact, and their feet wrapped around each other. When done eating, Leydon held Derstinna's hand. Periodically, he would kiss the back of her hand or bite and nibble at her wrist. He couldn't help it, almost as if urged by a primal instinct.

Dr. Hoen, as the professor introduced himself, asked, "Did you know what your partner looked like before you met? How did you know how to find one another?"

Derstinna glanced at Leydon. "You go first," she said. "I'm interested in hearing this as well! Because I just basically knew that, if I just waited, you would find me." Looking back at the doctor, she added, "I had this sense that he was looking, and a stationary target is easier to hit! Oh, and I just went first, didn't I?" Laughing, she kissed Leydon on the cheek.

"I didn't know what her face would look like," he said, putting his arm around her shoulder. "But she is more beautiful than I ever could have imagined . . ."

They were face to face. Derstinna peered up at him, neck craned slightly back. They were sharing the same air, the same emotional spark. He leaned forward and she met him halfway, brushing their lips together. And then he tilted his head and they were locked into a passionate kiss for the first time. Both got chills, and neither wanted to break the kiss. They pulled apart at last only because they had an audience.

"But I could clearly see her *aura* in my mind's eye," Leydon added breathlessly. "I knew that when I saw her, I would recognize her. The more I traveled, the more I could tell if I was headed in the right direction. And these last few days, I was guided by more than my feelings. My aura reached out towards Derstinna, showing me the way. I just knew I was headed towards her."

"Tell me the vision of her aura you had in your mind, was it so clear that you could have drawn it out color by color?"

"Yes, absolutely!" Leydon said. "I even dreamed of her aura."

"Me, too!" Derstinna added.

"Interesting." Dr. Hoen nodded. "Derstinna, did you know he was black?"

She shook her head. "Nope, not at all." With a smile, she added, "For a doctor, that sure was a strange question." Derstinna glanced at Leydon and said, "We are soul mates! We have known each other for a long time. Besides, look at him. He's gorgeous! So I'm happy that he's handsome, but his skin color means nothing."

"Sorry, sorry," Dr. Hoen stuttered. "That's not what I meant. I mean, did you have any idea that he was going to be black? For example, have you always liked black men?"

Leydon examined his own arm. "Not really black," he murmured under his breath. "More of a creamy milk chocolate, I'd say."

Derstinna laughed. "Nope," she said again. "In fact, this is the first time I've ever kissed a creamy milk chocolate man." She leaned in for another quick kiss from Leydon.

"But, like him, I also knew what his aura would look like. I have seen his aura all my life, especially in these last few months. There were nights when I would have dreams and just see the colors of his aura wrapping around me. I would feel so warm, so nurtured, so loved. I knew his aura. Besides, it's essentially identical to my own. When my parents died and I synergized with their energy, I started seeing past lives. I saw a life that we shared when my name was Kersti"—she turned to Leydon—"and your name was – "

"Logan," he finished. They repeated their former names together, savoring the old flavor.

They smiled, leaned together, and kissed again.

"I've been having the same experience for the last couple of years." Leydon beamed at Derstinna and said, "I clearly saw a time when you were already in a relationship, and I was totally in love with you. I recall saying that making love physically would probably disrupt our friendship. So I told you that I would rather know your spirit intimately – "

" – than my body intimately!" Derstinna finished, feeling tears swell in her eyes again. "Yes, I remember! I remember wanting you so much, but I was already married. I loved you for the rest of that life! You were so honorable, and I know how hard it was for you to walk away from me. Oh, Leydon, Logan, I wanted you so badly. I was afraid to even talk to you!"

"I noticed," he said sadly.

"I'm remembering the finer details of that lifetime. I know it was twice as hard for you. You were alone. I had a roommate in the form of a husband and, of course, I had my kids. I know the level of love that it took for you to walk away," she said woefully.

They talked for a few hours about all they could remember. Finally, Leydon said, "Derstinna and I have a lot of lifetimes to catch up on, and you will have to excuse us for now."

"Of course, of course," Dr. Hoen said quickly. "I apologize. This was just such an amazing experience for me!"

"I think that is true for all of us," Leydon said, wrapping Derstinna in another embrace.

Chapter 31

Together at Last

It occurred to him that this might feel strange, unnerving even, to be walking along together at last. But it was a most natural, peaceful feeling. Together. Her beside him, still playfully bumping shoulders on occasion, like she did to Logan in the hospital. Their hands were loosely held together and they spoke sometimes, but mostly their lingers talked instead in a whisper of energy.

"Do you have a place to stay?" Derstinna asked.

"No. I don't have a place to stay," he said grinning.

"I live alone, and I'm just a few blocks away. You could stay with me, if you'd like."

"That sounds perfect," Leydon laughed.

Derstinna tightened her grip on his hand, pulling him up the street. "Then let's go, silly! Stop dragging your feet." She lowered her eyelids till her eyes sparkled through long black lashes. Leydon's heart revved; it was the most seductive look he'd ever seen!

It felt so good to be holding her hand. As they walked, he kept raising it to his mouth, kissing, nibbling and gently biting her hand and forearm. He didn't know it yet, but she found it intensely arousing.

"You can call me Dersti. That's what my friends call me."

"Quite curious, isn't it? When we were together before, you were Kersti, short for Kerstina. Now you are Dersti, short for Derstinna. Funny, huh?"

She just smiled and stretched up to press her lips to his cheek. Then her lips traveled lower and briefly did something to his neck that robbed him of his breath. She pulled away, smiled, and kept walking as if nothing had happened.

While he regained rational thought, Leydon added, "Isn't this amazing, how we are remembering more of our past lives?"

Dersti nodded. "It feels like our combined energies are stimulating all the old memories. Back there when you were talking to Dr. Hoen, memories were flooding back to me. They're not all tidy and consecutive like my memory of this life, but bits and pieces are very clear. Here's an example: I remember the project we were on together with that scanner thing." Dersti paused, searching the scattered fragments of distant memories for something she'd remembered just a minute before.

"The Scrivner scanner," Leydon suggested.

"That's it! The Scrivner Scanner. I remember some of the people and some of the experiences so clearly. One I remember . . . very clearly. Like it just happened. Like it keeps happening. And I wish I could somehow take it back." She stopped walking and turned to face him. She reached out and took both of his hands into hers. "The day I told you I had to leave . . . I'll never forget it. I was so afraid that you would hate me forever. That you would never understand my heart wanted—*needed*—to be with you. Then I remember you saying that mothers have a sacred duty in raising their children. Even though the man I was bound to on paper was more of a roommate than a husband or lover, I felt I had to stay for my children's sake. Wait, something just . . . oh, Leydon, I just had a powerful visual come to me! Back in that lifetime, whenever I was meditating and praying I could see you kneeling and praying as if you were beside me. I could feel your love and support radiate out to me." Her eyes flickered into his. "I want you to know that feeling your love and support got me through many a hard day!"

Leydon pulled Dersti closer to his body, though not quite into a full hug. He allowed her enough space to lean backwards so they could retain eye contact. Both felt the excitement of touching one another.

"I remember," Leydon whispered. "after grieving your loss, I would meditate and pray for you every day. I would send you love and pray for your highest good!"

"It worked and truly touched me."

"What else could I do?" He pulled her against his body, against his chest, against his heart. "I have *always* loved you!"

They wrapped their arms around each other and shared a passionate kiss. Then his lips dropped lower and swept in on her neck, but she pulled away before he could mesmerize her. She grinned wickedly, knowingly, and took his hand with a seductively sweet smile to pull him along the street towards her house. As she led him along, he couldn't help but get excited just looking at her slender waist, her round and firm bottom, and her shapely, toned legs. She glanced back just as he was getting into the swing of her hips. Busted!

"What are you looking at?" she said with a giggle.

"Ooh, baby!" was all he could say.

The sound of his deep, sexy baritone sent a tingle winding along Dersti's spine, leaving her with a wonderfully warm, wet feeling where his eyes had been looking.

In another minute she opened the door to her home. Ouray was a small community, and everyone knew everybody. People had quit locking doors decades earlier. It was another paradigm shift in thinking. If someone needed something bad

243

enough to go through the emotional self degradation to steal it, they obviously needed the item more than its owner and were welcome to it.

Dersti turned around, bowed, and invited him into her house. Leydon swept inside and stretched both arms towards her while closing the door with a swift kick of his foot. She placed her hands in his and felt him gently pull her closer. They embraced, lips locked in a gentle, loving kiss. They were two bodies long denied one another that had longed for each other for lifetimes! They had been together in previous lives, but not for a long time. Their lips touched gently, sweetly, at first mere feather brushes but growing firmer, more passionate, with each touch. Her lips were full, soft and sweet. His were firmer and confident. Each loved how the other felt, tasted, smelled!

They were enthralled by their kissing. Time crept away to the dark corners of the room and watched them at a distance, each second blinking by and lengthening to minutes, hours. They could do this forever. Kissing was ecstasy! As his mouth moved against hers, one hand swept to the small of her back. He could feel her sweet bottom protruding out. His hand held her slender waist. His other hand massaged up and down her spine. Fingers webbed apart, he passionately stroked the firm muscles along each side of her spine. After massaging her back, he moved up to her neck. He massaged the muscles beneath his touch until they were butter and then let his hands drift to the top of her head to give her a good scalp massage. Then he went in reverse, massaging down her neck and spine again, all the while locked in a passionate kiss.

Dersti moaned into his mouth in pleasure. Her hands were wrapped around his back. His muscles rippled beneath her touch. As her arousal swelled from his kisses and wonderful massage, she slid her arms lower around his waist and pulled him into her pelvis. His hardness rubbed against her lower abdomen. Keeping him pressed close, she massaged the muscles of his back. She enjoyed slowly stroking up and down his back, both hands engaged at the same time. From his slender waist she gradually worked her way up to his strong, broad shoulders. She was increasingly aroused by the strength and power she felt in him.

Their kisses grew deeper, impassioned, tongues swirling around each other. Then the kisses grew sweet and gentle; their lips parted, and they shared little tongue tickles. With their mouths open, his tongue would flick against the tip of her tongue. Then he would pull his head back and gently run the tip of his tongue over her upper lip, then her lower lip, and finally gently slip his tongue back into her mouth where just the tips would meet. She would sigh and moan softly into his mouth and reciprocate, returning the favor. It was as if they both knew exactly what the other loved. They were loving, playful, and totally in the moment.

Leydon was a full eight inches taller than Dersti. He had to bend over in order to kiss her. Grabbing her sweet bottom, he swept her up and carried her over to the counter top in the kitchen. When he lifted her, she wrapped her legs around his hips and her arms around his shoulders. His strength was apparent in the effortless way he raised her and lowered her on the counter. With her legs wrapped around his hips, she could feel his hardness pressing firmly against her sacred spot. Dersti held him tighter with her legs, and Leydon wrapped his arms around her waist and pressed her up against the wall behind the counter, never once breaking the kiss. Inside, she melted! It was the sexiest thing that ever happened to her.

She was amazed how he seemed to know exactly what made her feel good. He was equally amazed at how wonderful she felt in his arms, so petite and yet his equal. Her smell and taste, unique and fresh and longed for over lifetimes, were driving him wild with passion. This was more than a kiss; they had become the press of lips, the exchange of rubbing flesh, intermingled tongues and souls! If this was all there ever would be—a kiss—he would stay a lifetime! A few times he nibbled on her neck, dissolving her into a moaning angel in his arms, but time and again he returned to her lips. God! The way it felt to kiss her! Every now and then he would rhythmically pull her against his pelvis. They still had every piece of clothing on, but never before had they made love so well!

After another round of neck nibbles and kissing, he released their embrace and straightened up. She still had her legs wrapped around his hips and was now leaning back against the counter top and wall. He smiled at her, making her dizzy with his gaze alone. His eyes flashed into hers as he gently reached over and took one of her hands in his, rubbing her hand across his hardness. "Look how I feel about you!" he said.

She smiled at him, a smile that sparked fire in his soul. After rubbing him for a couple seconds, she unbuttoned her own jeans and slipped his hand down inside her panties. "See how I feel about you," she whispered.

"Ooh, baby!"

Dersti felt his strong arms slide around her back and gently lift her into a standing position. Still locked in a passionate hug, they locked once more into a kiss. He had noticed her bedroom on the first floor when they walked into her house. Peeking through half-closed eyelids while still hugging and kissing, he walked her backwards towards the bedroom. She didn't know what he was doing at first, but she trusted him totally. It was a sexy experience, in fact, to be embraced in a hug during a passionate kiss while walking backwards with her eyes shut. When they got to the foot of her bed, he gently nudged her to sit down. In a single swift motion, Dersti sat and lay back. The sheets folded softly beneath her. Leydon joined her on the bed, knees and arms straddling her sleek body.

"Wrap your arms around my neck," he suggested. She did so, and he crawled on his hands and knees while she was pulled along underneath him until her head rested on the pillows. He gently pressed his body to hers and hungrily possessed her lips in another kiss. She was on fire with passion! Neither had been sexually active for several years because each sensed they were looking for one another. But neither could have imagined how beautiful and awe-inspiring it would feel to finally be together with a soul mate!

After two hours of kissing, talking, laughing, and generally being playful—sex, after all, is simply two adult bodies playing—Leydon was getting cramped! He had to take his pants off. He slowly stretched his lips into a sexy smile as he stood up at the side of the bed and did a little strip tease for her. He peeled his shirt off, allowing her to fully enjoy his muscular arms, chest and rippled abdomen. She was writhing with delight on the bed. He undid his belt buckle and his jeans. He turned so she could see his bottom as he shimmied out of his pants and underwear. When he finally whirled to face her, he simply stood there, naked and excited. A faint blush painted her cheeks pink, but she enjoyed how he just stood there for her to feast her eyes on. Not in a hurry. Not embarrassed. He was so much fun!

Dersti was getting so excited she could hardly stand it. When he climbed onto the bed to help her slide out of her jeans and underwear, she pressed her pelvis into his hands and wiggled quickly out of her clothing. He was kneeling in front of her, so she sat up in bed to allow him to pull her shirt off. Once the shirt was off, the wonderful vision before her eyes was one she would never forget. She wanted to lean forward, open her mouth, and let nature take its course. When she leaned forward, lips stretched apart, eyes eagerly glittering, he gently stopped her. "Baby," he whispered. "We are together now and will have plenty of time to play and explore. If it's okay with you, our first time together, I want to be able to kiss your sweet lips and watch your beautiful face as we make love."

Her heart melted. "Ooh, Ley," she said. "You know just the right things to say to me!"

He rested on top of her, and she tilted her pelvis forward and wrapped her legs around his hips. She reached down with her small, smooth hand and drew a single sharp breath. Then they joined together, and she turned to fire.

"OH GOD BABY!" they cried out simultaneously while peering into one another's eyes.

Dersti thought of it, but Leydon said it first as if reading her mind and desires. "Baby, do you want to pray with me?"

"OH . . . YES!" she said between moans. "I do! This is . . . well, it feels—"

"Sacred!" he whispered, with tears rolling down his cheek.

"Ooh, it . . . is! So much . . . so!" Her eyelids were locked tight, relishing the moment. When she slowly opened her eyes and saw his tears, she broke into a sobbing cry. "I knew you would . . . find me, I knew it! But I had . . . ah, Ley! . . . no idea it could be like this! In our daily . . . experience, nothing prepares you . . . for something like . . . ah! . . . this!" She reached up and held his face in her hands, gently rubbing his tears into his cheeks. A sudden vision struck them both; they remembered the past life in which Kersti had done the same for Logan in the cafeteria. Now Leydon started to sob, remembering how much he loved Kersti. How sweet it felt to have Dersti anoint his tears now!

"We are incredibly blessed," he said, sliding his hands under her head. He lifted her head tightly against the side of his own and, with his lips pressed to her ear, began to pray.

"Dear God!" he whispered, then nibbled on her earlobe. "We thank you so much with every ounce of our being that you brought us together in this time and place. To be able to share our lives together, we know it is a rare and sacred gift." They were close, so close, breathing one another's breath and growing lightheaded from the loving. "We ask that you continue to give us knowledge of your will and give us the power to carry it out," he continued, pausing as Dersti arched her pelvis towards him with an eager grin. "Oh, baby," he breathed. "Some might think it strange that we pray to you . . . ah, Dersti! . . . in the middle of making love. God, we know this is a sacred event. A gift from you, and it would feel disrespectful to not pray and thank you with our whole hearts. We thank you for everything you have given us, and we ask you to come and be present with us now, and always!" Leydon whispered in Dersti's ear, "Baby, do you have anything you want to add?"

She moaned softly. "No...ooh Ley...that was perfect my love!"

"Amen," they said together.

At that moment, they suddenly became aware of an intense golden light that entered the room and surrounded them. They remembered what the others had told them about the completion. That they thought it was another gift from God. That we just had to ask for it, and it was freely given. Both felt their spiritual energy build, spark and soar to new heights. The heat between their bodies intensified, and the energy chill raced along their spines. They felt their chakras opening. Their sexual energy was lifted to higher chakra levels.

Dersti gently rocked her pelvis in time to match Leydon's motions. Their lips danced together in the ecstasy of a thousand kisses while they gazed into each other's eyes. Dersti and Leydon could not take their eyes off the other, transfixed by the other's beauty and aura. After an hour of escalating bliss, they exploded into orgasm simultaneously. The look of ecstasy on each others face added to the intensity of their own orgasm. Like the other soul mates had told them, it was so incredible there were no words to describe it! Their physical, emotional and spiritual energies all culminated with unbelievable force during climax.

They were certain in that moment, and always afterwards, that they loved each other as much as humanly possible.

Yet what overwhelmed them most of all was not the bliss of physical climax – the intensity of Leydon's release or Dersti's powerful spasms, but they were awed by the feelings of love and innocence that pervaded the experience. Powerful emotions! Once felt for yourself and another, you were able to feel it for other humans and you were never the same again.

After praying again to thank God for this indescribable experience, they watched the golden-white light dissolve around them as they held one another. Each was lost in the feeling of holding a person loved for multiple lifetimes, gazing into the other's eyes, reveling in the softness of the other's skin, the curls of her hair, the way he smelled, the way she tasted, the way everything he said and everything she did while making love just naturally seemed to be the right thing for the other person to get maximum enjoyment.

Chemistry?

Gift from God?

The same energy pattern?

Who cares!

In the end, the details were inconsequential. What mattered was the fact that they just experienced the unimaginable, and it left them speechless. Plus, they both remembered the previous lifetime, so long ago yet close to heart, in which they desperately wanted to be together. Because of love, respect and honoring Kersti's previous commitment, they chose to love each other spiritually rather than sexually. Recalling that now made this experience all the more sacred. It was worth waiting lifetimes for this!

Dersti spoke first, breaking the quiet interrupted only by the sounds of soft breathing.

"I love you," she purred.

"Ooh, baby...I love you," Leydon echoed.

"What can be said after an experience like that?" Dersti asked softly.

Leydon gazed into her eyes with a smile. "Nothing," he admitted.

After several minutes of silence, she added, "Guess what?"

"What?"

"I think we've just honored Psalm 149."

Leydon's smile widened. "Refresh my memory, baby. What does it say?"

"Well," she said, grinning, "it goes something like:

Sing to the Lord, a new song
let God's children be joyful
let them praise his name with dance
let them sing praise to him with song and harp
for the Lord takes pleasure in his people
let the faithful rejoice in triumph
let them be joyful on their beds
let the praises of God be in their throats!"

"Wow, baby. I'm impressed!"

Dersti blushed. "Some passages I can recite word for word, and others I just have the general meaning."

"Was that word for word or general meaning?"

"Close to word for word. But I would say that we were 'joyful on our beds'!"

Leydon laughed. "I sure would say so! And we had praises for God in our throats."

Dersti giggled. "It's hard not to have praises when something like this happens."

"Amen, baby!"

"Amen," she echoed. Then she added, "Ley, did you feel the energy when the Holy Spirit entered the room with us?"

"Yes, and it was incredible! Did you see our auras?"

"Auras! My God," she said joyfully, "the colors and energy actually distracted me at times. How could I not see them?"

He laughed. "Me, too! Me, too." Then he cupped his palms around her face. She stopped smiling, and their eyes locked. "But, baby, you are so beautiful you had my full attention," he murmured against her lips. She beamed radiantly and lifted her head to kiss him.

"Oh, Ley, you keep melting my heart," she moaned as she kissed him.

"I'm not just saying it," he said, stroking her hair with his fingers. "You are so beautiful!" His gaze roamed up and down her body. And he meant it, too, for never had he seen someone as beautiful as her. Whether Kersti or Dersti or any of a thousand different names, she was always the most beautiful woman to his eyes.

Just the sparkle in his eyes each time his gaze flickered into hers made her melt. Desire began to bubble within her again. She could not believe how she felt with him.

"It was actually pretty easy for me to ignore what our auras were doing. I just had to look at you," Leydon said.

"Me, too," she admitted as her hand lazily caressed his muscular chest and arms.

"But you have to admit," Leydon began before pausing in thought. "Our energy patterns were enjoying it as much as we were," he realized. "Even now, the two little critters seem pretty happy," he said playfully.

They focused on their auras, awed at the stunning display. Blues, purples, greens and golden swirls of energy danced about, actually playing with each other. A purple

252

linger would streak out from Leydon's aura, only to be matched by a similar linger from Dersti. They would coil around each other, swirling in a brilliant DNA coil and dancing with one another, multicolored sparks arching between the two. Both strands of energy behaved as they were equal halves of a whole. They would mesh together, shoot out like DNA lightening, retract back into the body of the aura, then unite and *flash,* more lightening. Then a blue-green wave of energy would ripple from one aura and be matched by the others. Just as an ocean wave breaks as it reaches the beach, the tip of the wave arcing over the body of the wave, the corresponding wave of energy from the other person would interlock tips. Like a ying/yang symbol, the wave of energy would then ripple down the entire length of their bodies before the tips unlocked once more and each wave settled back to its original aura.

"Did you see that one?" Dersti asked excitedly, pointing at a swirl of color in their mingling auras.

"Which one? The ying/yang wave or DNA lightening?"

She laughed and added, "Isn't it amazing how the patterns are all stuff we see in nature? DNA strands, ocean waves, lightening and geometric fractal patterns. And it's all so beautiful!"

"I guess energy obeys the laws of physics, regardless of what scale it's on."

Dersti twirled a long strand of his hair on her finger. "You are so beautiful . . ."

"We are so beautiful together!"

"I love you."

"I love you too, Dersti!" Leydon said, kissing her.

"I feel so much love now that I keep hearing this in my head. It's weird, like someone is singing in my ear:

Love is always patient;

253

love is always kind;
love is never envious or arrogant with pride.

Nor is she conceded, and she is never rude;
love never thinks of herself, or ever gets
annoyed.
Love is never resentful;
is never glad with sin,
but always glad to side with truth,
and truth always wins.

Love bears up under everything,
believes the best in all,
there is no limit to love's hope,
and she will never fail."

"Corinthians 13 is one of my favorites, too," Leydon said, his voice quavering. When Dersti looked up at his face, tears glittered in his eyes.

She held his head with both of her hands and pressed a kiss to his lips. "I have always loved you."

And they rolled into another cycle of lovemaking, singing and praying and moaning till morning, and only when the golden dawn peeked through the windows did they curl their heads together on a shared pillow for rest. As the physical bodies slept, their auras continued to play . . . united at last.

Chapter 32

Gifts

"Are you ready?"

"With you?" Dersti teased. "How can anyone be ready when you keep coming up with new things to throw at me?"

Leydon smiled and tightened the straps around his shoulders. Glancing at Dersti, he sighed softly.

There is such a thing as loving someone to the point you would die for them, and this is an interesting lifestyle. The feeling of gratitude that you walk around with in your heart is a gift! All the love and acceptance you ever dreamed possible is palpable, so easy to feel. As if all the love you ever felt for everyone and everything dwells, swells, and blossoms in your heart. It's there within easy reach, with no blocks or mental machinations to stir hesitation in feeling love. You feel happy, eternally grateful. You smile for no and every reason.

"Come and help me," Leydon said, opening the force field door of the hovercraft. The door hissed open, and he and Dersti peered out upon the endless green plains carpeting the earth 5,000 meters below them.

There is intellectual knowledge of love. You know that is what you want to feel. And then there is emotional and spiritual knowledge of love. That "AH-HA" moment that floods your conscience when your heart fully opens to love. It is no longer an intellectual concept but a throbbing necessity, true and present, in your heart!

"Ready?" he yelled above the rush of wind.

She nodded and squeezed his hand.

You awaken in love to a glorious sunrise washed with creamy reds and smeared with orange. Your days are like a rose bush. You're aware the perfect rose may have a thorn, but you mostly gaze in awe and simply accept, that a thorn bush has perfect and beautiful roses! And you feel grateful for the roses, which glow and darken with mystery and passion in the crimson sunset of love. Then you sleep and dream upon pink clouds of love. Day after day, you feel gratitude for love.

Leydon dove first from the hov, followed by Dersti. Hard wind whipped their bodies as they sped to around 120 mph. Dersti, who had only been skydiving twice before, may have screamed. But her shriek of joy was lost in their earthly descent.

Love given by grace can be lost by ego. If you choose to stay in love and it is a choice, love becomes who you are. And love is not sheltered in any one heart; it spreads in ripples to the person who opened your heart to love and beyond, until those around you can feel the love that radiates from you! Once your heart feels the love of the beloved and senses how glorious love feels, you feel it for others. A glow surrounds, envelops, encompasses you.

Dersti held out her arms to Leydon. They linked hands and twirled together through the air, breathing the sky and the clouds and each other. Separating, both spread their arms and legs so the webbing on their suits caught the air. They glided down, spiraling around each other, watching one another's beaming smiles. The wind fluttered grinning cheeks, just as it ruffled the webbing of the suits allowing flight.

You feel it, and others see it. Soon the feeling of love spreads to even more distant others, for it is the most contagious feeling in the world. God created us in love, and our brains are hardwired for the feeling of love. It becomes a journey of exploring love in everything. From the soft lips of your lover to the curl of a rose petal. Love glitters in every living creation. Even within the perfection of the thorn.

As the ground rapidly approached they shared a quick nod of acknowledgment, both pulled their parachutes. What was the rapid, gliding flight of two flying squirrels, swiftly transformed into the slow, graceful descent of two dandelion seeds, floating at the whim of the wind.

*****

As months scurried along, Leydon and Dersti began keeping a list of all the synchronicity that had occurred. They teased each other that these were just coincidences, but everyone at their stage of spiritual evolution knew there were no such thing as coincidences. Coincidences were lessons the universe was teaching, and it was our choice to learn the lesson or not. To remain perceptive, or not. All knew the key to continued spiritual growth was being perceptive to what the lessons were. Learning is not the answers, but asking the correct questions.

They preferred the same foods, music, holographic entertainment. These eerily exciting discoveries became normal after a few weeks and did not make their list. What did make their list was having the same dreams. After thinking about the same complex problem during the day, they would continue to share it at night with one another. They began to see that while estrogen energy saw the world one way, testosterone energy perceived it slightly different. When they combined their energies and perceptions, life became ecstasy. The three of them found their relationship charmed.

The third, however, was not a child. Not quite yet. For now there was Dersti, Leydon, and the relationship. For the relationship was a separate entity that needed nourishment and attention, just as Leydon and Dersti did. They found that, together, there was nothing the trio could not handle with love.

There were still times, of course, when one of them would fall back into ego. Fault can be found in anyone and used as an excuse to leave love's temple. But when you love someone so much you would die for them, and your lives are interdependent and shared in symbiosis, somehow finding fault and having to be right is not as important as being happy. Leydon and Dersti believed in the saying, "Would you rather be right? Or be happy?"

They lay awake one night, discussing it in the dark, with whispers into one another's hair and the night air. If someone's ego has to be in control and *be right* all the time, it makes compromise difficult. That's what relationship skills are about: clear communication, acceptance that you can't change your partner, and learning compromise. When your ego does not have to *be right* and learns it's more important to *be happy*, it makes compromise much easier. When in love, and your partner makes a statement that could be confrontational, love allows it to be a point of curiosity. The nascent curiosity allows your ego not a chance to prove your opinion is right, but a chance to see your partners opinion and hence grow together in understanding and acceptance. But . . . darn those egos! Sometimes it feels so good to be superior to someone else, to sit in judgment. Sitting in judgment gives us power. It can be hard to remember if you want to be right or happy?

There were times when they both missed learning the lesson. The flitting feeling of superiority, however brief, still lay a balm to an aching ego. Within their relationship, they learned that the flip side to being superior was loneliness. When one pushed his or her control issue and had to be right, the automatic result was feeling distance from the other. No one wants to be with someone who always has to be in control, and they were fortunate to learn this lesson quickly. Their time frame for having to be superior, in control, be right, dwindled from days, to hours, then minutes. Eventually, they recognized it while it was happening and could laugh with each other. One of the things Dersti loved about Leydon was whenever they caught the descent into ego stroking, he would lovingly clasp her hand in his own and pull her into a hug. Then he would hold her, kiss her, and apologize if need be. More often than not, their love and chemistry would kick in and they would end up making love. Instead of proving who was right, they would rather be happy – together.

They also learned that when one was angry at the other, it sapped so much of their energy from their spiritual growth that it felt as if a parasite was attached to them and swiftly sucking their energy. They learned to pray together and ask "Casper" to help them. They soon discovered that if they asked for the anger to be removed, it always was. This was not the therapeutic approach of "help us work through our anger" or "help us understand it." Rather, they pleaded to "please remove the anger," and what was asked occurred. "Ask and you shall receive!" This allowed them to get on with what was important: love, forgiveness, and God's will.

There were rare occasions when one of them focused on being selfish and self-centered during the day and found himself or herself stuck in an unpleasant emotion such as fear. It was then that love was above all appreciated. The ability to come home, hug your soul mate, or make love ... and ask the Holy Spirit to give the gift of completion certainly had a way of setting priorities back to love, forgiveness and God's will.

*****

As time progressed, they found themselves asking for completion not only to feel pleasure but also to feel closer to God or to answer questions. Once while in completion they wondered about fear of failure to fully help others and both heard the now-familiar voice whisper back, "The perfect love of the Christ consciousness casts out all fear."

Leydon had an intuitive thought. "Dersti," he murmured into her ear, pausing from his fingers gently stroking her hair. "What if we have gotten this wrong from the start?"

"What do you mean?"

"All of us have been conditioned by preachers, the Bible and other stories that may—or may not—have been translated accurately."

"Okay?" Dersti asked slowly, uncertainly.

"Well, what did we just hear?" he encouraged.

"The perfect love of the Christ consciousness casts out all fear," Dersti echoed.

"Precisely. Well, we all thought that the second coming of Christ would be a return of his physical body. What if it's his *energetic* body, his *aura*, that's going to return! And what if that's what's been surrounding us and teaching us all along, way back when we first saw it during the Scrivner scanner experiments."

"It was so immense," Dersti whispered. "We said it was the Holy Spirit!"

"Jesus was fully human, meaning he had an aura. The halo people saw on Jesus was his aura centered around his crown chakra! So it would make sense that the Christ consciousness would come back to teach us because he was human in all aspects."

"By Job, I think you're onto something there, Watson!" Dersti said in her best Sherlock Holmes accent.

Leydon beamed and kissed her sweet lips. "Our energies would match better, since we are all humans!"

"So . . . the second coming could be a shift in consciousness. Instead of Jesus coming physically, it could be the Christ consciousness coming to help us!"

"Plus, they love us! I doubt they care what name we use to describe something as long as our hearts are sincere."

Glowing with love, Dersti said, "Soooo, let's try it!"

They hugged and prayed, only instead of asking the Holy Spirit to join them they asked for Jesus. They were immediately flooded by the golden-white light that was love incarnate. The thought of having the energy of Christ there with them along with the feeling of love was so overwhelming that they both cried together in joy.

Chapter 33

All Together Now

At this stage in human evolution, there were only two priorities. The first was healing childhood trauma and negative karmic events in your own life. Once you achieved your own inner peace, the second duty was helping others heal their own wounds. Most people had accepted that when one of us suffers, we all suffer. Areas on earth that were advanced spiritually experienced the most rapid decline in population and consequently gained the largest increase in spiritual energy. The people residing in these regions would help those less fortunate in whatever way they could.

The prospects of elevated spiritual energy and all the gifts that energy promised attracted people into seeking out and trying this way of living. Most religions were, historically, primarily occupied with promoting their own belief system, which they were certain held the only true answer. Ultimately, this led to numerous atrocities since religious followers believed they had to promote a certain belief above all others. Yet if such social systems clearly held a measure of violence, why were so many people attracted? These simple questions flowed out across the world and stirred wonder. Individuals originally drawn to such religious beliefs were now attracted to the new way of living because of the benefits it provided.

No man likes being told what to do. Show human beings a way and let them experience the benefits; this will attract more people to the belief than trying to promote a particular belief with force or coercion.

In addition, there were only several hundred thousand humans left at this stage of mankind's evolution. Though some forms of electronic entertainment and communication existed, almost everyone had some degree of elegant and efficient telepathic communication. The worldwide trend was that two soul mates would find one another and unite to become teachers. The spiritual energy achieved during completion guided soul mates within this teaching vocation.

Ouray, Colorado, had transformed into a spiritual center. Most afternoons would find the city's citizens gathered in the park to talk, listen and learn.

"Ready?" Leydon asked. Dersti nodded and slid her hand into his. They were preparing to share their experiences as soul mates, and many had joined together to hear the couple's wisdom.

Leydon stood before the crowd and smiled. "Dersti and I see life just a little differently," he began. "We have equal, but different, views. I guess estrogen and testosterone view life in unique ways." Everyone in the audience laughed, easily understanding the comparison.

"When we work together," he continued, "we can solve anything and are unstoppable. We work together to synergistically combine our strengths and grow together through love. One of mankind's major healing tools has been the ability to heal the childhood traumas that keep us from loving ourselves. Until you love yourself, it is difficult to love another. Beginning decades ago with the Scrivner scanners, then scanoids, and now seers, these advancements have given us efficient ways to heal thousands upon thousands of people.

"A child is born as love and innocence. When a child is abused, he or she builds walls of protection as a defense. As children grow with unresolved childhood traumas, they continue to carry those walls of protection as a defense around their adult bodies. Why? Because they have not learned a healthier way to live without defenses. That is what our past generations have been working on: learning healthier ways of surviving.

"We carry our defenses with us if untreated adults. The very defenses that were a survival tactic for us as children now hurt us as adults. We believe we enter relationships as adults, but only because we have adult bodies. Simmering deep within us, if untreated, are the emotional defenses of children. And like any defense, they naturally force the other person into the offensive role.

"The implications may not be immediate, but what happens when there's a problem in the relationship? The defensive person blames his or her partner because of the perception that the partner is the offender. When this becomes the status quo, a loving relationship is impossible to attain or maintain. Two people with defenses can only unite in utter chaos. However, after childhood traumas are healed and defenses become unnecessary, adults can take responsibility for their own behavior instead of blaming others. They can then openly communicate with the knowledge that growing in love is the goal. With the guilt and shame carried inside each of us resolved, we can begin to love ourselves and others."

Someone from the audience lifted a hand. Leydon acknowledged the man, who then calmly pointed out, "But you two have it easier than we do. You're essence partners, after all."

Leydon laughed. "I agree! Being partners gave us some benefits in the beginning, and the completion gave us a wonderful sense of love coming from God. But it was also a trap. At times, we both fell victim to the belief that we could only experience the love of God in one another's presence. Love is a gift given freely by God to all of us, and it may be experienced anywhere. It is our defenses that makes us believe that only another person can unleash the love within us.

"Love is there all along! It glows in our beating hearts, our every breath, and every word. Love is a gift from the beloved. The person you are *in love with* opens all of the visual and sensory cues that are inside you both from genetic inheritance and through environmental conditioning. The person you love has the perfect combination of traits that you like and find attractive. That person makes you *feel* you are in love, so your ego thinks your lover opened the love within you. But in reality, the love was always there. Your lover was merely the key that unlocked the door to your love —the love from God!"

Dersti stepped in place beside Leydon. His eyes flashed into hers, he winked, and for a moment she could not breathe. She winked back at him, took a breath and continued with a glowing smile. "In that lies the trap of the ego. Regardless of the path we take to find love, our ego will equate that path to the feeling that is love. It thinks the path and love are the same. The path could be love of a soul mate"—she nodded to Leydon—"or some other lover, meditation, sex, and in the early days, drug use. These are all different paths the ego may become trapped in. So you see, the ego connects to the path you take to seek out love and not to God-given love itself. The ego thinks the only way to feel love is through the path."

There was a pause as the audience members shifted quietly in their seats, murmuring to one another as the revelation trickled through their minds. Dersti observed them with a small smile and then glanced over at Leydon. He returned the smile, and his lips formed a kiss in the air. With a chuckle, she cleared her throat.

"For example," she continued, "if I first *felt love* while I was in a relationship, my path to love will have been through another person. Because of this, my ego will start to believe that the only way I will ever feel love is by being with another person. My ego has accepted the path of relationships, as the way to love. If I don't do the work within the relationship to choose to stay in love or hit a bump on the path—and there are always bumps along the way—my ego will tell me that this feeling of mine isn't love and I will end the relationship.

"And so my ego will take me from one relationship to another, and to another, and to one after that, and all because it thinks that love is the path of relationships. *Recognize* that whatever the path to love, it is just a path. Ideally, the path would disappear after it opens you to love. For example, once you fall in love with someone, and are enough of an adult to do the work necessary to stay in love, then the path to further relationships should close. You would stay in love. Yet too often, people believe it's the *excitement of being on the path* of relationships that is love and so have serial relationships in the pursuit of the ecstasy of falling in love. They soon are stuck on the path of relationships to find love and never reach the pinnacle that is love itself."

Dersti glanced at her partner. Leydon glided a half step towards her, eyes glowing with warmth. He praised her with a slight nod of the head, and she beamed. They used this signal between them – whenever one said something that gave the other a chill, they received a nod in honor. Each nod was a precious gift of love.

"What happens to most of us at a young age is we don't receive the love and nurturing we need to develop a healthy concept of love," Leydon explained. "We don't see healthy role models for love. The way a child's mind operates is that – he or she will create *fantasies,* out of ideas that don't make sense. They don't see healthy role models so they develop childlike fantasies of what love is. And what are these childlike fantasies of love? These are the defenses we were discussing earlier. These fantasies emotionally remove children from the abuse of not having known love in their youth.

"An example, if you will. Girls see their knight in shining armor coming to rescue them from danger! Boys see themselves as brazen heroes – the very knights coming to kill the dragon and save the princess. In their fantasies they all live happily ever after. Sound familiar?" he asked, nodding to the audience. "But in real life, both boy and girl walk down *the path* of falling for each other and so experience the ecstasy of falling in love. It is what happens after the romance wears off that is critical. If either the knight or the princess does something that is not written in the script of the other child's love story, he or she will think *this is not love* because this is not the childlike story of love that individual has crafted in his or her mind. So they end the relationship, only to recreate the same scenario in their next relationship.

"On the other hand, a healthy adult will talk with his or her partner and work on creating an *adult* version of love, which necessitates work, healthy communication, and a willing partner. It's also beneficial to have help from others who are successful in love."

His wide eyes flickered across the audience as he spoke, catching one bright gaze after another. All the while his fingers remained fused with Dersti's. When he finally paused, Dersti glanced up to meet his eyes and smiling gave him a nod. He bowed his head towards the audience, and she continued.

"That is one of the wonderful things about living in our time," she spoke softly, though even her softest murmur could be caught in the audience's eager silence. "Spiritual energies all around us are culminating to help us release our traumas and judgments. As we work through our negative energy patterns with the help of the seers and other healers, we release and heal our judgments. *Nothing* will end love faster than judging others! 'He's wrong, she's wrong, he did this, she did that' . . . such are the common rallying cries of those who judge others. It is only when you've worked through your own judgments that your partner can do something offensive and you still maintain your love because you and your partner will be able to talk things over instead of fruitlessly judging one another."

"We have both done hurtful things to each other," Leydon spoke, peering at Dersti until their gazes locked. She emphatically nodded in agreement, and chuckles broke out among the listeners. Laughing himself, Leydon added, "But we talk about it so we understand each other and will be less likely to repeat the hurtful behavior. We forgive one another if needed, but the love is still there! If you ever feel your love for your partner is fading, look to your own judgments. It's not the other person's fault. Your own judgments drag you from love's sacred temple . . . that is, if you have a treated partner!"

As more laughter floated up from the gathered group, Dersti rubbed her fingers against her partner's and continued, "When I talk to Leydon about the behaviors I perceive as hurtful, I always feel better regardless of whether anything real changes or I only imagine a change. Simply voicing my feelings is enough. Besides, I believe Leydon has never done anything to purposefully hurt me." She turned her gaze upon him until he returned the look.

"Never!" Leydon assured her. He leaned towards her and she met him halfway. They locked in a kiss that summoned soft sighs of wonderment from their listeners. Their auras glittered, and when they finally pulled apart Leydon added, "I love you and would never, ever hurt you." Redirecting his attention to the crowd, he said, "Every time she tells me something, I do my best to remember it since the last thing I want to do is hurt her. Why would I want to hurt the woman I love? But it takes talking to each other and work to keep love bubbling and delightful. That, and leaving the outcome to God. In other words, we must not sit in judgment. Yet the ego is full of judgments. It had to be so in order for our physical bodies to have survived these past hundreds of thousands of years. The ego is in a way corrupted, the result of a physical life of cause and effect. Pick some berries, eat them, feel better, live another day. We developed judgments about everything in order to survive, and each was a survival tactic that was absolutely necessary to keep us alive.

"Yet now we are in a different day and age! Holding onto our primitive judgments cages us in fear and keeps us from God. What Dersti and I have been trying to do is release our judgments. We try to operate exclusively on the basis of love and innocence," Leydon said.

Dersti stretched her arms and breathed deeply of the day's warmth and sunshine, "In the Bible," she added, "Jesus said, 'lest ye become like children, ye shall not enter the kingdom of heaven.' And what is it that children are like? They are *innocent!* They look at the world with innocence and wonder! Everything is fascinating and curious to see, smell, touch. The judgments of the world aren't built into their young minds. Love and innocence flow from the "I Am" presence within them. It is only as we grow from innocent babies into children, teenagers, and finally adults that we replace our innocence with judgments learned from our parents and the world. These are all hidden under the guise of growing up, but judgments destroy innocence. Leydon was talking about defenses—our judgments are our defenses! Every judgment is a defense we learned to protect ourselves. 'Lest ye become like children' in our adult life means healing and giving up judgments and defenses. If we do not, we will not reach innocence again because adult judgments block childhood innocence."

The very innocence she spoke of crept into Dersti's eyes as she gazed out at the crowd. The corners of her lips creased ever so slightly in a smile as she turned to Leydon. His eyes glowed with love as he pressed a kiss to her hand.

"I believe," Leydon added, stepping beside Dersti, "that there are only two willpowers in the world: the strength of God's will and that of my own. When I let my willpower have its way and sit in judgment of myself and others, the space that would allow God's will to be heard in my head is occupied. Because my ego is shrieking out its judgments at full volume, I can't hear the quiet voice of God's will. I think when God gave us free will, it became much easier to hear our own will because we are in physical bodies. God's will is spirit, and we have to keep quiet enough to hear it. When I heal my judgments and defenses, the space in my mind becomes quiet; only then can I hear God's will. And do you know what happens? I get what I was always looking for in the first place: love, peace and innocence."

"Love and innocence are our goal!" Dersti cried. "We have been working on our own judgments and defenses. For instance, we both thought we were luckier than most. Blessed more than most. But our egos were running the show when we first met. The fact that we had found each other in this world was a miracle. We were given the completion and have such amazing love for one another. Yet those notions were all ego traps because sometimes we thought such feelings came from each other instead of the Beloved. Ever since those early days, we have been working on releasing our egos. We know now that the gifts we have received came directly from God. Why it was given to us at this time and for what purpose is not for us to know. We have simply accepted it in our hearts with love and gratitude. The gratitude we feel for these gifts . . ." Dersti's voice dissolved into a choked sob.

271

"Whatever God has in store for all of us here will happen in God's time, not in our time. We will continue to do God's will. Love God. Love each other and wait for knowledge of his will," Leydon concluded.

He looked at Dersti as they stood together beneath the bright sky. Small rivulets of tears carved paths over the smooth landscape of her cheeks. Lovingly looping his arms around her waist, he enveloped her in a hug and brushed his lips against hers. He started to cry. Love and gratitude overwhelmed them both as they cried together. Innocence radiated from their eyes and hearts. While still embraced in innocence, they heard the audience gasp.

Leydon and Dersti's physical bodies were glowing brightly, and as they looked down at themselves ... slowly dissolving! In another second, their physical bodies were transparent. Light bent around them, highlighting their outlines. In doing so, the light refracted into all the colors of the rainbow like a prism. At first, just their heads had a halo of golden luminescence tinged with snowy white light. The audience watched the shining halos spiral lower until the couple's old auras were entirely replaced with bright, golden-white light. What were two physical bodies with their bright auras were now two identical golden-white globes of light. They were transmuting into energy.

As Leydon and Dersti watched their physical bodies melt away, they felt their energy levels surge. With a whisper of silent strength, they felt the Christ consciousness enter them. They felt connected to the Beloved as never before. They felt love and connection to everything as never before. All feelings of separateness were gone, and they loved one another deeply and truly and eternally. They felt love for *everyone!*

Moments after Dersti and Leydon's transformation was complete, the couple became aware of activity in the crowd. They watched as other developed souls surrendered

272

their physical bodies and transmuted into energy globes. No longer held down by physical bodies, all of the golden-white globes began to hover and glide about. The spheres wobbled about in the air for a few moments like small children learning to walk, but they quickly learned to control their movements and even became graceful in flight.

After a joyful hour of playfulness, someone suggested they pray and thank God for this new gift. Those with physical bodies stood on the ground with their glowing faces turned skyward and held hands, auras shimmering in love. Those newly released from physical form hovered above. Before they began to pray they asked for the completion and all were immediately surrounded with a bright, golden-white light that made them feel love, innocence and a connection to God and all those surrounding them. Everyone felt joy! They *played* and prayed the rest of the night in joyful ecstasy, and it was not until the next day when, in exhaustion, the physical bodies had to rest.

Leydon and Dersti drifted off in their new energy globes. Out of habit and curiosity more than out of need, they floated back to their home. As physical matter was no longer a barrier, they glided through the walls of their home with as much difficulty as clouds swirl in the sky.

The couple was curious about everything. This plane of existence was entirely new and unlike anything either had ever experienced before. As they passed through physical matter, they could see its energy pattern; however, it was not a matter of seeing energy since they no longer had eyes. *Sensing* energy became the new norm. Each type of atom, they realized, had a different energy and rate of vibration. Because every substance was a combination of different atoms, all physical objects had their own energy state that was perceptible. As the couple entered into physical matter, there was no feeling that something physical would stop them. There was only a sense of vast spaciousness and God's presence in all things. They sensed that all energy was God. Indeed, God was every neutron, proton, electron and subatomic particle. God was everything, everywhere.

Drifting around their home, Leydon and Dersti laughed and radiated more joy than ever before. Of course, talking and laughing were no longer done with vocal cords. They now had a telepathic sense through which they shared everything. It was much more effective than verbal communication; for instance, when they wanted to communicate with one another they simple had to focus each thought or emotion into a pulse of energy that immediately contacted the other person. They quickly learned that one of the interesting things about telepathic communication was that distance was no barrier. They could push a thought around the entire earth. If they opened it up to everyone, anyone who wanted could tune in to the conversation. When they opened themselves up to the worldwide link, it was mostly in a meditative thanksgiving of love and gratitude for the Beloved. Since everyone at this vibratory rate was immersed in the Christ consciousness, the prayers and meditation were very similar all around the earth. Deep love and gratitude for God flowed from all minds.

And it was beautiful! They had believed seeing auras was beautiful, but this was so much more. Everything was composed of light, vibration and color.

After floating about their home and exploring what different physical objects felt like, they learned that wood was different from metal or glass. They even devised a game in which one would drift through some substance and the other would guess what the material was based on energy feelings. Soon enough, they left the house without regret. There was nothing there for them anymore.

They murmured to each other through the new bond, although it no longer mattered who spoke first as they both felt each thought instantaneously.

"I love you, Dersti!"

"I love you!"

"We love everything now."

"Can you feel how there is no longer a feeling of separation?"

"Yes, but why did we ever feel separate? This is so indescribably comforting!"

"I'm not sure, but maybe that's what physical bodies do. They separate us."

"But it's an illusion, really, because our energy is all the same!"

"It didn't feel the same when we had bodies . . . did it?"

"It did when we made love! Remember when we couldn't tell where one of us started and the other ended?"

"I do!"

A pause. Then: "Want to go back to the physical realm?"

They roared with laughter and darted around one another in a glowing display of light and love. How anyone could prefer physical bodies to this was a mystery. This was so much more!

Drifting lazily about, they explored the energy of the outdoors. They learned that the rocks, minerals and gems all held a deep wisdom. Yet the wisdom seemed trapped within the crystalline atomic structure of its host material. If it was indeed all-knowing, it was regardless rigid and unchanging. Living things felt different because the life force held a different vibratory feel. It was comforting and nurturing. It moved and evolved.

They merged their energy with an apple tree. It was so very peaceful and a type of completion—a sharing of energies. They could feel not only the light and color within and between every cell of the tree but also the very life force of the tree. They felt roots chiseling into the ground. Water and nutrients absorbed through the roots. Branches and leaves caressed by the breeze. They were one with the leaves as they made nutrients from photosynthesis, which were used to make fruit, leaves, roots and wood. They felt the exchange of carbon dioxide, which the tree needed to live, with oxygen, which the tree knew all the birds and squirrels living in its branches needed to live.

It was an amazing balance of energies, and Leydon and Dersti were aware of it all.

They felt electromagnetic energy pour forth from the sun, the physical support and nutrients given by mother earth, and the energy of life within each cell. In their union with the tree they were surprised by the intelligence of their host. The tree was aware and happy of its place in the world and joyfully fulfilling its life's purpose. Growing, giving shelter to animals, releasing oxygen, making fruit, and even making wood so that after its death it gave something back to the cycle of life—all these the tree accepted. If not used as wood, the majestic being decomposed and enriched the soil. The tree felt it was perfect and all around it was perfect.

All life forms they merged with held that same infinite acceptance. From the towering tree to the worm and the birds, they all felt purpose and acceptance of that purpose. It was a gift simply to be alive.

Because all previous incarnations were accessible to him, when a lesson was needed it would suddenly flash into his consciousness. Leydon was at once aware of when Logan's dog Zeus died and his beautiful golden aura didn't stay with Logan. *It is different with animals,* he realized, just as he thought back then. Animals and plants are already connected to God so they felt the purpose, and accepted that purpose of their life. When they die, they return to the source.

*****

Although Dersti and Leydon no longer had physical bodies, they could still merge into completion. But it was different now. Their auras were no longer individualized with different colors; instead, they and the others who had transformed all looked very similar. Instead of being egg-shaped and surrounding the physical body, the aura had undergone a transformation of its own and was almost perfectly round. Clear light radiated at its center while golden luminescence sparkled from the edges. In this energy consciousness, they could see their old physical bodies from this lifetime and so much more! They could see every lifetime they had ever had, and each life had lessons associated with it. As they gazed back over the totality of their lives, they realized for the first time that each life was a page in a larger novel. There was an entire world library of novels, and each was a masterpiece!

The first law states that energy cannot be destroyed; it can only be transformed into another state of matter. Now they realized this new energy body was a different state of matter. It was obvious, too, that this body would require a much simpler upkeep on a daily basis. There was no need to eat or drink and consequently no need to eliminate waste. This energy body had the perfect instruction manual as it was directly connected to the Beloved. Whenever they asked a question, it was answered by a loving voice. Often the answer came through intuition and almost as if they inherently knew the right response. Sometimes a different energy body would merge with their own and relay the information – like turning the page of a novel to get more of the story.

They did not sleep but instead went into a type of meditative consciousness where they could feel the expanse of the universe. Feelings of love and nurturing were always present.

And always, they were aware of the quiet and intuitive voice they both had heard when in their physical bodies. They perceived it as their new conscience. Yet it had always been there, although so many times they had used their own judgment instead of listening to it. Now they knew quieting their ego-based judgments and allowing a quiet space for God to be heard was an essential part of the spiritual growth process.

Chapter 34

"One"

Diamonds danced in the sky above them as Leydon and Dersti swooshed through trees in a midnight park. The orbs glowed like twin suns, bright from joy and peace and wonder. Their lives were a colorful swirl of exploring the world around them, which was fresh in delights seen from a new perspective, and resting in a meditative state.

Yet they were not alone in their immersion into a glorious and transformed world. All around them, the earth's ecology recovered rapidly. Over the course of several generations, the population had plummeted from fourteen billion to only several thousand still in physical bodies. Without billions of people fighting over scraps, the natural beauty of the planet steadily returned. Most people left on earth were vegetarian. As the energy of people who died coalesced with those still living, many became unwilling to kill something in order to survive themselves. Even wild animals changed. No longer were they afraid of people, for they could sense the higher spiritual energy in men that made them friends, not threats. It was not unusual to see a bear and a human walking together in the forest, simply enjoying one another's company.

People still in their physical bodies were attracted to this new lifestyle. For most, It was not a difficult choice to make! Why choose to walk around on two legs and hold on to judgment, fear and ego like a lifeline if you could do the work needed to finally let go and transform into spirit. But it was still a matter of free will. If anything remained in the physical realm for one to experience, he or she was encouraged to do it.

Energy bodies still had work to do. Often hundreds would combine in a great completion where their united energies would pray in gratitude. The prayer was for "the highest good" for those still in physical bodies. Curiously, there was not a group of people waiting to greet and offer comfort to those who spiritually progressed, which was always the case in physical death. Because once one joined the Christ consciousness, all fear was gone and one became love's presence.

Each sunset led to morning, a thousand times around. Every day new souls left behind a physical legacy to ascend to the spiritual realm. At last there came a day when there were no more physical bodies left on earth. Thousands existed in Christ conscience as energy orbs circling the earth, and all the intimacy of love pervaded all relationships with each other and God. The feelings of love and gratitude was worldwide. There was no sense of time, for minutes and days and weeks are irrelevant when in bliss. Whether a year or a thousand years swiftly sped by no one knew save for God.

When a voice did speak, all heard it at the same time. It was a voice like the most melodious of songs, gentle and loving and so familiar. The voice all had become accustom to. It enveloped them in warmth and whispered, "You all are my beloved! Welcome home! Now the time has come to take the next step in spiritual evolution. When Jesuha said, 'No one gets to heaven except through me,' he was speaking while in his Christ body. As all of you now understand, it had nothing to do with a particular religion. It had everything to do with reaching this energy state.

"My children, all of you are now in your Christ bodies. The Christ body is a gift to you. I love each of you as much as I love Jeshua or any of the other ascended masters. Remember when he said, 'all these things I do, you shall do and more!' You accomplished many in physicality, and now you will do more! It is time to combine your energies. I will tell you when and with whom to combine."

No sooner had the words echoed into silence than energetic body after energetic body began to combine. Each carried along all of their many reincarnations, innumerable lessons all merging together to incorporate the knowledge that had been learned.

Hitler's energy learned what it felt like to be a Jew in a gas chamber. Custer learned what it felt like for the Native Americans to have their lifes destroyed. The Native Americans experienced their own revelation as they felt the arrogance and final disbelief of Custer at the time of his death. Trillions of lives combined, page after page, novel after novel, all sweeping together into a mass consciousness.

They had journeyed to a new plane of existence, for the earth was neither visible nor even energetically sensed. In the end, there were two energetic masses left. Each possessed half of the knowledge and energy of every human being. Yet within all of the energy, Leydon and Dersti still had a sense of their individuality. All the world's knowledge combined inside them. Each knew so much and could go back through thousands of lifetimes and remember what happened in every one. Each had the combined love of the world! They could see every moment. They could experience the energy and love of any person within themselves. They could travel from parent to parent and see how it influenced a particular lifetime, see what they *chose* to do with the experience, see each page of each novel. There were trillions of pages, all awaiting those who would simply open their souls! There was silence as they processed all this information. It was overwhelming, but it didn't stop there.

A moment or year or eternity later, the voice spoke again. "Adam, meet Eve."

Understanding and memory coursed through Leydon and Dersti. Those names sparked visions, long forgotten but always hovering as distant lifetimes of the three of them in the 'Garden'. They were overwhelmed with love and a sense of connectedness on a level never experienced before.

"All of the combined energy the two of you now have was given to you in the beginning," God explained. "We lived for some time in unison, joined by love and our deepening relationship. When you chose to partake of the fruit of knowledge, you also chose independence. Implicit in your choice was also independence of having a one-to-one relationship with me. This is why relationships in physical bodies have been so difficult for you. As you once discovered, estrogen and testosterone do view life differently. When we lived together, I was the love-glue that allowed union and understanding between you. Without me, you had to work very hard to learn acceptance of the differences between yourselves and continuously reaffirm a balance to stay in love. Before your choice of knowledge and our separation, we *were* love!

"Now you see that I did not 'kick you out of the garden.' It was your choice to leave, for you have always had free will. It was your choice to separate from love and relationship with me so you could learn it on your own. The earth plane existence is the path you chose.

"I AM and always will be, so I just had to wait and watch until you returned. For me, it has been the blink of an eye. All information was provided to you, including the way back to me. The "Energy Book" and scroll were correct. Each time a child was born some of the energy that was given to you was relinquished and given to the child. Generation after generation the process wore on, until at last there were so many humans and spiritual energy lay so thin that people took the path of self-will, which could only result in violence, judgment and war with each other and earth.

"I AM, so my love and desire for relationship with all my children has not and never will fade. Those who were diligent—Jeshua, Buddha, St. Germain, and all of the other ascended masters—found an escape from ego and back to relationship with me.

"None of this was done as punishment. I AM love and relationship, and I do not punish. I love you so much I gave you free will! I sent you Jesuha and other teachers to help you spiritually. Your *choice* was your punishment. Passion is the punishment. Yet it was part of your spiritual evolution. It's just one more *cycle*, He emphasized, gazing upon Adam, Leydon and Logan, and summoning Logan's memory of thinking lifetimes earlier about the cycles of earth.

"On the matter of Earth, she is alive and glorious! She possesses a consciousness of her own and incredible wisdom. What you call the atmosphere around Earth – is her aura! Her heart is a core of molten blood, which erupts in veins to the surface occasionally, but most important the magnetic blood protects her aura. In the original creation, she is the 'Garden'. You were given one another to care for and nurture each other. When you chose knowledge and independence, she realized that every other species lives in a relationship with ME. When the animals reach a homeostasis with the surrounding environment, there becomes a balance. I created her, Earth, and I listened to all my creations. She liked my idea of dividing spiritual energy upon each birth among the humans. Do you know why she believed spreading spiritual energy thin was a good idea? She thought it gave you a path through knowledge back to us—the creation before the choice! She was concerned that free will would deplete her resources without concern for long term consequences. Which is *precisely* what happened!"

"Energy that expands must contract," God whispered. "As people began to see the truth of what the world had become—overcrowded, violent, and blighted by famine, destruction and extinction—more people turned back to the spiritual path. As spiritual energy began to combine, humans saw the benefits of increased spiritual understanding and living within creation instead of against it. The path of knowledge led back to love and relationship. Humans reached a critical mass where even the last of the ego-driven became attracted to the spiritual way. All had free will, and the choice was theirs to make. Some were just slow learners!" Humor bubbled in the soft and gentle voice.

"That is the fruit of knowledge, my children! Every human must experience each aspect of physical existence that they wish to. Not all choose to, as my Son did. But all that wanted to—each had been a King and a pauper. A Queen and a prostitute. Be murdered and been the murderer. To be the loved and the despised. To be the abused women and the abusive man. After all who wanted to experience the knowledge of physical life, only then would humans have the humility to turn back towards a spiritual relationship with ME.

"It was interesting to observe your judgments of one another when the reality was *each* would *become* all he had judged! When all had experienced every aspect of knowledge, only then could you make a choice about whether to return to the original spiritual essence given to you. Some spiraled into depression—Vertig's, as you called it—and then were re-absorbed into my energy pattern. If life after life they chose self-centered and low or non-existent spiritual goals, then fewer loved ones passed on high levels of energy to them. It became a downward spiral with death as the outcome. Their energy is still with me, and if they do the work they can work their way up.

"Energy that expands must contract!" God repeated. "Your energy is indestructible; you are always with me! Feel the love and relationship within the three of us and hold on to innocence!

"You have always been spiritual beings! Beings of light! Of innocence! Of love! You chose to learn *knowledge* through a physical existence."

"And if we had not chosen the path of knowledge?" asked the soul that now knew itself to be Adam.

"My child, that is unimportant now," said the voice lovingly. "You are the pinnacle of my creation, and I know you are curious. You are the only ones I gave free will to. I will say that it is all perfect. You were created by me, just as Earth was created by me. You evolved together on Earth with her energy. Once the path of knowledge and independence was chosen, you had to grow to huge numbers, devastating Earth in the process. This was necessary so you would obtain the knowledge that independence away from me, away from my presence, will always limit you. But, that's not what I'm about. I AM LOVE AND RELATIONSHIP!"

Before either could ask another question, the voice whispered, "We have one more thing we need to do."

"Yes?" asked Leydon and Dersti, Logan and Kersti, Adam and Eve, and a dozen other lifetimes all at once.

God said, "What was one, that became two, must once more become one."

Darkness flooded all around them, and nothing was visible except two great supernovas of energy. With those words, the two energies began to merge. As the outer bands of energy met, there was a peaceful acceptance. The energy swelled, intensified in brightness and size, and it was complete synergism. When the centers finally met, the energy mass quadrupled in size. It was radiant and beautiful and had become ONE! Once both energies were together again, all questions they had were answered. All was known instantaneously. At last, at long last, they were complete. Every energy pattern that had ever existed on earth felt all of God's love and innocence.

Then, without the voice's prompting, the mass started to shrink.

Slowly at first but swiftly building up speed, the energy imploded and increased in density. Soon less light was visible. As the mass shrunk in size, it went through the full range of the color spectrum—red, orange, yellow, green, blue, indigo, and finally just a deep violet that gradually faded to black.

All was one. There was darkness. Stillness.
A deep void. Unfathomable.
Timelessness.
There came the sound of a deep breath, and the voice that all people hear—the quiet, intuitive voice we hear only when we are quiet enough to listen—said:

"LET THERE BE

LIGHT!"